TIGER IN THE BLOOD

VIRGINIA RUSSELL

MP
Mistry
Press

NATIONAL
LIBRARY
OF AUSTRALIA
A catalogue record for this
work is available from the
National Library of Australia

For Frank

Entrance into the City of Amoy.   Engraving by S. Fisher from a drawing by Thomas Allom c.1840

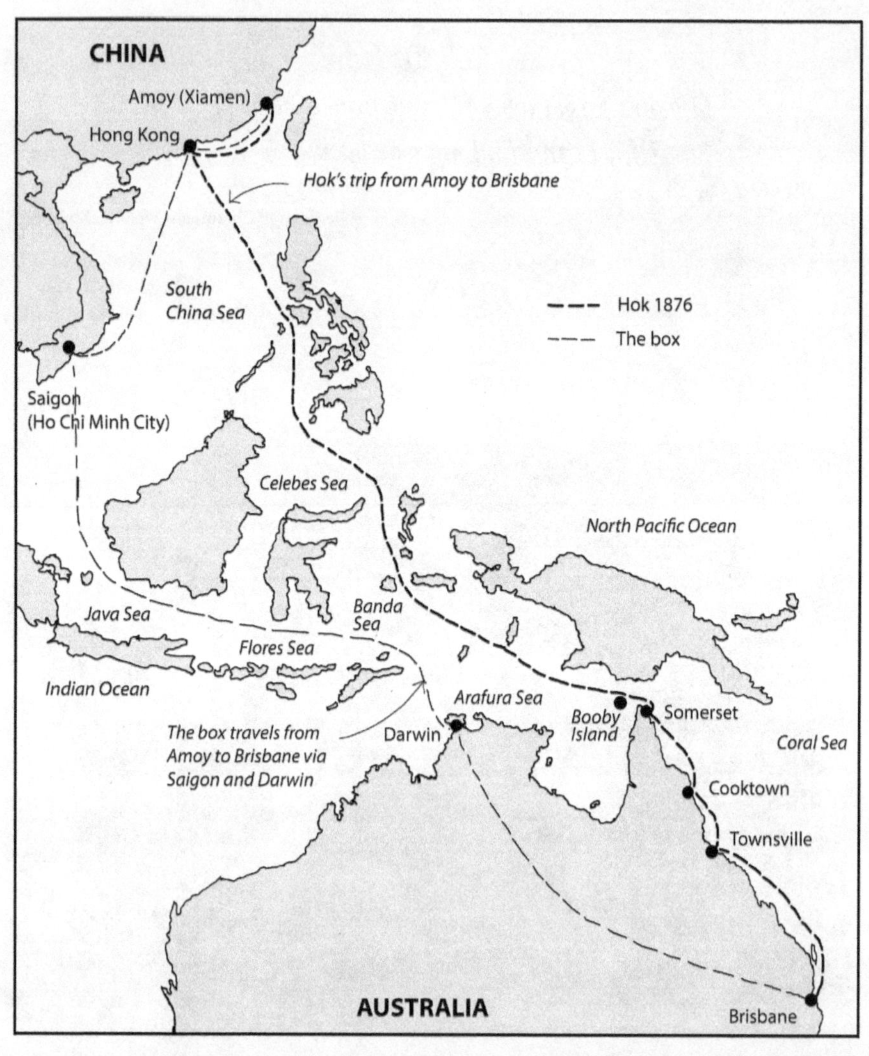

MAP 1 : From China to Australia

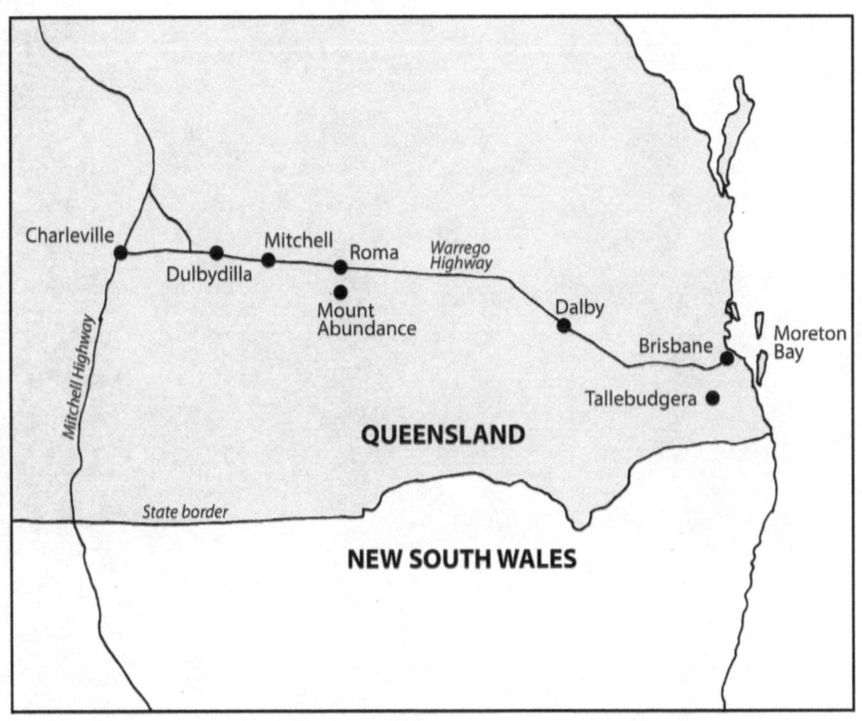

MAP 2 : From Brisbane to Dulbydilla (present day)

ONE

1: Hok

Boggo Road Gaol, Brisbane, Australia: 1886

I was hanged yesterday, hanged by the neck until dead.

They say I killed the baker. And it's true I didn't like him. I was ready to go home, and he took advantage. That gambler borrowed money from me and was never going to pay it back.

All the same, I didn't shoot him for that.

2: Eirene

Queensland, Australia: June 2019

Frank was in his favourite place, his head bent low over the stove. The silver streaks in his once ink-black hair had multiplied and hanging loose over his black jeans was a Nick Cave Nocturama tee from 2003. I smiled. My father's collection was legend—always hand-washed and hung inside-out in the shade to dry. However old they were, they still looked like new.

"Where's Mum?" I asked.

"Working." He nodded his head towards Ronnie's study. "She'll join us later. Breakfast?"

"Sure."

He cracked some eggs into a small glass bowl then reached for a wok off the rack above the stainless-steel bench and poured in half a cup of oil. When the oil was shimmering, he slid in the three unbroken golden yolks surrounded by a sea of glistening egg whites. Deep in concentration he sliced three bright red chillies and cut two stalks of spring green onions into horse ears. The pan spat and crackled. Easing a wide spatula under the raft of eggs he lifted them out onto a side plate and poured off most of the oil. Then he slid the eggs back into the wok.

"I love the way you get that crispy bottom."

He grinned.

"Years of practice," he said, setting a charcoal-glazed handmade bowl down on the square-cut wooden farmhouse table.

In the middle were three sunny yolks embedded in a circle

of egg white and edged with a lacework of crispy brown. Strewn over the top were the red rubies of chilli and scattered emeralds of chopped spring onion.

"Eat up, I want to show you something."

"What is it?"

"Later," he said. "Eat first." He handed me the oyster sauce and watched with a silly look on his face as I wolfed the lot down.

"Coffee?"

"Yes, please."

And Frank hustled around the kitchen just like he used to when we arrived home from school. Not much had changed. The house was light and bright as always, its gallery-white walls enlivened by Frank and Ronnie's eclectic art collection. They built the house themselves—just ten minutes north of the New South Wales border, in Tallebudgera Valley, Queensland. My sister and I arrived a few years later and the simple three roomed shack grew incrementally.

The house nestled comfortably into the landscape, its simple corrugated metal roofs hovered above like spreading wings and gathered each new addition into the fold. In the heat of summer, the huge timber-framed sliding glass doors opened wide onto the slatted timber deck. But it wasn't summer now. Outside, low-hanging clouds embraced the hills and clung to the sides of the valley. That morning everything was battened down.

"Here." Frank passed me my coffee. "Come with me," he said.

I followed him down the passage past Ronnie's study. This was her machine for working in where Veronica Law, the journalist, fine-tuned her renowned essays on the modern world. The door was firmly shut.

"She's been locked in there since five," Frank whispered as he opened the door to his sanctum. It was a complete chaos. Books were shelved higgledy-piggledy; his LP collection was stacked in piles on the floor and architectural models gathered dust on the top shelf. In the corner next to his Mac was his drawing board, a survivor from the pre-digital past.

"What's the big secret?" I asked.

Reaching into a cupboard Frank pulled out a dark-red box with brass handles on the side and an oblong brass lock plate on the front. It was about the size of one of those handyman tool boxes, but taller and a bit more squat in shape. The front and sides were a dark red lacquer, originally shiny and smooth I guessed, but now dull and dented, crazed and scratched. The lid was the same red lacquer, its sides curved up to a flat top. On each side of the box were faint scenes of women in trailing robes painted in gold. The back was a dull black.

"Wow." It looked seriously ancient.

"I want you to have it," said Frank. "Add it to your collection."

"What collection?"

"Those wooden things you're collecting."

"Hardly a collection, just a few things I like." I ran my hand over the top of the box. "Where did it come from?"

"From Jimmy … when he died."

Frank lifted the lid to reveal a shallow tray holding a few old photos. He handed me the top one. Our grandparents, Jimmy and Mei, stood next to their five children, all stiffly upright, all in white shirts, their uniformly shiny jet-black hair brushed flat.

"Which one is you?" I asked.

"The youngest … there," he said, pointing down the row to the smallest.

He picked up another photo, one of Jimmy standing outside a low white building.

"That's how I remember Pa," he said, "he always wore those baggy army surplus shorts. When he went out, he just changed that dirty old white tee for one of his favourite Hawaiian shirts. He's standing in front of the bakehouse."

Jimmy stared proudly at the camera with a master of all I survey look.

"It looks tropical. Darwin?"

"Yes. That's where we lived. It was different then before Cyclone Tracy flattened everything.

"Must have been scary.

"It was. I never want to spend another Christmas Eve like that."

"How did you manage, wasn't everything blown down?"

"Not quite. The business district escaped the worst, and we lived at the back of the shop. It was still damaged though ... no power, no water, and food was hard to find."

"You stayed on then?"

"We hung on for a while but then Mei, Jimmy and I took a flight out to Alice Springs. The rest of the family stayed on to help feed the people in the evacuation centres and rebuild the town."

"You didn't go back?"

"No. Jimmy decided we should move to Brisbane so I could finish my schooling and go to university. He had high hopes for me."

"How do you think he came to have the box?"

"He said he carted the damn thing around ever since his father died. The damn thing. That's what he said. All the way from Saigon to Darwin ... and then here."

"Saigon?"

"That's where Jimmy trained as a French pastry chef. He was born there."

"No wonder I don't feel Chinese."

Frank gave me a quizzical look.

I scrambled for an explanation, "China is such a long way back—generations back, on Jimmy's side anyway."

Another raised eyebrow. I grinned back at him. "Can't help the way I feel."

I looked back at the box, "Anything else in there?"

Most of the front below the lid was cut out like a window, square on the sides and bottom and curvy on the top. Behind the cut-out was a black board slotted into grooves on each side. Frank slid it up to reveal another compartment—musty smelling and chock full of papers. I picked out a letter from the pile, it was addressed in Chinese characters.

"Can you read this?"

"Are you kidding? No… ." He frowned. "Well, I can recognise a few characters, but not enough."

"So who do you think the letters are from?" I asked.

"No idea, must have been something to do with Jimmy, or maybe Mei? Just keep the box safe and in the family. OK? Don't worry about the letters." Frank's slender shoulders gave an involuntary shudder, and before I had a chance to look further, he gathered everything up, put it all back in the box, and gently closed the lid.

"Let's not disturb the spirits," he said.

It was after eleven when I drove down the winding tree-lined driveway back towards the city. The slow crunch of gravel under my tyres reverberated in the dark silence. On the seat beside me was the box.

3: The die is cast

Tee Hok Siong: Amoy, China, 1876

Hok gripped the damp wooden rail tight, his eyes on East Anchor Island lighthouse fast fading into the distance, his body alive with a mixture of excitement and dread. The wind lashed every which way around him as he said goodbye to his homeland, and if he did have any salty tears to shed they would have been whipped away instantly. Sand sprayed up from dunes lying here and there amongst the rocks on the barren coast; between ridges piled high with grey-black stone boulders were distant glimpses of lush crops of sweet potatoes and rice. On top of the highest hills pagodas towered like farewell beacons.

He'd left the village that morning in the dark, even before the grey twilight of dawn. Ma had cried, and Ba had wished him luck. His brother, his sisters, and Aunt Yangyang waited their turn to say goodbye as older sister stepped forward. She bowed, her black hair falling forward in shiny wings, and palms up, presented him with a jade amulet.

"Good fortune," she'd said. "Don't forget us."

Goodbyes over, he slung the amulet around his neck, Ma had handed him his bundle of clothes, and he had set out for the docks.

The decision had been made in haste. Ba's elder brother was a merchant in the town, and it was he who had summoned Hok a short week ago.

"You must go son." Ba had said. "See what your uncle wants."

Glad of the diversion the young man had left early the next morning striding along the well beaten dusty road. It was a rare chance to escape the daily grind of working the family's fields. In summer the heat rained down upon them; the rest of the year the weather was kinder, but the work was still back breaking. Now it was spring—the trials of the rainy season and the steamy heat would soon be upon them.

When the sun started to burn, he took care to walk in the shade of the spreading banyan trees on either side of the rough track. He smelt the town long before he saw it. Once through the north gate the buildings closed in around him, the dirty crooked streets narrowed in places, barely wide enough for two men to pass. The city hordes hustled by, travelling musicians competed to be heard, and gongs sounded in every direction. His feet slipped on the uneven granite blocks, wet with who knows what stinking mess. The stench was dampened by the sweet and savoury aromas wafting from the street stalls, whose owners accosted him at every turn. He climbed yet another set of winding stone steps. Beggars hassled him, pulling at his sleeves. Half-naked coolies dripping sweat jostled past with their heavy loads, startling him with their warning grunts. Nearer to Uncle's house the street widened. Two panting runners hefting a silk–clad mandarin in a sedan chair knocked into him as they jogged past. He dodged this way and that to avoid the crippled ragged beggars and yapping dogs.

Uncle was about to eat breakfast, relaxing after a few hours of business on the docks. He welcomed his nephew, "Come in, come in. Have you eaten?"

Hok stepped into the dark shuttered interior. As the heavy door closed behind him the tumult from the street outside cut to a faint murmur. Between slurps of congee Uncle asked after his brother and the family.

"And the crops … how is the season going? Do you have enough water? Eat … eat, don't be so polite nephew. You must be hungry."

The food spread out before them was enticing. An array of pickled cucumbers, salted turnips, fried peanuts and other titbits surrounded a large bowl of congee. Hok, too, was soon slurping the rice porridge down. He hesitated until his uncle had taken some of the steamed taro cake before taking a rather large helping for himself. The cake they ate at home wasn't as tasty—this one was soft in the middle and crisp on the outside with fried shrimps and plenty of chilli. *Ho-Chiah*. Good to eat!

Once breakfast was over the flood of polite questions ceased. Uncle's face took on a serious look as he smoothed his commodious blue shirt over his expansive belly. He reached back and drew a sheet of paper from the box behind him. "Your father has a big family. It's hard for him. And you, you're a hard-working young man, you must have ambition."

Surely, Hok dared to hope, Uncle was about to ask him to join the business. But no, that wasn't it.

"Last week I met an agent, a good honest businessman. He wants to engage some healthy young men to work in Australia."

Hok could neither read nor write, but still he had been optimistic. Being sent to Australia was not the future he had dreamed of. He swallowed hard and tried to brighten his face as Uncle talked on.

"You must know … the Amoy men who go overseas have much success. They come back with plenty of money. Look at Tan Bing he has his own business now. Only five years and you can come home a rich man. You will get seven silver dragon dollars for each month and a new suit of clothes each year."

"Yes Uncle," he responded to his uncle's steady gaze.

"When you come home you will get fifty dollars. This will not be hard work; they need shearers and cooks for the big sheep farms in the west of the Queen's land."

"Shearer? What is shearer?"

"In Australia they have many sheep. The wool of the sheep is cut by the shearers and sent all over the world to make clothes and blankets."

"I not know how."

"You know how to eat don't you?" Uncle said looking at the empty plates in front of them. "You can be a cook."

Hok gave a weak grin.

Back out in the street he wandered along dazed and confused. Thwack! thwack! thwack! He felt the lash of a whip on his back, and only then did he hear the shouts to get out of the way. Ai–yo! Ai–yo! Clear the road! Two dark skinned ragged looking thugs with whips were clearing the way for a mandarin's retinue. Street urchins hired for the day carried large sign boards announcing the great man's importance. Hok skittered out of the way, pressing his back flat against a wall. The four bearers passed by sweating and heaving. The poles of the sedan chair rested between their shoulders and curved low with the weight of a large, very fat, official.

At last, the clamour of the town was behind him. To his right clusters of green trees grew between smooth stone boulders mounded up like so many giant eggs piled on top of each other. On his left a flock of egrets skimmed along the shallows to surround a group of brightly painted fishing boats. At the end of the estuary was his village.

He strode past the temple gates but then stopped abruptly and decided to go in. Standing before the richly decorated altar his thoughts were a jumble: Should he follow Uncle's bidding? Would he be fortunate? What was his fate to be? He knelt and bowed three times.

Moon shaped divining blocks lay amongst the remains of candles and sticks of incense. He reached for them, passed them around the incense burner, knelt, and cupping the blocks between his hands, he asked his question. He threw them into the air with a deft turn of hand, his eyes following eagerly as they fell to the ground. The blocks gave their answer, "Yes,"— he should go. He threw them up once more. Again, the answer was the same. With dogged perseverance, and not sure what answer he was looking for, he tried again. Once more the ground rang with the sound of the falling blocks. But this time both blocks fell round side down. An uncertain answer. Were the gods laughing at him?

Leaving the temple, his straw sandals scuffed up the dust as he hurried past the fields where his grandparents' urns lay. As a child he had spent many happy times with grandmother. Everyday *an-ma* had strapped the chubby cheeked Hok Siong to her back and carried him around as she worked. From his vantage point high on grandmother's shoulders he had peered out at the world, eyes wide, his ink black hair sprouting from his head like fresh un-mown grass. He was safe and content.

When he could walk, he steadied himself by grabbing the folds of her loose trousers as she cooked. If he got bored, he would tug on her clothes pestering her till she handed him a special treat, always with a warm smile. He remembered, too, fishing in the estuary with his grandfather, and their whoops of joy as they hauled in the nets full of thrashing silvery fins.

Now only Aunt Yang-yang lived with them. When she was a blushing seventeen Yangyang had married Wen-fei. Dressed in a sinuous silky scarlet wedding robe, her dark eyes sparkled happily over the edge of her fan. But then she committed the unforgivable, she failed to produce any sons. Wen-fei took other wives and the family punished Yangyang for her sins in every way they could. Life could not get any worse. Clutching at survival, escape was the only option. She arrived back at her home village, humiliated and sad. Luckily Wen-fei didn't drag her back and punish her. He was engrossed with the birth of his number one son, too busy to pursue his recalcitrant and barren first wife.

Hok Siong's family home was one of the largest in the village, it had four rooms and a loft. Grandfather had worked hard—the tiny cottage he grew up in had expanded, sprouting up and out, just like the two pomelo trees he had planted in the yard.

Aunt Yangyang slept by the fire and was the first to rise every morning. She limped around in the hushed morning stillness, folding her bedding, kindling the fire, and sweeping the earthen floors.

They led a simple life, but always had plenty to eat. Rice and sweet potatoes grew lush in the fields. Ginger, and groundnuts too. Exuberant sugar canes fluttered their grasshopper green leaves in the breeze. In the heat of summer, the village dogs tunnelled between the cane stalks and lolled around in the shade while Aunt Yangyang kept the children happy with cane juice and cake.

One day a tall stranger came by. First, they heard the shouts from the workers in the fields, "Go away stranger!" Ten-year-old Hok Siong and his friends could not miss this bit of excitement. They surrounded the tall man with the funny clothes as he kept on walking towards the village. The old men lifted their bamboo pipes out of their mouths, and stared, smoke drifting in the breeze. Even the blind ones turned their heads in the direction of the stranger.

The whole village was there. Ba, Ma, Aunt Yangyang and the children crowded around with the others to view this strange apparition. Scrawny dogs and fat little village pigs circled around, excited by the commotion. Ba told Aunt to bring tea and cake. The stranger spoke a little language, and he exchanged a few words with Ba as he drank his tea and ate the cake.

He was the first of the red-haired devils—the *ang-moh*—to come to the village. Soon he was followed by two more and they set up in a rented house. They talked about *Ia–So* who died to save them all. They said that the villagers should obey his sacred rules and flourished their black books high. On Sundays they invited people to come for singing and reciting together. Ba went once to see what was going on. One of the red heads stood on a platform and talked loudly, waving his arms around and shaking his finger at them. Ba came home shaking his head. He said, "They want us to stop looking to our ancestors. How strange is that?"

The next morning Ba stood before the family shrine and set extra incense sticks smouldering away; he placed bright shiny orange persimmons in bowls on each side and fresh spring flowers in the vases. Forget the ancestors? What an extraordinary idea!

Hok and his friends were fascinated and scared at the same time by the strangers. They played pranks, knocked on the front door and then hid in the bushes, stifling their laughter until one of the black clad strangers opened the door to no one. Then they ran away as fast as they could to escape retribution. When Ba heard he was angry.

"You are disrespectful. They are good men, even if their ideas are strange. Your brothers will imitate you. It's a bad example."

Then a terrible thing happened. On an endless summer's day Hok and his friends chased a crowd of the younger ones through the corn field, waving sticks and threatening to beat whoever they caught. It was just play and they didn't really mean it, but Hok's little brother believed them. He stayed hidden until the shadows fell over the fields, too frightened to come out. Ba and the others searched till they found his pathetic mangled six-year-old body. The tiger slunk away unwilling to face the barrage of lanterns. Ma and Ba forgave him in the end, but the memory sat like a stone in Hok's heart, however much he tried to forget. Now he only had four sisters and no brother.

Shaking his head to dispel the scenes of that horrible night Hok walked on, and at last arrived home. He reported to his father everything that Uncle had said.

"What do you think Ba? Should I go?" he asked.

His father leaned back, put his hands on his head and closed his eyes.

Hok stood by the side waiting patiently. He had the habit of cocking his head on one side when listening, his eyes bright and enquiring. His well-formed eyebrows arched lightly above two brown eyes flecked with green and shaped like almost-round almonds. Between high cheekbones his nose was small, an upbeat nose. When he smiled, which was often, his eyes lit up and his mouth stretched wide towards his shapely but slightly asymmetric ears, the left being a little higher than the right. Usually quick to turn a serious moment into a joke, he knew better than to joke about this situation. He waited.

The low sun slanted through the open door and danced over the room. Hok's father smoothed his hands from the back of his head down to his neck, elbows jutting out on either side, before turning to look at his number one son.

"Yes son, I do. I know it will be difficult for you. But every day we struggle here. Your sisters …"

His voice trailed off, but Hok knew what he meant. The family had four girls, and no marriage offers. It should not have been so difficult to find husbands for them; the village was overflowing with an abundance of young men. But everyone was poor. Taking a wife into the family meant finding a bride price, and another mouth to feed. What hope did they have?

It was settled then. He was going to Australia. It was his duty, and Hok felt proud to be chosen to help the family.

"Watch out," he said to his sisters. "I'm going to come back a rich man. You'll be able to hire a sedan chair and four coolies to take you into town." He even bragged about building a new huge house for them all.

But in the quiet of night, he remembered the tricks they had played on the black-clad, bible-carrying *ang-moh*. Soon he would be going to a country full of them. It was an exciting yet scary thought. Some who had made the journey to Australia had returned with pockets of gold and money to burn, like Tan Bing, now a prosperous merchant with a beautiful wife and four children. But others, he knew, came back as bones to be buried with the ancestors. Which would it be for him?

4: Sunday with Billie Holiday

Brisbane: June 2019

Billie Holiday was having a gloomy Sunday as I wandered around the apartment making coffee. It was a few weeks since Frank had called me down to Tallebudgera, and the Chinese box now sat square and handsome on the side table. It looked at home.

On one side was the cage doll I'd lugged all the way back from France, and on the other was a time-worn, white-painted, nineteenth century English prancing wooden horse. The aesthetics of an object means a lot to me and the red box was unquestionably old, battered, and beautiful. History dripped from every warp and scratch.

Our apartment was in a re-modelled old sugar refinery, and the presence of the past was never far away, always hovering in the air. In my imagination the ghosts of men in singlets toiled away dripping with sweat in the sickly-sweet atmosphere, the clang of machinery assaulting their ears. That battered red box, too, exuded an aura of the past that I simply couldn't ignore.

What secrets was it hiding? Curious, I pulled out the photographs and then the pile of letters from the second compartment. Underneath was a bundle wrapped in brown paper and tied up with string. I lifted it out and spread everything out over our huge dining table.

I should explain—I said 'our' table because I share the apartment with my younger sister, Dee.

Dee's real name is Aphrodite and as for me, they named me Eirene after the Greek goddess of peace. For that we blame Frank's nostalgia for the hippie days of peace and love, together with our mother Ronnie's love affair with Greek mythology. Naturally Dee hates her name and only divulges it when absolutely, and I do mean *absolutely* necessary. Me, I'm okay with mine. Still, our names might seem incongruous to some, as our ancestry or part of it, is, on the face of it, obvious. Ethnically speaking we're half-Chinese from our father's side. The other half is a mongrel heritage and usually too complicated to explain. So, we're part Chinese, part Welsh, part English, and part whatever—but naturally I consider myself all Australian.

It's surprising Dee and I get on so well as we're completely different. I'm usually found lazing around in no-fuss jeans and runners, and I drive a gas-guzzling ute called Maud (yes, I know, I feel the guilt, believe me). Dee wears colourful dresses, high heels, and drives a sporty little car more suitable to the affluent suburb we live in.

But Dee is hardly ever home, and that day I had the place to myself. Well almost. Just then Celeste wrapped her tail around my bare legs reminding me of her presence. She sat back looking at me through her critical wide open cat's eyes while I dished up her breakfast, then she padded silently into the kitchen to eat it.

"Sorry Celeste," I said. "Breakfast's late. But you were fast asleep on the bed when I saw you last."

I cranked up the volume as Billie moved on to a slightly more cheerful *All of me—why not take all of me?*

The string around the brown paper bundle took a bit to undo, I disentangled the knots and inside were some old age-yellowed newspaper clippings and a small circular carved pendant made of pale jade. I curled my fingers around it. It felt smooth and warm in my hand, not cold. Scrawled across the top of one whole page of a newspaper was a name—Mr John Holland, 76 Cristal Street. I smoothed my hand over the paper to iron out the creases. It was page three of the *Toowoomba Chronicle and Darling Downs General Advertiser* dated Wednesday, 17 March 1886. A pencil mark highlighted an article near the bottom of the second column.

The Dulbydilla Murder:

Regarding the case of Tee Hok Siong, the Chinaman who was sentenced to death at Roma, on Wednesday last, a correspondent to the Courier pleads for further inquiry into the case of the unfortunate man. He points out that no one saw the prisoner with the gun on the night of the murder; that the fact of caps and shot of the same size as those used in the murder being found on him next day was not very conclusive evidence as these things are made of certain sizes only, and thousands might have had the same size in their possession. The deceased said the prisoner had committed the deed; but he must have been greatly weakened by loss of blood when the police arrived, and perhaps not in his right mind, besides which he may have had some dispute with the prisoner beforehand. The prisoner's statement that had he known the police were after him he would have cleared out, must be viewed in the light of his imperfect knowledge of English.

Strange. Over one hundred years ago. And where was Dulbydilla? I had no idea.

I read the next clipping, a rather sobering account of Tee Hok Siong's execution by hanging. According to the journalist, he was a small slight man with straight black hair and an intelligent face, and, although he was despondent at times, he had resigned himself to his fate with Oriental stoicism. The prisoner had spoken calmly about his approaching death, but vowed he would return to earth, and when he did, he would wreak revenge on those who had spoken against him and perjured themselves.

What the hell—what did this have to do with our family, with me, or Frank, or my grandparents Jimmy and Mei? I looked out of the window, an indulgent second cup of coffee in hand. A feeling of distaste crept over me. I didn't want to be reminded of my Chinese roots. Especially not with something like this.

Growing up, Dee and I had no conception that we were different, not until some idiots from school started calling us names. The taunts echoed around the playground. We got *Hey Chop-suey!* and *Ching Chong Chinaman*, and it hurt. We even got *Chop, chop, chop off your tail*, which must have come from a long way down through the generations—it put me off plaits for life. Even worse they shouted China-*man* even though we were two adorable little girls. At least that's what Frank always called us.

"How are my adorable little girls?" he used to say when he arrived to collect us from school.

In the early days Frank and Ronnie used to take turns at working from home and we never knew who was going to pick us up from school until one or other of them appeared at the gates, either in the Toyota Land Cruiser, or in the ancient bone-shaker Vee-Dub. Our indomitable parents swapped vehicles as often as they took turns with the child minding and cooking.

On the days when name-calling was rife, we cringed in embarrassment when it was Frank who stood waiting at the school gates. We hurried him off up the road, Dee on one side and me on the other, hands gripped tight, dragging him along and pretending that we just wanted to get home quickly.

But we never said a word.

Ronnie would have marched up to the school and made a big embarrassing fuss. While Frank—well Frank would have given us an interminable talk about how nothing was wrong with us, it was the others who were ignorant. "You should turn a blind eye and forgive them." That's what he would have said.

Despite the name calling, and though I wouldn't ever be caught dead shouting *aussie aussie aussie*, I have never thought of myself as anything else but Australian. The box and its contents were no more than a curiosity. An interesting curiosity, but nothing to do with me.

The apartment fell silent as Billie Holiday finished her greatest hits. Framed by the open window a small fishing boat chugged its way down the Brisbane River. A few pelicans bobbed and flapped in its wake while a cluster of seagulls swooped and swirled endlessly above. I dragged my eyes back to the table and rifled through the rest of the contents. The other newspaper articles were reports of the arrest and the trial. Among them were the letters that Frank and I had found. The envelopes had all been carefully slit open and I gingerly drew a few of the letters out. Vertical rows of Chinese characters covered the flimsy paper. Some of the characters were in a shaky hand as though written by someone unfamiliar with putting pen to paper. I folded the pages back up, crease for crease, and studied the envelopes. The stamps were all Australian.

Looking up I saw that the light had changed. It was later than I thought, and I'd promised to meet up with Maddy. I jumbled it all back in the box.

Driving to the restaurant my stomach reminded me that the day had consisted of far too much coffee and not enough food. Luckily the place was buzzing, and service was quick. My hunger pangs abated, but still Maddy and I tussled over the last spear of burnt broccolini in black bean butter. I won.

"We must meet up more often. I've hardly seen you since the wedding," she said as we parted, adding a quick, "Sorry it didn't work out."

"Too long, can you believe it was five years ago? Ancient history now! How's John?"

"He's fine. Take care ... and stay in touch," she said waggling her finger at me.

We'd all been at university together, Maddy, John and I. We'd met at the tennis club, and though we were all in different faculties, we supported the same causes, and were all fiercely competitive tennis players. I studied visual arts specialising in photography and my dream was to be that young Australian artist who surprises everyone by having an exhibition at the Tate Modern in London. Some hope! I soon found that I'd need to earn a living first. So photography was on the back burner, but graphic arts encompassed the need to be precise and creative at the same time which suited me.

Back home the phone rang as I struggled with the key. I pushed the door open and scrabbled deep in my bag. It was Ronnie.

"Hi Mum."

"Hi, love. How are you?"

"Good. Just been to dinner at Happy Boy—with Maddy."

"Nice. How is she?"

"Nothing new, same old." Just then Celeste wandered out of the bedroom arching her back. I ran my hand across her smooth fur and along to the tip of her tail, silently mouthing 'yes I'll feed you soon.'

"What are you up to?" I asked Ronnie.

"Busy as usual. I'm writing a new piece."

"Anything interesting?"

"The unseen poverty of struggling middle Australia."

"I thought we were doing all right."

"Not really. There's inequality, increasing poverty, and the expanding casualisation of the workforce—the gig economy. And I see the poverty as not just rooted in monetary terms but in ideas and aspirations."

"I know what you mean."

I poured myself a glass of wine with one hand and, phone in the other, I wandered across to the window, drawn by the sound of the late-night walkers cutting through the stillness of the night. A lone bat cruised soundlessly over the moonlit, wavery, black depths.

I told Ronnie about the box.

"I'm pretty surprised Frank gave it to you," she said.

"He said he thought I would appreciate it. Told me to keep it for the family, for posterity, I guess. What do you know about it?"

"Nothing really. After Jimmy died, all I saw was a quick glimpse as he hustled it into his study, never to be seen again. It was a busy time, and we had Mei to look after. What do you make of it?"

"It's beautiful, but it's the stuff inside that's really strange."

"Uh-huh?"

"On top are some old photos of Jimmy and the family, but then under that is a bundle of clippings about a murder someplace I've never even heard of. The murderer was Chinese, and he was hanged in Brisbane Gaol. Must be the old Boggo Road Gaol, I guess."

"How bizarre. When?"

"The eighteen hundreds, 1886, way back."

"Anything else?"

"Some letters but they're all written in Chinese characters, I can't read them, and Frank couldn't either. We looked at them, but Frank closed the box up before we got to the clippings underneath. Do you think he knows anything about the murder?"

"You'd have to ask him. He's never said anything to me."

Now, our mother Ronnie likes nothing better than to get her teeth into some mystery or other. That's why she's such a good investigative journalist.

"How about getting the letters translated?" she said.

"Could do."

"One of the guys at the paper might be able to help. He's not been there long but he's our Asian expert, good at translating."

"Might be interesting," I said, and immediately wanted to take the words back. I didn't really want to know any more about it. But now I'd unleashed Ronnie.

"Okay, good," she said. Perhaps sensing my reluctance, she immediately changed the subject. "How's Dee?" she asked.

"She's driving me crazy. She's never home. You know she has a new boyfriend?"

"Don't be too hard on her. She has a gregarious nature. What's the boyfriend like?"

"His name is Patrick. He's OK I guess." I couldn't see her face, but Ronnie's amused smile at my lukewarm approval travelled across the ether to me.

"Got to go," I said. "Work tomorrow. Say hi to Frank. ... Yes, I'll come down again soon."

Next morning at our usual Monday meeting Will announced a new project, a high-end art book.

"I need a brilliant concept for the cover and the overall design," he said.

"It has to be shit hot," he said looking at me. It was what he always said, and I didn't have any problem with that. I like perfect too.

5: Leaving

Tee Hok Siong: May 1876
They sailed halfway to Hong Kong before bad weather forced them
to take shelter and anchor off Nan'ao Island. Night fell. Below decks
the motley collection of passengers set themselves up for a night
of gambling, and in the crowded quarters a heady mix of tobacco
and opium fumes made it hard to breathe. Hok couldn't bear it. He
scrambled back up the narrow stairs to the top deck and sought
shelter under a broad strip of canvas stretched tent-like over a spar
from one side of the deck to the other.

In the lee of the island the gusty winds were subdued but the
canvas still flapped and snapped above. Resting awkwardly against
the bulwark he tried to sleep, but it was impossible. He slid down
until he lay flat on the weathered wooden deck next to his bundle of
clothes. His head ached and he was alone. On a calm night the deck
would be crowded with bodies but not on a night like this. He had
never slept alone before, and never on a ship. It was an adventure.
But Australia? It was so far away.

At daybreak he ventured below deck. Most of the passengers
were still sound asleep. They were lying in heaps here and there,
as if tumbled and tossed by the winds during the night. Their
foreheads glowed in the early light and their pigtails lay about in
wild confusion. Some had the unmistakable signs of the habitual
opium smoker. Wan and haggard, their breathing was quick and
disturbed.

The sun clawed through the clouds bathing the ship in a pale morning blush. The heaps stirred, unwound, stretched, and rubbed their eyes. A breakfast of rice, fish and vegetables awaited those who had paid for it.

Two long days later, they reached Hong Kong and disembarked. A colleague of Hok's uncle met the ship and hustled Hok along the docks to the RMS Singapore.

"No time to waste," he said, "Captain Peake is keen to set sail this afternoon."

The Royal Mail ship, Singapore, left Hong Kong harbour in the midst of a strong north-east wind and pelting rain. The steam brig was long and lean, and both masts were fully rigged to take advantage of the wind. Square sails pillowed off the fore and main masts while triangular staysails whipped and strained off the bowsprit which cleaved through the raindrops above the elegant concave curve of its clipper bow. Wisps of smoke from a central funnel indicated that the engines were running on slow ahead. It was the early afternoon of the eighth day of May 1876.

Hok Siong was one of two hundred and thirty-six passengers in steerage, all bound for Australia. The Singapore carried the Royal Mail; 66 bags of sugar; 52 packages of opium; 64 bundles of rope; 166 packages of hemp; 27 boxes of porcelain; 24 chests of drawers; 12 trunks; 89 packages of dried fish; 17 bundles of bark; 74 packages of vegetables; 7,291 bags of rice; 2,556 crates of tea; 30 packages of tobacco, and her human cargo. It was an iron hulled hybrid steam-sail vessel, a giant compared to the coastal steamer, but below decks the steerage quarters were the same—packed, stifling, and odorous.

Most of those who boarded at Hong Kong were bound for Cooktown and the Palmer River goldfields. There, they believed, was a fortune waiting for every one of them.

"Where you come from?"

Hok turned his head sharply to see the speaker, a young man with a friendly face. He spoke the language of Amoy, and his head was wrapped in a turban, just like the one that Ba usually wore.

"I come from Kang-thau. My name is Tee Hok Siong," Hok said, his voice a little husky from lack of use. He'd barely spoken to a soul since he left home.

"I know it! Kang-thau, nice village. Pleased to meet you. But where are you going?" the young man asked.

"I am going to the Queen's land, to a big sheep farm in the country," Hok replied, with a grin.

"I am Lee Yunlong. I'm going to get rich in the goldfields of Australia!" Yunlong said, his confidence matching his name—Cloud Dragon.

Hok was encouraged by his new friend's boldness, and, united by language, the two of them banded together like long-lost brothers. Down below they grabbed bunks next to each other. But by midnight they were in the middle of a storm. The ship plunged up and down with the high seas. They were unlucky. It was barely the beginning of the typhoon season, and all should have been plain sailing.

In the cramped and dark confines of the steerage quarters two hundred and thirty-six frightened souls fought a losing battle to retain the scanty contents of their stomachs. Below the battened hatches and in almost total darkness, they battled for room to move. Hok wedged himself into a corner next to Yunlong and pressed his shaking limbs against the surrounding walls. He tried to think of distant things, times past. Anything to stop his ears being assaulted by the sound of the iron hull smashing down onto the ocean. Anything to block the howl of the wind screaming on all sides. Anything to stop thinking about his lurching stomach.

The next day was no better, the wild dark sea crashed over the decks and seeped through the hatches. Hok and Yunlong clambered up on deck, but the wind almost tore the clothes off their bodies. Again, the wind died, and again the storm returned. The foresail split and thwacked down on the deck timbers. They scurried back below as the canvas flopped and swirled about in the invading waves. The ship rolled heavily, and the engines laboured on slow speed. At night they heard a mighty clap as the scanty sails that the captain saw fit to hoist were ripped apart and torn from their masts. Two hundred and thirty-six shards of humanity moved from fright to terror … and beyond. They were broken vessels drained of hope. Exhausted, and abandoned to their fate, at last they slept.

It was two days of hell before the typhoon passed. New sails were hoisted and soon a cheerful rhythmic throbbing sound indicated the captain had ordered full steam ahead. The next fourteen days were less terrifying but the stench below decks was unbearable. Their bunks exuded a damp rotting smell; the reek of their fetid clothes mingled with the stink of vomit and the evil smell of the primitive toilets. Yunlong and Hok Siong escaped to the open air of the crowded upper deck. Hungry, they shovelled down bowls of rice and pickled cabbage. Hok was grateful for the dried titbits Aunt Yangyang had packed for him.

"Here, have some. I have plenty to share," he said handing the precious packages over to Yunlong.

"Thanks. … The giant is enjoying his food." Yunlong angled his head in the direction of a huge man from Chefoo who was sitting not far away from the boys, accompanied by his manager, a short spritely German, and a harried looking Chinese assistant. Zhou, the Chefoo giant was bigger than anyone they had ever seen before. His feet were twice the size of theirs and he was big in every sense of the word. They had watched him below decks as he tried to get comfortable. He could not stand up straight; his only options were to move crouched over in a back-breaking stoop, or to crawl around on his hands and knees. If he lay down on his bunk his legs dangled down, and his massive feet stuck out blocking the aisle causing much amusement. After a few days he resorted to curling up on the floor like a monstrous caterpillar.

Now they watched in awe as he scoffed down fourteen bowls of rice and vegetables, gleefully counting them off one by one on their fingers.

"… thirteen … fourteen!" they said in unison as the giant put his bowl down firmly and shook his head at his Chinese assistant, who was poised to deliver yet another helping.

"Enough! Go!" barked Zhou's German manager to the assistant, who scowled and leapt up, shooting a dirty look at the German's back.

Word had got around on the multi-lingual grapevine that the trio would soon be making a fortune presenting *Choukiczee the Chinese Giant* in the theatres and halls of Australia and New Zealand. The German spruiked his protégé to any of the saloon passengers who came near, handing out leaflets and exhorting them to attend the levees in Sydney and Melbourne, where they would hear amazing stories and see the giant splendid in the elegant silks of a Chinese mandarin.

"According to that big talking German, Zhou is seven inches taller than Chang," Yunlong said, "and the tallest, stoutest, and heaviest man in the world. A living Colossus—whatever that is."

"We get to see for free," Hok said with a cheeky grin.

"We are fortunate," Yunlong agreed. "But that foreign man has been talking up big. He says the Nian rebels captured him east of Shanghai about ten years ago and forced him to fight with them."

"Unlucky."

"Yes. But then he befriended the giant Zhou. Together they plotted their escape from the rebel camp and managed to get back to Chefoo safely."

"So, the German got lucky in the end?"

Yunlong laughed. "A tall story. I don't believe it. As if the rebels would have let that rich foreigner live. Their motto was, 'Kill the rich and aid the poor.'"

"Still, here they are on their way to Australia," Hok said looking over at the giant who sat, knees bent up to his chin, contemplating the watery horizon with a mournful look on his smooth face. Then the German came over, tapped the giant on the shoulder and pointed to a speck on the horizon. Over to the right where the blue of the sea met the blue of the sky was a white mound.

"A white whale?" said Hok straining his eyes to see.

"No—it must be an island," Yunlong said as they drew near. A few tufts of palm trees sprouted from the white whale-like hump.

Before long soft green mounds of multiple islands looped across the sea like a dragon's tail. Dense green bush ran down to the turquoise waters; here and there white strips of sandy beaches vied with the white fluffy clouds above. A few smoke plumes drifted in the southerly breeze from one of the islands but there were no other signs of habitation—no buildings peeked out between the exuberant green leaves, and no people could be seen.

They rounded yet another island. Before them lay a looping crescent of sand, and behind the bay, to the southwest, the land stretched to infinity.

"Australia!" The murmur travelled like a continuous rolling wave around the ship.

TWO

6: Hok

Boggo Road Gaol, Brisbane, Australia: 1960s

They hustled my body away in a cart, but my soul stayed tethered to the place where I drew my last breath, this wretched gaol.

Time has passed—much time. Every day men come with their picks and shovels, and every night there is less of the old gaol left. The noise and dust are unbearable. When darkness falls the other doomed souls roam around screaming, moaning—unsettled, uneasy, lost.

All that is left of number one cell block is a pile of rubble, but we have nowhere else to go. I prowl around hungry to escape.

7: Coffee with Christian

Brisbane: July, 2019

It was dark outside the office and light rain had turned the streets a shimmering black. I stared back at the computer screen and shuffled an image up a few millimetres, then nudged the text across just a fraction more. It had to be brilliant—exceptional even. The final draft was due in less than a week's time. The place was so quiet I jumped when the phone rang and looked around guiltily. But no one else was there, just me, alone, sitting in a pool of light, surrounded by shadows. I put Ronnie on loudspeaker, not to waste a second.

"Good news," she said. "Christian is happy to translate the letters. He said he could come over and pick them up if you like. He lives not far from you, near Brunswick Street. When will you be home?"

"I don't have time," I told her, hand on mouse. "I'm busy. Next week is the deadline for the final draft."

But Ronnie can be pretty persuasive.

"OK," I agreed reluctantly, "What about Saturday?"

The apartment buzzer sounded right on time. With a name like Christian, I had imagined some middle-aged pale nerd with a PhD in Asian Studies—balding maybe.

"Hi," he said. "You must be Eirene, Ronnie … your mother, she talks a lot about you."

Ushering him in, I ducked my head to cover up my surprise.

He was young, slim, and dressed in inner-city black. Dead straight black hair, undercut at the back and gathered in a loose ponytail on top. And he was Chinese. Well, that actually made sense—for an Asian translator.

He could have looked effeminate—with that hair—but the rounded shape of his face and the curve of his slightly broad nose exuded a sense of strength and reliability. Not that that impressed me. I'd had it up to here with good-looking guys. Too vain, too self-obsessed, and who wants to look like the dowdy half of a couple. And Christian? Who calls their kid Christian?

"It's all there, in that box," I said, waving in the direction of the side table.

"Nice! It's a scholar's box, pretty old too." His black eyes looked steadily back at me from under two perfectly arched eyebrows. He bent down to stroke Celeste, who had woven herself around his legs.

"She likes you."

He smiled.

"How old? The box," I asked.

"Could be a couple of hundred years."

"A scholar's box. So it's the olden times equivalent of a student's backpack?" I said. I don't think my brain was working quite right at this stage. I was a little thrown by his appearance.

"No, not that kind of scholar." He ran his hand slow and smooth over the top of the box, as if asking it to share its secrets with him. "A scholar was a *shi dafu*, a civil servant of the emperor."

"A pen pusher?"

"Kind of. The favoured ones became court officials, and the rest were sent to far flung parts of the empire as administrators."

"Banished?"

"Uh-huh. Quite a few got into political strife and were exiled even further into the rural wilds. They often ended their days as drunken poets."

He turned the box around and we studied it together.

"Yes. I'm pretty sure it was part of a scholar's belongings, used to store and transport all his important objects," he said. "You ought to get it appraised. Should be worth a bit. It's strange how it's wound up here … in Australia … in Brisbane."

"Even stranger when you see what's in it!" I moved the box onto the table, opened the lid and lifted the board between the front opening and the side wall of the top section.

Look what's in here," I said, pointing to the bottom compartment.

"May I?" he said. I nodded and he lifted out the papers and letters. He picked up the pendant.

"This looks like a good luck talisman; it has the dragon and phoenix pattern on it."

I prayed he wouldn't give me a lecture on the meaning of the symbols on the talisman—I hate information overload. It worked. He didn't. I made a mental note to look it up myself.

He read the clippings, smiled a little at the photos from the top section, then examined the letters.

"It looks like these were all posted from Australia to Amoy. It's called Xiamen now. It's an island city in South Fujian. The foreigners called it Amoy because that was the way the name sounded in the local dialect. … My family came to Malaysia from that area way back when, and they still speak Hokkien, or a form of it."

"Right." I nodded, but I had no idea what Hokkien was … I would look that up later too.

"Do you speak any Chinese?" he asked.

No getting around that one. "No," I confessed. "Frank, our father, never spoke it at home. We learnt to say a few things to our grandparents, Jimmy and Mei, but it was hardly a conversation. Bad huh?"

Feeling like an imposter I changed the subject, "How about I make us some coffee, I *can* do that."

"Thanks, that'd be good." His voice was soft with just the hint of a residual accent.

"Coffee coming up then. How do you take it?"

"A latte if you can, otherwise just a flat white would be fine."

He shuffled the letters and gave me an earnest look, "You know, don't feel bad, Chinese is a bloody hard language to learn. Someone once said that learning Chinese is a five-year lesson in humility. According the American academic, Moser, what that really means is that after five years your Chinese will still be abysmal, but at least you will have thoroughly learnt humility.

"No wonder I've never tried."

"And then, even if you did learn to speak standard Mandarin Chinese, you still wouldn't be able to understand Cantonese, or Hokkien, or Hokkla, or a lot of other dialects."

"Really?"

"But the characters, they all mean the same thing, doesn't matter what dialect you speak. The words just sound different when they are spoken."

"Interesting."

I busied myself making coffee, wishing all the while that I was more skilled as a barista. Our espresso machine was fearsome and Dee's domain for anything more complicated than my usual long black. For some reason I wanted to impress, so with a bit of luck, and a lot of concentration, I managed a glass of my best attempt at a caffè latte.

"Nice table," he said, leaving the quality of the coffee undefined.

"Isn't it. Recycled tallowwood. Cost a fortune but we love it."

"We?"

"Me and my sister, Dee. We came into a bit of money after our grandparents Jimmy and Mei died, and we pooled resources to get all of this," I said throwing my arms about.

Christian's eyes roved around the apartment, taking stock. I wasn't offended. It's something I do myself, a surreptitious look to check out the books on the shelf, the pictures on the wall, and the state of the kitchen. You can tell so much about a person by the objects they surround themselves with. His eyes lingered for a while on another expensive purchase, a striking aboriginal painting of a crescent moon and a star, shining out from a dark background.

"I bought that five years ago," I answered his unasked question, "when I landed my first major project. It's a Mabel Juli. Probably couldn't afford it now, she was not as well known then."

"Warnum? East Kimberly?"

"Yes, it's a moon dreaming story of forbidden and unrequited love. I like her brother's work too, Rusty Peters."

His eyes moved to a rather moody black and white photograph I'd taken of Ronnie, her face half hidden by a curtain of hair.

"One of yours?"

"Yes, I'm trying to get a portfolio together for an exhibition. That'll probably be in it."

"Great. Can you send me an invite."

"Sure, but it mightn't be for some time, Will keeps me busy. Will, my boss."

"You're a graphic artist, right?"

"Yes. Studio three thirty-three. We mostly do high end art publications. Promotional handouts, books to accompany exhibitions, auction catalogues, that sort of thing. Actually, I need to get back to the office this afternoon. Deadline next week."

"Sure. Do you mind if I take the letters?" he asked. "I'll bring them back with the translations. I'd rather take some time over it."

"No problem."

I gathered up the letters and handed them over. Christian shuffled through them and then, just before he left, he handed one back to me. "I know you can manage this one, it's in English."

"OK, thanks. I'll get to it." I tossed the letter on to the table, grabbed my bag and followed him out the door.

The office was dark and silent when I locked the door four hours later. And so was the apartment when I arrived back home, dark and silent. No Dee—just her denim jacket draped over the back of a chair. She'd been home then.

The letter was lying on the table where I'd left it. I studied the envelope. It was sturdier and larger than the ones Christian took away with him. The stamp was for two shillings and sixpence, it was reddish orange and postmarked Brisbane. A banner across the top of the stamp read Queensland and in the middle was a rather stylish oval portrait of what must have been a young Queen Victoria, wearing a crown, some seriously heavy drop earrings, and a simple looking necklace around her elegant neck—probably plain old diamonds, worth a fortune. The handwritten address read:

Tee Ai–ling, Kang–thau Village, Amoy.
c/o the Rev. H. Carmichael,
London Missionary Society,
Amoy, China

Frank had said never mind about the stuff in the box, and maybe he was right. So far the contents had been pretty depressing. A murder and a hanging. Did I really want to read the letter? But what the hell, might as well get it over with I thought, and pulled out the thin sheet of paper.

17.6.1886

Dear Miss Tee Ai–ling,

I have asked the Rev. Carmichael to kindly deliver this letter to you and trust that he will explain all that is in it, painful though it may be. Your brother, Hok Siong, asked me to write to you. Unfortunately, I must now pass on the sad news that he has passed away. Please accept my humble condolences.

So, the amulet and the newspaper clippings must have originally
been enclosed in the letter to Tee Ai-ling in China. And it seems
likely that Mr John Holland was the correspondent to the Courier
pleading for further inquiry into the case. But what did any of this
have to do with our family? Why was all this stuff in the box. It was
a horrible story. Hanging is a barbaric way to die. I shook my head
… must stop thinking about it.

The door buzzer jolted me back into the immediate present—
the pizza I'd ordered. After I'd eaten more than enough, I poured
another glass of pinot, and reached for my laptop. The challenge of
a mystery to be solved was taking precedence. I wasn't my mother's
daughter for nothing. I needed to figure out who the mysterious Mr
John Holland was, and why all that stuff was in the box.

I typed "John Holland Cristal St"—nothing. "John Holland

Dullbydilla"—nothing. Then "John Holland China." I scrolled down and came across: *Travels in the Celestial Empire, or Adventures in China: Holland, J. H. (John Harold)*. The link was to a book published in 1889 in London. About the right era, I thought, but was it the right John Holland? I clicked on full view and searched through the chapter headings *Foochow, Kulangsu, Amoy, Swatow, Hong Kong* then some more general titles, *Temples and Religion, The Chinese Disposition, Modes of Transport, Emigration,* and then, further down, *A Man from Amoy.* That could be interesting.

"What are you doing up so late?" Dee bounced in and I closed the laptop quickly.

"Just looking something up."

Dee was a social butterfly at night, but by day her life was pretty serious. She worked for the Public Prosecutions office as a lawyer. Some of the cases she had to work on were horrific—no wonder she had to balance her life with a different persona on the weekends.

"I just had the best time. Patrick and I went to … ." And on she went, my unstoppable sister.

She didn't ask about the letter lying open on the table, and I wasn't ready to tell her about the contents of the pandora's box that Frank had bequeathed me, not yet anyway.

Next morning Dee and I were lingering over a rare Sunday morning breakfast together when my phone rang. Ronnie again.

"I wondered … what would you like to do for your birthday?"

"I don't know. I haven't given it much thought. Nothing."

"It's your thirtieth."

"I know. Not sure I want to celebrate that."

"Oh, but you should. Shall we have family dinner here, or at your place?" And with that Ronnie took charge. I reluctantly agreed to a birthday dinner at our place in Brisbane. Ronnie and Frank would stay the night.

"What's up?" said Dee, a hefty slice of toast and marmalade poised in front of her mouth.

"Ronnie. Ringing about my birthday."

"The big three oh?"

"She's taken over again. We're having it here. Next minute she'll be telling us who to invite and what to cook!"

"Stand up for yourself Sis."

"Why does she have to be so quintessentially perfect all the time … and so clever … and so controlling?"

"Come on … you know you take after her."

"I do not. How can you say that? She makes me feel so inferior."

"True. You are inferior." She had the grace to grin.

"Oh, touché! Well, I probably am. But I wish people wouldn't keep saying, *Your mother is so wonderful*. I hate it."

"Come on, Ronnie is Ronnie. She can't help it."

"When people say that to me, *Yes, yes she is*, I say. But what I think is…yes, she is wonderful, and clever, and smart. But I could have done with less perfection, and more … "

"More what?" Dee looked bemused.

"Remember when we were kids? Why did our offerings for the school cake stall have to be the very best?"

"They were, weren't they?"

"Would it have mattered if we'd done the icing by ourselves and got it a bit smudged? We could have messed around, and stuffed things up. We could have had fun, laughed about the icing all over our faces and the wonky cake. Frank would have said, *I bet it will taste delicious anyway. Someone will buy* it. And if no one did, he would have."

"But that's the way Ronnie is, Sis, a perfectionist to the core. You have to get over it. OK, I'm off. Meeting some friends for lunch. Want to come?"

"Thanks, but no. I've promised myself a day of leisure. No more thinking about work. No more pressure. I'm going to take it easy."

"Leave you to it then."

Winter weather in Brisbane can be glorious and it was too good to stay inside, so I took myself out for a brisk jog. As I pounded along, I couldn't help my mind returning to the letter and the story in the box. Were we related to Ai-ling? And to her brother? The box belonged to our grandfather, Jimmy, so the relationship would have to be from his side of the family, not Granny Mei's. I wracked my brains to see if I could dredge up anything from the past, from our visits to the grandparents. Nothing came to mind. For a moment I was back there, in that rather ugly little brick house in New Farm where yeasty baking aromas intermingled with the sweet earthy smell of the plaited strings of onions hanging on the back porch.

As soon as we arrived Jimmy would take us out to the back garden to eat peas straight out of the pod. I can still see him standing there in his Chesty Bond singlet, sturdy and stolid looking despite his saggy-skinned ageing body and his floppy mane of white hair. He was king of his domain, pointing out rows of feathery carrot tops and the bean pole tepees, all running straight as a die between furrows of black earth.

"This one *peh-chhai*, white cab-bagee, this one *ang-chhai-thau*, red *chhai-thau*, car-rot," he would say pointing out his favourites. Birds flocked in as he tilled the soil. They crowded the fruit tree branches, swooping down, hustling, and squawking as soon as they saw a worm.

After admiring Jimmy's garden, we were hurried inside to sit on plastic stools, to sip tea and eat Jimmy's pastries while Granny Mei regaled us with another of her funny stories. She always laughed uproariously at the punchline. Her broken English was no barrier, mostly we understood her perfectly, and if we didn't, we laughed anyway.

Now I had two mystery people, Tee Hok Siong and Tee Ai-ling. Were they related to us? Too late now to ask Jimmy and Mei. And I didn't think the usual route of searching for our ancestry on-line was going to work. Even if the records existed, I couldn't even recognise the characters of my own surname, let alone theirs.

But first another challenge was coming up, I had to survive my thirtieth birthday.

8: Australia

Tee Hok Siong: Australia, 1876

"Cooktown next. Maybe one more night," said Yunlong. His excitement at reaching Australia sent Hok into despair; he wished he was going to the goldfields too. Instead he would have to travel on alone.

Night fell, and they anchored in the dark sea between an island and the mainland. Sleep did not come easy, and Hok woke reluctantly to the clanging, grinding sound of the anchors being raised and the engines starting up. They were barely afloat before the anchor was dropped again in a small cove. Somerset Bay, their first stop in Australia. Scattered in the cleared land around the bay were a few two-story buildings and a number of huts. There was a flurry of activity on the shore as boats were readied and launched. As they came near Hok was surprised to see some of the crew were blacker than anyone he had ever seen before.

Four passengers boarded, all first class, the lone woman gathered up her skirts before she made her ungainly climb up the ship's ladder. The steamer's crew lowered some ten crates of cargo into the boats below and that was it. By the time seven bells sounded the RMS Singapore was already well down the coast.

The hubbub of excitement on board swelled, but the afternoon sun was low in the sky even before they managed to reach Cooktown. Yunlong had to wait out another night at anchor before his adventure could begin.

Hok slumped on the rail as a watery morning sun rose above

the horizon behind him. He watched the hordes from Hong Kong gather in high spirits further down the deck, buoyed up by the promise of riches for the taking. Clutching their meagre belongings nearly two hundred hopefuls clambered down the sides of the ship to the waiting rowboats for the two-mile trip to shore. Amongst them was a jubilant dragon, Yunlong, bound for the Palmer River goldfields.

At Townsville they offloaded more cargo and a few passengers. Below decks the steerage quarters were more bearable now that the numbers were thinning and though Hok missed Yunlong's friendly face, he began to look forward to arriving in the English Queen's land. His optimism rose when he discovered that two of those left on board, Tan Wei-ting and Lee Kong, were engaged to be shepherds on the same farm station as he was. It would be a leap into the unknown, all that any of them knew was that they were going out west and that they should disembark at a place called Brisbane. But at least he wouldn't be alone.

They lined up to have their heads shaved. The barber was from Hong Kong and hoped to start up a business in Sydney. Somehow, he had managed to find a pail of hot water and, wielding his cut-throat razor with expertise, he shaved off the black stubbles of hair surrounding their queues. Their foreheads were restored to a burnished smoothness.

The thick squally weather came back long before the ship reached Morton Bay, and worse, below decks one of the passengers bound for Sydney had dysentery. He rolled around groaning and clutching his stomach. Hok Siong couldn't wait to leave the stink of the ship behind. But the bay was heaving. The ship anchored but had to stand by until the afternoon before the sea calmed enough for a handsome little paddle steamer to come safely alongside, carrying with it the health and customs officers. Hok watched the government officials warily. But all was well, and Hok, Wei-ting and Kong grabbed their bundles and clambered down the ladder onto the deck of the river boat. They had barely settled before they heard the clanking sound of the RMS Singapore's anchor being winched up. Too much time had been lost with the bad weather.

The paddle steamer chugged past a few low swampy islands before the bay transformed itself into a looping watercourse. Hok scanned the banks of the broad brown river; mangroves lined the water's edge and behind were unfamiliar tall trees with dull silvery green leaves. A few more bends and it all changed; swathes of vines hung jungle-like from lush tropical trees just like the tangled vegetation in the hills behind his home village. It was thirty days since he had left his family behind in Amoy. When would he see them all again?

Over on the right bank a lone man in a horse and cart jogged along a dusty road. Small buildings appeared amidst the undergrowth. At a curve in the river a slate roofed house stretched along the top of a hill. Its elegant and generously wide verandahs looked out over a scattering of trees on a grassy slope which flowed gently down towards the riverbank. They rounded another bend, and the trees thinned. A few boats chugged past. Soon a jumble of city buildings and the masts of sailing ships at anchor closed in around them. One more bend and the steamer came to a halt.

A crowd of people stood dockside. Hok's anxious eyes scanned the throng. Standing back a little was a slight figure with slicked down black hair, sporting a striped waistcoat and a pencil behind his ear. Hok could just make out some of the hastily written marks on the chalkboard the man was holding—the familiar characters of his name: 鄭 福 祥. Tee Hok Siong. Once on dry land Hok and the others hustled through the crowd until they were standing next to the man. He introduced himself as Mr Bauer's number two.

"Mis-ta Bow-er," he enunciated slowly and rather loudly. Hok had no idea what the man's following words meant, but reassured by the sight of his name on the chalkboard he stood silently waiting with the others. They held tight onto their scanty possessions—

Wei-ting, like Hok, had a cloth bundle strung swag-like on his back, while Kong had a woven bamboo basket bound with rope dangling off his shoulder pole—and when they had all been accounted for by the immigration officials, Mr Bauer's number two led the three of them not far along the dock to a warehouse.

"My name is Mr Olsen, Mr Johnnie Olsen," he said, as he ushered them past a wall of old sacks in a corner of the big shed. Behind the wall were five men, unmistakably countrymen. Three were sitting cross-legged in a circle playing cards, while the other two lay in hammocks, slung between timber pillars. At one end was a makeshift kitchen, a bag of rice and some vegetables.

"You sleep here. Wait for me. I come back," said Mr Olsen. "I'll take you three to get your outfits tomorrow. Those others," and he waved a hand in the direction of the five, "they're off to try their luck in the tin mines. Six-Mile Swamp, that's where they're going."

One of the card players looked up long enough to notice the bewilderment on the faces of the three new inhabitants of the shed and was kind enough to explain what Olsen was saying.

Next morning Mr Olsen led them to Jackson's store in Edward Street for their new outfits. They viewed the unfamiliar clothes with suspicion. They would have preferred to keep on wearing their own soft shoes, loose pants, and tunic, but there was no choice. Hok was given a blue shirt, moleskin trousers, a leather belt, boots, and a cabbage-tree hat. Payment was to come from his future wages, of course. He wound his queue around his head, crammed the hat on top, and followed the others out. He felt stiff, uncomfortable, and hot. Under his arms he carried a bundle of his old clothes, together with a new waistcoat, a jacket, and a blanket.

Walking back to their quarters near the river they marvelled at the passers-by. Women sailed along in their bell-shaped skirts. Some were dressed in silks rivalling that of the grandest mandarin. A young man strutted by in a buff-coloured outfit, a silver topped cane in his hand and a fine straw hat on his head. Nearer the docks a rough looking gang lounged outside a public house. The men's shouts were unintelligible, but their jeering laughter made the meaning clear. Heads down, Hok and the other two scurried past. They had arrived in an exciting and different land—a distant part of the British Empire—the colony of Queensland, but not one of the newcomers was curious or brave enough to venture out beyond the warehouse again. They would wait.

Just after dawn the following day Mr Olsen led them through the empty streets to the Brisbane Terminus. They walked through the fresh red brick arches of the newly built station to the railway platform as a train drew into the station dragging four carriages behind it. The big black engine hissed and whistled. Smoke ballooned in clouds around them. It was a frightening sight. Never had they seen such a thing, a great black breathing iron monster. But they had come this far, there was no turning back. Mr Olsen bundled the three of them into a compartment and there they sat, straight backed and wide awake, either in anticipation or fear, their bundles by their side.

"Do not move, do not get off, do not talk to anyone. Stay on the train, maybe ten hours. The afternoon sun will be going down in the sky. When you get to the end of the line, that is Dalby. You get to Dalby; you will see Mr Callan. Remember that, Mis-ta Kal-lan. Mis-ta Kal-lan, don't forget. Show him your papers, he will look after you the rest of the way. Savvy?"

With the help of Olsen's elaborate hand gestures, they managed to understand most of what he had said. They would not move; they would wait till the sun was low in the sky and the train reached the end of the line.

The train gradually climbed to the upland downs away from the coast. After five hours the view opened out. Below them was a rolling sea of green, and in the distance a string of hills fading to a misty blue. The small bundles of left over rice from last night's meal filled their stomachs but did little to ease their anxiety. But gradually nervousness gave way to resignation as the train chuffed along. Eyes glazed over as the unfamiliar empty landscape unfolded, heads slumped backwards, forwards, and onto the next man's shoulder. At last a squeal of brakes and great cloud of steam announced their arrival at Dalby.

Sure enough, Mr Callan was there waiting on the platform. He led the three of them, by now starving, to an eatery nearby. The owner was Chinese, and the food was good. After they had eaten, they followed Mr Callan around the corner to a bullock dray piled high with provisions bound for various stations along the way.

"We can't waste good daylight hours," said Mr Callan, even though the sun was already dropping low on the horizon. And so they set off for their first camp half an hour away, a small clearing by the side of the road. The eight bullocks were unyoked and hobbled, and soon the flames of a small fire leapt from the midst of a pile of blackened stones. Mr Callan's sidekick threw them a sheet of stiff canvas to lie on and a few blankets. There they lay, Hok, Wei-ting and Kong, staring up at the huge expanse of sky and listening to strange animal howls in the dark distance.

"Dingos," they heard Mr Callan say to his companion.

At daybreak they woke to a cold, unfamiliar frost, and the constant chattering of swarms of small brown birds swooping here and there overhead. They helped round up the bullocks and harness them to the dray, and on they went.

The nights were cold, and the days were hot and dusty. It had been a wet autumn though, and the occasional dip in the track was still a boggy mess. Hok and the others lent a shoulder to give the bullocks a hand heaving the cart out of the mud.

They marvelled at the strange animals who paused to observe them, standing tall and still before bounding away. Flocks of pink and grey birds shot out from the silvery leaves of the black-barked trees, disturbed by the thumps and clunks and snorts of the lumbering bullocks. Between patches of green grass, the odd clump of trees seemed to promise shade, but the sparse leaves gave only the faintest semblance of respite from the cloudless sky.

Hok listened to campfire stories of spearings, and thefts, and murders, making out a few words here and there. One night they saw a few shadowy figures on the opposite bank of the creek. Mr Callan looked alarmed, "Blackfellas," he said, and stood like a statue, staring into the darkness with his rifle ready. Nothing had come of it, but the incident gave birth to a nameless dread—the fear of a hidden danger lurking in the shadows.

They travelled on and slowly the relentless dull-green landscape gave way to dusty Mulga scrub interspersed with patches of red dirt. Bounding the track were piles of cut branches stripped bare of their leaves. Before camp each night the three of them helped cut more piles of Mulga for the bullocks. In the barren landscape it was often the bullock's only sustenance. Some didn't make it. Occasionally they came across the hump of a dead beast laying right where it had fallen, surrounded by flies, and a sickening odour.

The endlessly flat landscape stretched out in all directions until, at last, after six long days, a hilly mass emerged through the distant haze—Mount Abundance. Without a doubt, if only they had known what the word meant, all three of them, Wei-ting, Kong, and Hok, would have hoped it meant an abundance of good fortune for them.

9: The Celestial Empire

My phone flashed. The message was brief: *Finished. We need to talk. Tomorrow at 3? Your place? C.*

Matching his style, I typed: *Sure. See you then, E.*

"You look like the Cheshire cat. What's up?" said Will peering over the piles on his desk.

"Nothing," I said, not sure why I was smiling. Christian was obviously not my type.

Friday was always busy, and it was late when I got home and opened my laptop. It had been more than a week since I'd read the letter Christian had left for me, but I hadn't read John Holland's book. I found the link I'd bookmarked at the chapter entitled *A Man from Amoy* and started reading. At least I'd have something to add to the conversation the next day.

TRAVELS IN THE CELESTIAL EMPIRE
or ADVENTURES IN CHINA

CHAPTER 14: A MAN FROM AMOY

Back home in Queensland, Australia, in the summer of 1886, I happened to be out west in the country town of Roma, on business. Everywhere was abuzz with news of a murder trial. I was at a bit of a loose end as I had finished my concerns there and my railway train to Brisbane would not leave until the next day. I resolved to attend the trial. After a hearty breakfast I made my way up to the Roma Courthouse.

This could be the trial of Tee Hok Siong. Interesting.

At the front steps a large crowd jostled around eyeing the still closed door. A great number of the crowd were Chinese. Amongst them I saw my old friend Tim Long Sing, the publican of the Roma Hotel, and Yang Ben Sue who owns a general store here. The door opened, and, after a certain amount of pushing and shoving, we made our way into the courtroom. I settled myself onto one of the wooden benches in the front.

On trial was Tee Hok Siong, a cook from Mr Falconer's bore site at the Black Waterhole, Dulbydilla. He was accused of murdering Charlie Ah Fook, a baker.

It was Hok Siong then! Good old John Holland. Let's see what he says:

After the jury were seated the prisoner was led in handcuffed. Though he appeared wretched, and was obviously unsophisticated, he did have an honest look to him.

Over the hum of the fans swirling above I could hear murmurs from the room "Min-nahn ren" and "Ha-mun ren." Having spent some time in China I knew this meant a man from Amoy in Fuh-kien province. People think that John Chinaman speaks one language, but I know for a fact that the Peking fellow cannot understand one from Amoy and one from Canton cannot understand either of them. Here in the colony of Queensland a great deal of the Chinamen come from Canton, but not the accused.

I have had the pleasure of visiting Amoy on tea business on a number of occasions in the past and I found it to be a most vibrant and energetic place. It is one of the five treaty ports and the first major port north after Hong Kong. From the moment I arrived I formed a fa-

*vourable impression of the people. As many have remarked, the Amoy
coolies are hardworking and willing to work for small remuneration.
Great numbers were encouraged to take their chances in Australia
during the 1850s and onwards. They were sought after to work on the
sheep stations and in the sugar plantations there. Others took their
chances on the goldfields.*

*The trial was in its second day, and the jury filed back in after
being locked up overnight. Mr Forbes was announced as representing
the defendant. He said the Crown had just a few moments ago employed his assistance for the prisoner and he had not even had time to
read over the evidence from the previous day.*

*An interpreter was sworn in the customary manner with celes-
tials, by blowing out a match. It seemed that the court had had diffi-
culty finding not only a defence lawyer but also an interpreter.*

It seemed a bit odd, no legal representation and no interpreter till
the second day. And blowing out a match, I hadn't heard of that
before. But hunger overcame me before I could read anymore. I
scrabbled around in the cupboards, found some fettuccini, and put
a pot on to boil. Pasta it would have to be. I went back to the book.

*The arresting constable was re-called for cross examination and
Mr Forbes, for the defence, asked about the evidence given the day
before on the subject of the supposed confession of the prisoner. Constable Kelly had repeated the prisoner's words as "If me knew you
were after me, I would have cleared out when I done it." Mr Forbes
suggested that the prisoner had meant, "Supposing I done that, I clear
out." The suggested interpretation was denied by the constable.*

*Not having been in attendance the previous day I was at a loss
as to what to think, but I did form the firm opinion that, whatever the
actual words Hok Siong said, he was more likely to have meant he
hadn't cleared out, because he hadn't committed the crime. His state-*

ment should have been viewed in the light of his imperfect knowledge of English.

Exactly. That sounds feasible I thought. But hadn't I read those words before? I found the clipping from the Toowoomba paper. The same phrase. So the correspondent to the Courier had to be Mr John Holland and that was why his name was scrawled on the top.

There were several other witnesses who seemed to contradict both themselves and Constable Kelly on a few points. This, however, was not explored by Mr Forbes and at five o'clock Mr Forbes addressed the jury for the defence.

He made the point that, when asked who shot him, Charlie Ah Fook was in great pain and may have been confused. It had been a dark night, and visibility was low. He added that in the dark all Chinamen look the same, and that, "They are something like cats, which in the dark are always grey in appearance."

I found this argument rather weakened the case to any thinking man, for it seemed that there were only seven or eight Chinamen in the town, and they would have all known each other.

What kind of defence was that? Like cats in the dark? Weird.

"What do you think about that, Celeste?" I said to the fluffy lump dozing on the couch. She didn't answer.

Steam was billowing out from the pot on the stove. I threw in the pasta, smashed two cloves of garlic and chopped some parsley. A splash of olive oil into my favourite little frying pan, then the garlic, a half a teaspoon of red pepper flakes and I was ready. Fettuccine, garlic, chilli, parsley and a sprinkle of parmesan. I plonked the bowl down in front of my laptop.

Cats in the dark—what's next?

Mr Forbes said that the Canton Chinese had a hatred against the Amoy men and that the trial ought to be looked upon more as a persecution than a prosecution. He claimed there was, in fact, every probability that it was a trumped-up charge. He urged the jury not to be carried away by any feelings of malice, but to review the evidence with intelligence, and come to the conclusion that however strong the case might appear against the prisoner there were missing links which would justify them in acquitting him of the heinous crime with which he was charged.

The prosecutor had nothing to add, and his Honour gave his summation to the jury. Ten minutes later they returned their verdict—Hok Siong was guilty.

That was it then. Sentenced to death.

I rubbed my eyes. There was more to read, but I'd had enough for one night.

Christian arrived at three the next afternoon. True to the style of his abrupt email, he didn't have much small talk.

"Here. I've printed out the translations," he said, pulling a few papers out of his bag and handing them over to me.

"Thanks."

"The letters are from Hok Siong to his sister, Tee Ai-ling. They look like they've been written by a scribe—the text and the signature are in a different hand. I'm assuming he could write his name at least. A few have stamps on them, some not. They may have been sent back with others returning to China.

"Any clues about a link to our family?" I asked.

"No. The first letter is dated 1876 and is postmarked from Roma. He says he has arrived in Australia and is working on a sheep station—the trip from Hong Kong was rough, and he was glad to arrive in Brisbane. The others are brief, but he sounds miserable. Long hours, and very hot, he says. Then in the last letter he says he hopes to be coming home soon."

"So, nothing?"

"No. ... how did you get on with the other letter?"

"Good. It was from a Mr John Holland, and written after the execution. It was sent to Tee Ai-ling via the London Missionary Society in Amoy—telling her that her brother was dead. He said that he thought an injustice had been done. The talisman was enclosed, it was all that Hok Siong possessed at the end, no money, no nothing."

"A well-travelled talisman. Hok must have brought it with him to Australia, then it went back in the letter to Ai-ling, then back here again in the box."

"It seems a bit cruel, but he also enclosed the newspaper clippings in the letter."

"So that's why they're in the box."

"I guess so. ... I looked him up—that John Holland."

"Find anything?" Christian asked.

"He wrote a book about his travels in China. And I know it's him because one of the chapters is about Hok Siong."

"Really?"

"It turns out that this Mr John Holland was in Roma at the time of Hok Siong's trial. He took an interest because he had business dealings in Amoy and knew the area well."

"Send me the link and I'll have a read."

He accepted my offer of a glass of wine.

"I really like your apartment. Next to the river too, couldn't be better," he said, looking around.

"Thanks. It helped to have had industrious and frugal grandparents. We love it."

He stood silhouetted by the light from the window behind him, looking, just for that moment, like he was from some ancient dynasty.

"I'm curious about why all this stuff is in the box," he said.

His dark eyes regarded me from the shadows of his backlit

silhouette. It was one of those moments when I itch to whip out my camera, but of course I didn't. I mentally framed the shot—Christian and the window asymmetrically on the right and the brick wall taking up almost half the frame. A tricky exposure.

"It's got to be related to your family, surely?" he said.

I shook my head. "Maybe. But I don't have any idea what it's all about."

"Pity."

"Except … we know that Jimmy carted the box from Saigon."

"To Brisbane?"

"No, the family didn't come here till later. To Darwin… and then here."

I picked up the family photograph.

"There's Frank … Dad. He's the smallest. And there's Jimmy. He was a baker, originally apprenticed to a Frenchman in Saigon. He used to make the most amazing pastries for us when we were kids. His bread was the best too! We were introduced to *Bahn Mi*, chilli and all, from a young age. Somehow I didn't make the connection, *Bahn Mi* and Vietnam until Frank told me recently. Well, what would we know, we were just hungry kids."

"What do you think prompted the move to Darwin?"

"Apparently not long after Jimmy and Mei were married the French started to pull out at the end of the Indochina War. The future was uncertain, so when Jimmy heard about a bakery for sale in Darwin, they took the opportunity to escape.

"After Cyclone Tracy Jimmy and Mei moved to Brisbane with our dad, their youngest, so he could go to university here. They always said Frank was the clever one."

"That talisman really is well-travelled then. From China to here with Hok Siong, then back to China in John Holland's letter, then to Saigon in the box … "

"Then to Darwin, and back here again," I said.

He stood silent for a moment. "But what part of China did

Jimmy's family come from?" he asked. "Was it Amoy—Xiamen? Because that's where the letters were sent to. And that's where Hok Siong must have come from."

"I'll ask Frank. But maybe Jimmy inherited the box from someone else, and over the years our family's stuff was just piled on top of someone else's history."

"You can't escape the past," he said on his way out. "It's immutable."

I rolled my eyes heavenward but said nothing.

10: Arriving

Tee Hok Siong: Queensland, June 1876

The bullocks huffed misty gusts into the morning air as they left the campsite and headed west.

"Only a few more hours. We'll be there around midday—sun up top," Mr Callan announced pointing at the sky directly above him.

After six gruelling days along the bullock track from Dalby, Hok welcomed the promise of a relief from the miles upon miles of emptiness. This was a strange country indeed, where were the people? Behind him the rising sun began to lighten the sky. Its hidden glow burnished the edges of the diminishing dark silhouette of Mount Abundance.

At last, there it was, the homestead. They had arrived. In a strange quirk of fate, at almost precisely the same time, the first sod was turned for the extension of the railway line west of Dalby. Though Hok had no way of knowing it, that railway line was to lead him to misfortune. But now, unaware of anything but the present, he looked around in eager anticipation.

A rough log fence surrounded a conglomeration of tin roofed buildings, some no more than shacks. In the centre was the homestead, sturdily built with shady verandahs all round, and encircled by another fence. Inside the fence was an oasis of green grass, a few trees, and some squat rounded bushes. Striding down the path towards them came two *ang-moh*. One of the men took charge of Wei-ting and Kong and led them off to shepherd the large flocks of sheep on the station. If they were lucky, they would learn the art of shearing, then, once they finished their indenture, they could earn big money.

Hok followed the other man to a low-slung building about ten paces behind the homestead—the cookhouse. Inside, moving nimbly from pot to pot, was a small figure with a shiny, sweaty face, and a glossy black pigtail wound close around his head. He was dressed in the same dirty moleskins and blue serge shirt as they all were.

"I am Mr Burton, the station manager, and this is Cookie," said the *ang-moh* to Hok. "You work here. Cookie tell you what to do, show you where to sleep. All good?"

"Good, good," said Cookie, looking up from checking the contents of a steaming pot.

"*Lai, lai, lai*, enter, little brother," he said to Hok.

The station manager walked off, striding across the red dusty expanse separating the cookhouse from the homestead. Hok moved further into the cookhouse. It was little more than a shelter really, open on three sides, but shaded by the overhanging eaves. At one end was a huge hearth, and above it a wide chimney scooping up the smoke and steam from the cast iron pots ranged across the hearth. In the middle of the cookhouse was a battered wooden table with black rough-cut legs, its planked top was bleached white, and its edges smoothed with constant scrubbing. Two younger men stood working away chopping onions and peeling potatoes.

"This one here, him call Jifeng, and here is Chhiong," said Cookie.

Jifeng and Chhiong lifted their perspiring faces in acknowledgement, then lowered their heads back down to their work.

The smell that Hok had noticed when he first set foot on the new land was everywhere. It was an unmistakeable odour that tainted the air; it leaked from the strangers' skin and from the cooking pots. It was the stink of butter eaters, and mutton fat.

"Come, little brother, I show you the bunkhouse," said Cookie.

Dismay hit the fledgling cook with a thump when he saw where they were to sleep. It was no better than an animal shed, the walls were unlined, just rough slabs of timber. Their village house was ten times better than this! At one end, a piece of dirty calico divided Cookie's bunk from the others. The only cheerful touch was a small shrine opposite the central doorway. Mounds of brightly coloured fruit sat on either side of three tattered and worn scrolls pinned to the wall—the three pure ones. Incense and candles were spread out over the red paper cloth covering the table, just like at home.

The day passed in a blur of strangeness until at last it was night. Hok stretched out on his bed, hands behind his head, and contemplated his fate. The rhythmic snores from Jifeng and Chhiong were a comfort, but still he found it hard to sleep. He lifted his head to look out of the nearby window. The full moon cast its white light like frost on the dusty stubbled grass. It reminded him of a poem that Ba used to recite when he'd been drinking and was feeling mournful. Hok lay his head down and thought of home.

At dawn he worked in the garden, tending the vegetables, and then helped prepare the midday meal for the homestead. Every afternoon after a short rest they cooked the evening meal, not just for the family but for the overseers returning from a day in the field, and for the shepherds when they brought a flock in for dipping or docking. Hok learnt to cook roast mutton, cottage pie, chicken pie, beef ragout and many hearty variations of stew for the workers. And Cookie made sure his helpers had good Chinese food, using their allowance of fresh meat and plenty of leafy vegetables from the garden.

Soon he didn't notice the buttery, muttony smell anymore because, by then, he smelt the same. He got used to wearing the strange clothes too, and if it wasn't for the dream of going back to China, he would have cut off his tail. Instead he wound it tight around his head and jammed it under his hat or wrapped it under a loose turban.

Sometimes he was told to smarten up and deliver the meals to the homestead. The manager's wife insisted on calling him John. "Missus, me no John, me Hok Siong," he protested but it did no good. Then he discovered that she called them all John—Cookie, Jifeng, Chhiong—and now, he too was John. John Chinaman.

Best of all Hok loved working in the gardens early in the day with the drops from the morning watering balancing lightly on the leaves. It was good honest work even if, when the sun rose higher, the sweat ran over his brow to lodge, stinging, into his eyes, and the bandana around his neck became drenched. He felt at home, surrounded by the lush green of the vegetables, and the watery sounds of the creek. But outside those few acres it was an alien land.

Once a month, on a rotation, they were allowed to hitch a ride with the provisions dray into Roma. On his first trip Hok asked around for a scribe and managed to find one. Big sister Ai-Ling had been a much better student than he'd been, she could read more than her name, and so it was she he addressed his letter to.

Elder Sister,

Please tell Ba and Ma that I am well. I reached this place six weeks ago. The voyage was rough, and I was glad to arrive safely. This place is a long, long, way from the sea, there are many sheep, and there is much land. The work is not too hard, I work in the kitchen and in the gardens. The cook master is from Tong'an and is kind to me. Sometimes when the shepherds come in there are lots of mouths to feed. Sometimes I am asked to serve the master's family. The dining room gleams with silver but outside is dust, dust, and more dust.

I think of you all.

Your brother, Hok Siong

After a few months Hok became used to life on the station and began to feel more comfortable. Then came a break in the routine.

In September Cookie took Hok and Chhiong with him to another cookhouse, in a far paddock next to the shearing shed. For the few weeks it took to transform their mob of sheep from fat, woolly blobs to skinny, blood flecked, bewildered creatures, shorn of their warm coats, Hok Siong helped to keep the bellies of nearly two hundred shearers, roustabouts, and musterers, full.

Shearing season stretched from August to December in the Maranoa. The shearers were welcome, but everyone was happy to see the backs of them before Christmas. None of the farmers wanted their sheep to suffer with a full fleece in the searing heat of summer, and they all vied for the most favourable weeks between September and October.

"Budgery tucker," Hok heard one day as he cleared the breakfast table. He looked up to see a dark-skinned young man sitting easy on top of his horse. The young man gave the novice cook a thumbs-up and threw out a cheeky grin from under a battered hat as he rode off, loose and elegant on his skittish, side-stepping steed.

There were a few natives working on the station, but Hok mostly observed them from afar. Two girls worked in the homestead, all shy and giggly. And three or four roustabouts were at the beck and call of the manager—they were men really, but the manager called them all boy, "Boy!—Come here boy!" he would call. Sometimes Hok didn't know if he was calling the men or the dogs.

Hok nodded and went on wiping the table clean as the young man rode away.

A few days later, "Good food," the young blackfella said again. "Name Billy. You been here long?"

Hok relaxed and answered. He decided that Billy was probably not about to spear him in the dark.

The shearing was over by mid-December and Cookie's mob returned to the homestead. One evening they were clearing the kitchen after dinner when the sound of a galloping horse broke the silence. Loud shouts came from the yard. It was Billy with one of the

Amoy shepherds slumped on the saddle in front of him.

"Been speared by blackfellas," said Billy, looking just as worried as the rest of them.

With a shock Hok saw that it was Kong. They lifted the injured man down and moved him onto a bed. Cookie cleaned the wound and applied a poultice of strong-smelling herbs, bound in place with strips of cotton bedsheet. They all hoped for the best.

"I ride over to them fellas … check on the sheep," Billy explained. "The sheep make a big row, and I see them two lying there. One, him dead finish, and I bring this other fella here."

Kong had been injured, did that mean that Wei-ting was dead? They had both been so excited about their new life in Australia, when Hok first met them on the ship, and now? Hok shook his head and winced hearing Kong's groans of pain.

Billy downed a big bowl of mutton stew, then walked to the dam with Hok.

"You know them blackfellas?" asked Hok, his voice shaking with anger and despair.

"Na, I didn't see them, but I know they mob. Not my mob. My mob over the other side."

"Why they do this thing?"

"Before, this all their country. They hunt and fish everywhere. Then foreigners come. Fences all over the land. Nowhere left to hunt. They angry, and sad, and hungry. Yeh, they angry."

"But why you here? Why you no stay with your mob," Hok asked.

"They all gone, my mob. Just a few old fellas left. I five years old when the police kill my father. I see it with my own two eyes." Billy held up five fingers and then pointed two fingers to his eyes. He shook his head and thumped his chest, once, twice.

He didn't have the words to communicate the horrors of that day to Hok. If he had, he would have told of the commotion in the camp when a small boy, one of their kin, had been injured. The boy had startled the station manager's horse, and in a fit of anger at being nearly thrown, the manager had jumped down and hurled a stone at the boy, knocking him unconscious.

Billy would have told Hok of the elders' anger at the injury inflicted on the defenceless child, the muttering around the campfire, voices rising and falling, as they discussed the incident. He would have told how his mob gathered near the station as night fell, chanting loudly to make their displeasure known. And how at daybreak twelve troopers from the native police arrived; and how the troopers, their white master, and the stockmen from the station, got together and opened fire on the tribe.

Billy's mother grabbed his hand and dragged him away. But not before he saw his father running for the creek as the mob tried to escape, not before he saw his father's body flung in the air by the blast from one of the guns and heard his mother's grief-stricken keening scream. He could have said all that, but all he said was:

"It was bad time. But all passed now."

Hok was no stranger to vicious retribution, he had seen prisoners suffering, yoked with cangues around their necks, unable to feed themselves. He had heard of many beheadings. But the thought of seeing his own father shot before his eyes horrified him.

"Who shoot Ba… your father?" he asked.

"Maybe white fella, maybe blackfella. Those police blackfella from far away, not belong here, some they badfella too."

Hok could see that Billy was shaken by the spearing of the Chinese shepherd.

"Too much trouble here," Billy said. "Maybe it will be me next. I can make good money bounty hunting—kangaroo, wallaby, pademelon."

"Will you go?" Hok asked.

"Maybe."

And that was the last time he saw Billy. "Gone walkabout," was the only answer Hok ever got when he asked around.

THREE

11: Hok

New Farm, Brisbane, Australia: 1979

Time passes. An eternity. I see a line of bright lights tracing through the darkness. I take courage. I follow the lights down the hill to a wide gently flowing river and cruise along its silvery path.

A cloud of bats surrounds me; on silent wings they sweep gracefully around the bends. I follow their looping trajectory. Moonlight shimmers on the water. A sense of home is in the air—warmth, food, and light—I hear the faintest burbling sounds drifting on the soft breeze.

I hear laughter.

I plunge away from the river towards the sounds in the distance. At first they are muffled, but then louder—there is more laughter. Faint words float on the breeze. My ears strain to hear. My dead eyes strive to see.

Light spills from the windows of a small brick house with steep steps leading up to the front door. Above is a red good-fortune banner. The house feels welcoming. I float through the front wall, and into a small, cluttered room.

A dusty red box sits alone on a small table in the corner. A warm feeling floods over me. I calm my tortuous, writhing body and ease myself into the comfort of its walls.

12: Three Oh

Brisbane: August, 2019

"Just a quick call," Ronnie said. "How are you getting on with Christian?"

"Good."

"I thought about asking him to your birthday lunch. I'd like Frank to meet him."

"Could do," I said.

There seemed no point resisting the Ronnie juggernaut. But did she have some hidden agenda? If so, I knew the reason. It had been a long time since my divorce.

I hesitated, then said, "Okay, good."

"I'll ask him then," Ronnie said.

"Yeh, good," I repeated like a robot, all the while trying to subdue a kaleidoscope of memories. All those widowed nights while Dave was out playing. And then when the band didn't have a gig, me coming home from work to a house full of smoke and beer cans. In the morning I'd have to pick my way between crashed bodies, and squeeze past the drum kit just to get into the bathroom.

Then I landed a great job with an exciting group of graphic artists, and I needed more structure and space than a musician's free-style life allowed. It took us a while, and not a few arguments, to realise that we were incompatible, and by the time we had untangled the threads of our marriage, the apartment, the parents, and our own hearts, three years had passed.

"How's the sleuthing going?"

Ronnie's voice broke into my rummage through the bottom drawer of my life history.

"What do you mean?" I asked.

"The box."

"Oh that." I dragged my mind back. "One of the letters in the box was from a Mr John Holland to the sister of the man that was hanged. And there was also a newspaper clipping of a letter, most probably written by him to the Courier, suggesting that he thought the man could have been innocent."

"What do you think?"

"I've got no idea. But Christian thinks there must be some connection to our family."

"Was that because of the letters?"

"No, they didn't give out any clues. Except that we know that Hok Siong's sister was living in Amoy. It's a place called Xiamen now, on the coast about halfway between Shanghai and Hong Kong. Would Frank know anything about it?"

"He might."

"Do you think he knows anything about the murder?"

"He's never said anything," she said. "You should ask him yourself."

"I'd rather forget about it. Don't say anything. What could a dead illiterate murdering Chinese cook have to do with us?"

"Sure. Whatever you think."

"And Ma … if you must ask Christian to the lunch, tell him not to say anything either."

"Okay."

She sounded a bit disappointed.

"See you soon birthday girl," she said.

My eyes had started to avoid looking towards that red box; no longer did it exude the vibe of ancient mystery. Now it seemed to hold some type of evil spirit. Was that why Frank wanted to get rid of it? I wondered. Surely not. If that was the case, he wouldn't have given it to me. It's all ridiculous, I thought—better to forget about it.

But the next time I opened my laptop there it was again, *Travels in the Celestial Empire*. I've always hated leaving things unfinished. Might as well finish reading it, and then forget it. Okay, Mr John Holland, let's get this over with.

On my return to Brisbane, I wrote to the executive council and sent a copy to the local newspaper, setting out my view that a great injustice had been done.

I determined to visit the prisoner if it was at all possible, and through some useful connection was able to obtain an appointment for visiting. The day was bright and clear, and it being St Patrick's Day, the town was full of people, some waiting for the parade and some on their way to spend the holiday at Sandgate, or on a steamer in the bay. The omnibus stopped immediately outside Brisbane Gaol which, at first glance looked more like an English country estate within its own grounds. I approached with some trepidation and entering through a grand archway I was greeted by the prison Governor, Captain Jekyll. A large burly warder was assigned to take me to the main cell block which was accessed through an open courtyard featuring a rather in-congruous circular flower garden. My guide informed me that under this flower garden was a vast underground tank, from which the water supply of the gaol is drawn. On entering the cell building we were in a lofty, well ventilated, atrium, lit from skylights above. The cells were lined up on either side in three tiers. Bolts, and locks, and bars were everywhere; the strong walls and the still quietness were all testament to the grim reality of the place.

I was led upstairs and along a light iron walkway with the open cell doors on my left and the central atrium on my right. All the pris-oners, except for the condemned man, were in the yards below. Our footsteps echoed in the vast space. At the end behind a barred grille, was the prisoner. A warder was stationed outside the cell, which was guarded day and night, so I was told.

The iron barred grille was unlocked and relocked, the two warders stayed outside the cell, and I was locked inside with the prisoner. I managed to greet the condemned man in his own language, which was a great surprise and delight to him. I told him of my travels in Amoy and said that I fancied I had been through his village. Though I couldn't be entirely sure, for we had tracked through many villages, clusters of maybe 200 houses cheek by jowl, surrounded by large banyan trees. Above, huge boulders interspersed with bristling pines lined the mountain sides, while below, in the fertile valleys and ravines, verdant hillside terraces rose one above the other, covered with wheat, barley, rice, sweet potatoes, ginger and sugar canes.

Hok Siong was a slight fellow, as is usual with the people of Amoy. His forehead had sprouted into a wiry black fuzz with a stub of hair at the back where his queue had been chopped off.

I asked him if there was anything I could do for him. He requested that I contact the priests from the Taoist temple in Brisbane, the Temple of the Holy Triad.

I was well aware of the Breakfast Creek temple as I had been present at the opening ceremony little more than two months earlier, and I had some small acquaintance with the chief personages. I agreed to help and left the prison in a subdued frame of mind.

Unfortunately, the condemned man's request proved to be elusive. Not one of the men involved in the temple agreed to see the prisoner. One, a prominent businessman in Brisbane, had often acted as a court interpreter. He too flatly refused. I was not surprised as I had some familiarity with the customs of the Chinese people. I do realise that for a Westerner some practices may be easily misunderstood, nevertheless, I believe it is not the crime that causes one to lose face. The crime lays in being caught, or in being convicted. That is what turns one into an outcast and causes all to look upon one with scorn. Hok had, face to face with me, vehemently denied committing the crime, and I believed him. But he had been convicted, and according to the

Whew, grim reading. I noticed he wrote that despite his submission the executive council ordered the execution. So he must have been the one who wrote to the Courier.

The past is immutable, Christian had said. Maybe. But what we believe is the truth depends on who's doing the telling, doesn't it? Perceptions change according to the point of view. I wondered how true John Holland's account was. Not that we'd ever know.

I shut down the laptop. OK, done. Now forget it, Eirene.

The day arrived. Three oh, thirty. I said it out loud through the mist of my morning shower. It's only a number, I told myself, don't get so uptight about it. Reluctantly I dressed for my birthday lunch. My usual working gear of jeans, runners and a loose three quarter-sleeve tee was not going to cut it today. In my wardrobe were two dresses, a black midi for winter and a flowing layered print dress for summer. I threw on the black and tarted it up with black ankle boots and some chunky tomato red earrings. I smoothed my hair down and tied it in a loose knot while I contemplated whether to add a slash of red lipstick. But I hate the taste, and lipstick is just not me—have to do, I said to my reflection.

Dee was in the kitchen putting the finishing touches to a Middle Eastern feast and before long Ronnie arrived with a deliciously decadent, dark chocolate Queen of Sheba cake, complete with candles—not thirty I was relieved to see.

Ten of us sat down stretched out on each side of our long table—Frank, Ronnie, Dee, Will and Kathy from work, three of my long-time friends, and Christian. I was embarrassed, though flattered, by the fuss. I had a glass or two, and once we reached the coffee and cake stage I relaxed and began to enjoy myself. At one end of the table Christian and Frank were engrossed in an earnest conversation about Zaha Hadid and her architectural legacy, while the rest of us amused ourselves by telling embarrassing stories from our childhood. No one brought up the subject of the murder in the box.

In the middle of the night, I woke up groggy with sleep, bathed in the white-hot glare of my reading lamp. I must have fallen asleep and forgotten to turn off the light. I squinted. Through narrowed eyelids the room looked strange. I heard, no, I *felt* a voice. That did it. I snapped upright, fully awake, eyes wide. Nothing. Everything looked normal. The book I was reading had fallen to one side of the bed and lay half open on the crumpled doona. There was just the faint sound of light rain outside. My heart pounded, the voice had sounded real, but not so I could understand any words. Come on! I told myself, be sensible. You've just had too much to drink, that's it. Of course there's no one there. Lights off, covers smoothed, thirst quenched, I gave my pillow a good shake, lay still, and finally slept.

But then it happened again a few nights later. Everything was the same, well almost. This time I hadn't left the lights on in a drunken haze and I wasn't so frightened. But why was it happening? I'm too matter of fact to be seduced for long by anything bordering on the mystical, surely? Was my mind playing strange games with me?

Christian rang thanking me for the birthday dinner and I couldn't help telling him about the visitations. I hid my embarrassment by making a joke of it.

"I think this hanging thing is freaking me out. Am I an idiot or what!"

"You know it's the *Gui Yue*, the ghost month, don't you?" he said.

"Never heard of it."

"Your ancestral education was a bit short then. It's been a part of Chinese mythology for hundreds, no, thousands of years."

"What is it?"

"The gates of hell open up and wandering spirits come out from the underworld and roam the earth seeking food and entertainment."

"They do?"

"They're called hungry ghosts. They have long needle-thin necks, making it difficult to swallow, so they are always hungry. Many types of homeless and lost spirits can manifest as hungry ghosts. In the Taoist tradition it is believed they can be the souls of people whose deaths have been violent or unhappy. These are *Yuan Gui*, ghosts who have grievances, some are hanged ghosts or drowned ghosts."

"Really?" I was sceptical.

"On the night of the full moon some people put out food to appease the ghosts and burn incense to ward off any evil spirits. Some have a feast and leave a seat empty at the table for a ghost ancestor. At the end of the festival, to make sure all the hungry ghosts find their way back to hell, people light their way with floating lotus flower shaped lanterns. When the lanterns go out, it symbolises that the spirits have found their way back."

"You don't believe in all that, do you?"

"Maybe not, but it *is* a rather colourful way of thinking about past lives, and the redemption of lost souls. I don't see any harm in it. And who knows, maybe the spirit of Hok Siong is haunting you?"

I shivered. "That's absurd. There's no such thing as ghosts. And anyway, I'm not interested in all that Chinese stuff."

Silence from Christian.

"And why would I be haunted?" I said. "The box belongs to our family, but who knows where the grisly story inside came from? It probably has nothing to do with our family."

"Are you sure?"

I wasn't sure, but I surprised myself by answering angrily, "No, I'm not, but I'm damned sure I'm going to find out."

13: Surviving

Hok Siong: Queensland, 1880
Hok persevered, he worked hard, amongst the dust, and dirt, and heat of the Maranoa.

At night he looked to the dark sky and was a young boy again gazing up at the stars. Up above the Cowherd and Weaver Girl shone, one on each side of the silvery river, just as they had at home in the village. Grandmother had liked that story. Every year she led the children outside to look up at the sky while she told them about the star-crossed lovers.

"The Cowherd was a simple mortal, just like you," she said. "But the Weaver Girl was the daughter of sky gods. The boy and the heavenly girl loved each other dearly, but the goddess found out. She was angry and banished her daughter to the heavens. The heartbroken cowherd followed her. He hurried, but before he could catch up, the goddess created a heavenly waterway to separate them forever.

"Look up," grandmother said. "See the two brightest stars on either side of the silver river, there they are, the lovers. But don't despair children," she consoled them. "Some kind-hearted birds took pity on them, and the weaver girl's parents relented—once a year, on the double seventh, flocks of magpies fly up into the sky to make a bridge over the river of stars. The lovers race over the bridge to embrace, united for one night only. Be happy for them!"

Each year on the seventh day of the seventh month, Hok took heart when the lovers were re-united. He felt homesick and lonely, but the story gave him hope that one day he would be together again with his family.

His letters home often skirted around the truth, as things did not go entirely smoothly. On one of the monthly expeditions to Roma to collect provisions Hok was enticed into a game of fan-tan. Almost a hundred Chinamen crowded into one of the shacks on the outskirts of Roma, pushing and shoving and shouting, and gambling their lives away. They were all from Guangdong, but language was not a problem for Hok, it was easy to follow the chants. You won or you lost.

Good-hearted Cookie warned him over and over, and tried to stop him going into Roma, but Hok wouldn't listen. It became a habit, an exciting interlude in the humdrum of daily life on the station. But he lost more often than not. Money lenders were abundant, looking for a chance, and he became not only addicted to the game but indebted.

One night the temptation to get even with the house became too much for one of the frequent losers. He blabbed to the police. Of course the local police knew everything that went on in the town, and they usually turned a blind eye. But that night with nothing better to do they crossed the river, raided the place, and arrested all they could grab.

Hok managed to climb out a window, and the near escape was enough to jolt some sense into him. He vowed to never gamble again. His five years indenture was nearly over, and he was entitled to fifty silver dragon dollars. This was good, but he was in debt for almost all of it. Ashamed, he wrote to his sister that he had been offered a good opportunity and was going to stay on. He had no option, he signed up for another five years at the station, paid back his debt, and never gambled again.

The shame lingered and clung to his body; a miasma of despair enveloped him. But soon another disaster followed. Cookie, who made the production of every meal an acrobatic performance,

Cookie, who was always jumping around like a cricket, leaping here and there, Cookie slipped and fell.

They picked him up and lay the injured man on his bed. He stroked the wispy grey hairs on his chin, winced in pain, but told them all not to worry. "I good, I very good. No worry. You go cook, I very quick get better." Except that he didn't. The doctor from Roma came to put a splint on his leg, but an infection took over and that was the end of it.

"My bones stay here," he said with almost his last breath. "I happy here," he told them.

The station owner and his family joined Hok Siong and the others as they laid Cookie to rest on the small hill to one side of the vegetable garden. Hok felt uneasy. How would Cookie join his ancestors? But that was his wish. No one knew anyone from his family. What could they do?

They made sure to inscribe the characters of his name and his village on a grave marker— just in case someone came to find him. They burnt his belongings, and, to help him pay his way into the afterlife, they threw a heap of joss papers folded to look like boat shaped gold ingots on the fire too.

Life continued on the station as usual, but without Cookie.

Jifeng was elevated to chief cook, and the three of them managed what four used to do. Over the next three years the on-again off-again drought took hold. A sombre mood overtook the station. Sheep lay dying in the fine powder of dust that lay everywhere. Hok's eyes were clogged with it, it crept into his ears, his nose, and his pores. He was continually thirsty.

Christmas Day came, and they cooked the same strange food that they cooked every year. They started before dawn; the plum pudding took four hours to cook. Not once must the water be allowed to stop boiling. And if it boiled dry it would be a disaster. The sweat poured off them as they stoked the fire for the roast goose, two hours in a camp oven. Hok busied himself making butter sauce for the plum pudding, apple sauce for the goose, and a clear soup to begin the meal. He carried the soup tureen to the house, and, careful not to spill a drop, placed it on the sideboard. The dining room was festive with candles, and flowers, and red ribbons, the scent of sherry was in the air, but the mood was sombre and subdued.

Hok hurried back to the cookhouse wondering if the rumour he had heard was true—that the station was to be sold. It was no secret that half the stock had been lost to the drought, that the price for wool had gone down, and the banks were refusing to lend more money.

Not long after Christmas, Jifeng, Chhiong, and Hok were clearing up after the midday meal when they saw the manager walking over towards the cookhouse, his every step raising a cloud of dust. When he took off his hat Hok knew that what he was going to say was serious. And it was. The station had been sold. It was a rumour no more.

"The boss … he … we … he couldn't hang on any longer. Sorry boys, you will have to go. The new boss has his own cooks, you savvy?" he looked at them one by one with a concern they had not seen before, checking that they understood. "Not to worry, you will all be paid. Two weeks then you must go."

Jifeng had suspected as much, "I've been talking to a fellow at Surat, he needs a cook. And maybe a kitchenhand," he said nodding to Chhiong. "But you Hok, what will you do?"

"Me? I was going to leave in a few months anyway. I'm going home." Hok's face split into a grin. "Don't worry about me," he said.

He was not sorry. His second five years was up in June, now he could go back home early. With a cache of money hidden in the pouch tied around his waist, he hitched a ride to Roma. This time he was determined not to mess things up. He would find his way to Brisbane and buy a passage back home.

He changed his dragon dollars and pound notes for Australian minted sovereigns and booked into one of Roma's many hotels. He would not go to Chinatown, no more fan-tan. He would stay far away from any temptation and catch the morning train to Brisbane. He felt light-headed in anticipation. He allowed himself one drink in the bar.

Long Sing the publican looked him up and down while pouring a finger of whiskey into a not too clean glass.

"You look for work?" he asked.

"No, I'm going home."

"You're a cook, aren't you? Good money to be had."

"Where?"

"That water boring plant at Dulbydilla. They want a cook."

"Where's that?"

"The end of the line, near the railway camp, out west, past Mitchell."

"No, I'm going home."

"It won't be for long. They found water here in Roma pretty quick, and in Mitchell too. They been drilling for a while now in Dulby, must be near finished."

Hok looked doubtful.

"Just a few months and you can go home with more money in your pocket. Go see Mr Harley Griffith at the Royal Hotel."

Hok struggled with the thought. Should he go? Just for a few months, weeks even? He had money, but all the same, more would be better, he wanted to make his family proud.

And at eleven o'clock the next morning, after unleashing his cheeky charm on the woman at the front desk, Hok found Mr Harley Griffith in the smoking room of the Royal Hotel. Twenty minutes later he was employed again.

It was early in February. The next day would be the dawn of a new year in the Chinese calendar—the year of the dog, and Hok's twenty-ninth year. He bustled around the town spending a precious few pounds on a bed roll and two tarpaulins as he had been instructed.

New Year celebrations were muted in Roma. Long Sing hung three red lanterns out front of the hotel and invited a few local dignitaries to a feast, but Hok found it hard to celebrate.

Still in this wretched place, he thought with a sigh, regretting the delay in going home. Ten years ago, he'd left his homeland a callow young man. He'd survived, but he had no wife, no family, and no real friends. Billy had never returned, and Cookie was dead. He was lonely.

"Two months, that's all, and I go home. Get on that ship, and go back home," Hok said to Long Sing.

He straightened his waistcoat, adjusted his hat, and downed his last drink. He settled his bill, threw his swag over his shoulder, and walked out the door, headed for the railway station and the 8:00 p.m. night train to Dulbydilla, to Mr Falconer's bore.

14: Strange Ways

Two weeks after my birthday I got another unexpected call from Christian.

"How about meeting up for a bite, or something? We can catch up on your mystery."

"Su…ure," I said slowly. What had I said to him last time? Something about being damned sure I would prove that my family had nothing to do with the story in the box. And had I done anything? No.

He ignored my hesitation and we arranged to meet up at the Old Government House coffee shop. Christian was helping a PhD student at the university with some translations, and our studio was not too far away.

He arrived a few minutes after I got there, dressed in regulation black. Why is it that even the most unlikely men look good in black? It's one of those mysteries of the universe. But then, Christian didn't even need to try. A double happy. I smiled.

"What?" he said.

"Nothing."

We ordered, spinach pie for me and a chicken and roast vegetable panini for him.

"Have you found any family connection to Amoy? Did Frank know anything?" he asked.

"No. I don't know. I haven't got around to asking," I confessed.

"There must be a connection somewhere, otherwise why were

the letters and all the other stuff in the box?"

"I guess you're right, but I've been busy."

I was embarrassed. I'd done nothing to find out—did we have not just a black sheep, but a murderer in our family? He gave a nod as though he'd expected that answer. Annoying.

"When I met Frank at your party I detected a trace of Hokkien, the language of Amoy, in the way he spoke. A few expressions, his way of stringing words together. Something … ." I frowned. "I didn't say anything. Ronnie warned me," he quickly added.

Then thankfully he changed the subject. "Have you seen the exhibition at the QUT gallery? It's Ann Wallace."

The waitress took our empty plates.

"No. Is she a Brisbane artist?"

"She is," he said. "I saw some of her works at GOMA last year focusing on Goodna, the old mental hospital, down the river. This new exhibition should be interesting. We could check it out. Have you got time?"

I did. "Why not? It's on my way."

We downed the last of our coffees and walked the short distance to the gallery.

Strange Ways was the exhibition title, and the name was apt, Ann Wallace's works had a strange unsettling surreal quality to them. Each image seemed to have a narrative that extended before and after the frozen moment in time.

"They're right about the 'eerie sense of looming danger'," Christian said, reading from the handout.

"I thought they were terrific, really good," I said.

We stepped out of the gallery into hot bright sunshine.

"This way," he said, "I have to pay homage to my favourite trees."

We walked side by side down the steps towards the Botanical Gardens into the deep, dark, shade of the ancient fig trees. Their vast spreading branches dripped with aerial roots. As soon as the roots found solid ground they became twisted pillars buttressing the spreading limbs which stretched out further than one would have thought possible.

Above us the leaves waved as if hit by a flurry of air. The ferns on the other side of the path curved over, bending in the direction of the wind. The rustling leaves sounded louder as a stronger gust enveloped us. Small, round fruit fell from the canopy above and bounced on the path, sounding like the heavy drops of rain that herald a sudden thunderstorm.

"Is that a storm coming? Rain?" Christian said.

I glanced ahead at a couple walking out in the open beyond the trees. They didn't seem to be ducking from rain drops, nor were they hurrying to find shelter from the oncoming storm. We emerged from the shadows into a blinding light; the heavy heat of an early summer sun beat down on us from a clear blue sky, and all was still.

"That was weird, almost like a ghost, or the spirit of the trees."

"I thought you didn't believe in ghosts," Christian said giving me a small poke in the ribs.

"Maybe I do, and maybe I don't," I grinned back at him.

Walking back to the office I thought about that poke in the ribs. It was kind of nice.

I needed to prove that the murder couldn't possibly have anything to do with us and the first step was to find out what Frank knew. So the next Saturday I headed down south.

Frank listened intently while I gave him a brief version of the story—the murder, the execution, and the letters.

"I should have looked at that stuff before I gave it to you," he said, a concerned look on his face.

"So," I asked, "do you think it has anything to do with us?"

"I've got no idea," he said shaking his head.

He stared off into the distance, silent, his face a blank canvas. I knew he was rattled, I'd seen it before. Usually so calm and optimistic, this was the way he dealt with conflict, by withdrawing into himself. If you didn't know him well you wouldn't pick the difference but we all knew when it was best to leave him alone with his internal struggles.

I felt Ronnie's hand on my shoulder.

"Come and see the garden," she said.

We walked down the steps and into a dappled leafy shade.

My mother is a bit of a Vita Sackville-West disciple when it comes to gardening, she has all the right books, and nothing gets planted without a plan. Naturally, she has a white garden, a walled garden, and a wild garden, all three perfectly executed. Ronnie is all about style. Even if you came across her at work in the garden she would look as though she was straight out of a Vogue magazine—like a 1960s film star on safari, Lauren Bacall maybe. What she lacked was a troupe of labourers, but she managed with the help of my ever-obliging father and, for the heavy work, a young broad shouldered local called Marcus.

The garden was lovely though, and worth all the effort. From the semi-formal top section paths snaked off down into the valley. Flowering shrubs and ferns blended in seamlessly with the native bushland. The path opened up to a little pocket of moss-green lawn flanking the meandering creek. A stone bench beckoned.

"What do you think that was about? Frank, I mean."

"No idea," Ronnie said. "Maybe he's insulted by the idea that the murder might have something to do with his family."

"He did seem a bit spooked by the box when he first showed it to me."

"Was he?" Ronnie looked off into the distance. After a few moments she said, "Could he be reflecting an attitude that Jimmy may have passed on? Some dark and mysterious dread passed on by osmosis. Jimmy might have known what it all meant, but never said anything about it."

"Now you're getting deep. Could be … . Maybe I shouldn't

have asked him about the murder."

"Better to leave him for now," she said. "He'll talk about it when he's ready."

We retraced our steps and found that, in the intervening half an hour, Frank had returned to his normal self—we had drinks and dinner and talked about anything but that bloody box. Instead, my indefatigable parents kept me entertained with their latest exploits: glam camping at Kakadu and visiting my uncles and aunties in Darwin.

"You should see Uncle Ho now," Frank said. "He's got a tribe of grandchildren and keeps them entertained with his 'magic' tricks. The trouble is he's always getting them wrong. The kids die laughing, which only encourages him."

"It was hilarious." Ronnie smiled.

"And Uncle Sammy. He's in his seventies now but insists on *helping* at the family restaurant. Even though he's handed over the management to Mei-Ling, your cousin, he's still there every day— just checking."

"What about the aunties?"

"They're good, both running their own businesses in between coping with a tribe of their children's children. They send their love."

I headed back to Brisbane the next morning feeling a little depressed. Frank sounded so happy to be back with his family. Why did it make me feel so left out, so alienated?

At Uni there was a sort of reverse racism, where our Chinese background was something exotic. This made me feel uncomfortable, as though I was masquerading as someone I wasn't. I wanted to be the same as everyone else, to belong, not to be different, not to be unusual, not to be noticed. It didn't happen.

Ronnie didn't help. Just like the others at Uni she found everything about the Chinese culture *so* interesting. When we visited Darwin as kids, Frank's family was more like a doctoral thesis research project for her rather than a gathering of the clan. We ran wild around the neighbourhood with the cousins, getting dirty, having mock fights and scraping our knees, while Ronnie put the family under a microscope. You could see her mentally chalking up every strange happening or conversation for later investigation.

But that's always been her way. The intellectual approach. Is it any wonder I tried so hard to bury the half of me that was Asian. But then there was Frank. I loved him dearly; was I rejecting him too?

While getting ready for bed, I remembered the amulet buried in the lower compartment of the box. Christian had said it was some sort of a good luck charm. I could do with some of that. Threading a cord through it, I hooked it over my head and slung it around my neck. It felt right.

15: Mr Falconer's Bore

Hok Siong: Dulbydilla, February 1886

Hok peered through the train window into the darkness. The weak light of a half-moon revealed a sandy wasteland with patches of wild scraggly bush. Another barren landscape—no houses, no people, no gardens. How different it was from the countryside around his village, which was forever lush with vegetation, full of colour, movement, and life. He drifted into an uncomfortable sleep until, clang, hiss! He jolted awake as the train came to a grinding halt.

He stretched his aching neck and looked out. A small crowd was gathered on the station platform even though it was the middle of the night. A horse and buggy stood waiting to one side. But no one seemed to be expecting the new cook for Mr Falconer's bore.

Hok found a dark corner behind the railway station and settled down to wait till daybreak. The pink-grey dawn revealed a straggly collection of shabby buildings sprawled back down the line beyond the railway station. On the slopes of a creek a patch of green signalled a market garden. Not a soul was in sight.

Under rusty roofs of corrugated iron, the walls of the buildings on either side were hastily cobbled together with sheets of bark, gin cases, kerosene tins, and fragments of bullock-hides. White painted signboards announced each establishment, all by the same hand it seemed. The first letter of each word was in red and the remainder in black, although the paint had been partly washed off, and trailed down in red and black streaks. When this had happened it was hard to say, since it didn't look as if there had been any rain for a long time.

Hok couldn't read the signs, but he could see about nine or ten hotels or bars, numerous stores, and traders of all kinds. The town had sprouted out of nowhere—it was a border town, ramshackle, but thriving, a frontier town, a town full of strangers. Here there was no history, no past, and probably no future. A sweep of wind blew billows of yellow dust up from the beaten earth track as he trudged along. What had he let himself in for?

Further down the rutted dirt road the smell of baking enticed him to peer into one of the buildings.

"Welcome stranger," came a voice from inside.

The greeting was in the southern dialect of China. Peering in he saw a figure behind a counter piled high with loaves of bread and buns of all sizes.

"I am Ah Fook," the man said. "Here they call me Charlie. And you are?"

"Tee Hok Siong, from Amoy," Hok kept it brief. He knew a few of the southerner's words but after that he had to resort to a cobbled together pidgin English. He lifted his head, inhaling the delicious aroma of fresh baked bread.

Charlie's broad face cracked a grin as he handed Hok a sample, "You look hungry. You try, you try. Very good to eat," he said. "You know the secret, boy? Potatoes. I mix'em up with flour. Make bread soft."

In between taking mouthfuls of the cushiony bun, Hok Siong asked for directions. He smoothed out a crumpled much thumbed paper on the counter.

"Ah, Mr Falconer's bore. It's that way, back behind the railway yard. Not far," said Charlie. "You're the new cook for Mr Griffith, aren't you, boy?" he asked.

Hok nodded, "Yes."

"I'll be seeing you again soon then," said Charlie.

Hok picked up his bundle, and set off back down the road towards the railway yard. Soon he could see the water bore in the distance, a metal structure held upright by guy ropes, surrounded by men and piles of debris. A few horses stood by, harnessed to work the drill. By the side of the bore was a blacksmiths forge, ready for the running repairs that were always needed where machinery was involved. Beyond was a collection of dusty, begrimed, once-white, canvas tents, some large enough to stand up in and others with just enough room for a swag.

It wasn't hard to find the cookhouse. A brick and tin fireplace stood at one end of the simple gabled shelter of corrugated iron held up by a framework of rough-cut logs. There were no walls, but the eaves were widespread enough to provide shelter from the belting sun and all but the worst driving rain. A mutton carcase shrouded in muslin and a meat safe swung from one of the beams, pots and pans from another. In the centre was a long worktable. A huge cast iron pot stood on a griddle on one side of the open fire, and on the other side were two tripods with billies hanging from them. Staggered stacks of dirty dishes teetered at one end of the table, and the fire was down to its last embers.

One of the men broke away from the huddle of workers around the bore and came striding across the dusty stubbled expanse towards Hok. Mr Griffith was barely recognisable. He was no longer the man about town that Hok met in Roma. His clothes were rumpled and dirty. Every crevice of the hand that lifted off his battered hat was deeply ingrained with machinery oil and his fingernails were rimmed black. He launched into a well-rehearsed spiel, all in pidgin English.

"You cook good, you okay. Allee day six o'clock breakfast. Dinner, middle of day. Supper, seven o'clock, night-time. Then clean up, all finish. No trouble. No gamble, no fight. Payday Saturday."

Hok listened carefully while Mr Griffith explained what was expected. For the mid-day dinner—mutton stew with potatoes and cabbage, or salt beef boiled with carrots, and plenty of bread to soak up the juices. Breakfast was to be porridge, followed by eggs and fresh damper, with a fry up of left-over potatoes and sheep kidneys—or bacon if there was any. Sunday dinner was to be roast mutton or lamb, followed by a boiled suet pudding, and supper everyday was leftovers. Englishman tucker. He could do that.

When the formalities such as they were, were over, Mr Griffith returned to the drilling site. Hok chose a spot as close as he could to the cookhouse to lay out his bedding. He had his swag and the two canvas sheets he had bought for a few precious pounds in Roma, one for under and one to be rigged up in case of rain. But there was no sign of rain. Smoothing out the dry dirt, he removed a few stones and tufts of desiccated grass, laid one of the canvas sheets down, and rolled his bedding out on top.

The dirty dishes indicated that the workers had already scrambled up a hasty breakfast for themselves, but the midday meal was due in a few hours. Hok found some salt beef in the hanging safe, a few carrots, some potatoes, and some cabbage. He stoked the fire, set the pot to boil and hurried back to the bakery. The hungry well-borers would need bread. The baker greeted him warmly.

"Come in, come in. We meet again," Charlie's chin hairs were streaked with grey, but seeing him leap up off his stool, anyone would think he was a much younger man.

"Yes."

"Four loaves? The usual?"

"Thank you."

"You are number nine Chinaman here," said Charlie. "There is Ah Sing, and Ah Sow, he has a general store. Yung Kee is another storekeeper, and Ah Gow is a cook at one of the hotels. Ah Sue has the market garden by the creek, and there are two others in the railway camp."

They were all from the far southeast of China, and Hok would be an outsider. What did it matter though—soon he would be going home. He hurried back to the camp, grateful that he didn't have to cook damper for the midday meal.

That night he lay down in his unfamiliar bed, looked up at the starry sky, and immediately sank into a deep sleep.

The next day was a haze of hard work. He scrubbed the kitchen clean and in between producing meals got himself organised. Night fell and wild drunken revellers flocked the town, spending their Saturday pay-packets as though there was no tomorrow.

On Sunday Hok trailed behind the rest of the camp heading for the dusty yellow grass of a makeshift oval. It was cricket day— gangers and their labourers versus the rest. Most of the town's inhabitants were there, some sporting black eyes, and some hangdog after the night before. For what else was there to do to celebrate the end of a hard week's work in this godforsaken spot in the middle of nowhere? Some were indulging in the hair of the dog. Selling liquor on a Sunday was against the law but that didn't stop the ten or so pubs in Dulbydilla from bending the rules. After all what would the Sunday cricket matches be like without a bit of sly grog?

Hok stood at the edge of the field, a little apart from the others, who were all barracking loudly for their respective teams. There were a few women among the crowd and, as he stood there feeling out of place, a young woman sauntered over in front of him. She smiled provocatively and flounced away.

"Watch out for that one, boy," Hok heard a voice behind him. "She's trouble."

Hok looked back at the man, and seeing a kindly face, tentatively returned his smile. He took another quick glance towards the fast disappearing young woman and turned back to the game. The shearers at the station used to play this strange game of cricket, always with lots of hollering when the ball hit the kerosine tin behind the man with the bat. This time there were three sticks instead of the kerosine tin. The players ranged around the field waiting; their eyes followed the ball as it flew looping high up into the air before one of them scrambled to make the catch.

On Monday morning after breakfast Hok made his way to the market garden near the railway station. Mr Griffith had told him to pick up whatever produce he needed. "Just tell them I sent you," he'd said.

Hok was surprised to see that the woman behind the counter wasn't Chinese.

"I'm Molly, Moll to you," she said with a smile, "Ah Sue's wife."

"I am Tee Hok Siong," he introduced himself with a small formal bow. "Am cook for Mr Griffith."

"Good morning Tee Hok Siong," the woman said with a slight dip of her head. "And what will you have today?"

As he scanned the table laden high with all sorts of fruit and vegetables, a glimpse of movement caught his eye. Standing in a doorway at the back was another woman. Hok couldn't see her face but the light coming from behind her lit her hair in a fiery halo around her head.

"Who's this then?" the woman said.

"This is Tee Hok Siong," said Molly, "the new cook Harley hired for Mr Falconer's camp."

"Pleased to meet you," said the apparition. She stepped closer and Hok saw she was the woman from the cricket match. She wiped her arms dry with a towel. Her skin was fair but with the rosy glow that comes from a light touch of the sun. Her eyes stared straight into his. They were not quite blue and not quite green. They were, Hok thought, the most exquisite eyes that he had ever seen, and she was the most beautiful golden exotic creature in the world.

"Yes," he said. He couldn't think of anything else to say. He felt his skin flush and looked pointedly down at the vegetables. He felt stupid. Why had he never learned to speak the foreign devils' language properly?

She laughed. "See you round then," she said nodding her head in his direction as she swished back through the doorway.

"That was Kate," said Moll. "She takes in washing. Does it out the back and helps me in the shop sometimes."

Hok did his best to calm himself. Studying the produce assiduously he took his time and eventually selected a nice big pumpkin, some carrots, a mass of onions and a selection of greens and stowed them away in the cookhouse cart.

"Thanks," said Moll. "I'll tell Ah Sue you called by. See you next time."

"See you," he repeated, hoping it was the right response.

Next stop was Ah Fook's bakery shop. Charlie was effusive in his welcome but soon launched into a long story about lending money to someone who was going to pay him back in a few days.

Hok shifted from one foot to the other and glanced out the door. He thought he knew what was coming. He wanted to escape but Charlie wasn't going to hand over the bread order until he had finished what he had to say.

"The thing is," Charlie said, "I need money. I need money now. I must buy provisions. Flour, salt for my bread… and for my pastries, sugar, eggs, and butter."

Then the inevitable question, "You can lend me some money?"

"You need money?"

"You can lend me? I pay you back."

Hok was trapped. He was an outsider and refusal would make him even more of one. "You pay me back when?" he asked.

"Soon, soon. I pay my provisions now, sell my bread, and next week I pay you back. *Mou muntai*, no problem."

Hok pulled out the leather pouch he kept tucked away next to his body and surreptitiously extracted eight gold sovereigns. Charlie lifted his forefinger and beckoned—one more, two more.

"Is much money, Charlie. I need money back soon."

"No problem boy," Charlie crossed his arms and leant back.

"I go home soon."

"I speak true," Charlie rested his hand on his chest and fixed his gaze on Hok as though daring a challenge.

It *was* a lot of money, and the minute he handed it over Hok knew it was a mistake. But, too late now, he thought, it's done. He resisted the temptation to run his hands down the sides of his waistcoat. Better not let Charlie know he had another fifty six sovereigns sewn into the lining.

That night, after he had finished all his chores and lay down Hok allowed himself a small soft whisper, "Kate." And with that one word all thought of the unpleasantness with Charlie was gone.

Hok had been surprised when Kate flounced past him at the cricket match. He'd been entranced when she locked eyes with him at the shop. And then he became hopelessly bewitched. Most days when he arrived with his little two-wheeled cart to pick up vegetables there she was at the back of Molly and Ah Sue's shop, up to her elbows in suds. From Molly he heard about her two children and the husband who had left her. It made no difference to him.

He had often dreamt of arriving back in Kang-Thau laden with money, and marrying Yang the fisherman's daughter. They had been promised to each other though they had exchanged no more than surreptitious smiles as was proper. Now, he could barely picture Yang. He remembered the yellow robe she wore on feast days, but her face was no more than a generic one, a combination of all the girls in the village, this one's smile and that one's blushing cheeks. It had been ten years, and who knows, maybe her family had given up any hope of him returning and had married her off to someone else.

Kate liked to laugh, and he dreamt up little amusing stories to tell her. At night he lay looking up at the endless starry sky racking his brains to remember anything faintly funny he had heard in the past. He laboriously practised telling it in a language she would understand, over and over, until he was confident.

He started saving scraps of left-over food and extra tidbits for her. She was surprised at first but accepted the gifts with an amused smile. One night he was bold enough to walk up to her tent at night after supper with his gifts. She didn't seem to mind, though she kept her distance and thanked him with a formal bow. It was hard to deny the excitement she roused in his body. If she just looked at him Hok was flushed with happiness. He had thought of Yang often, and yearned for the intimacy of marriage, but never, never, had he felt such feelings as he was experiencing now.

He was in love.

FOUR

16: Hok

Brisbane, Australia: 2009

I hear a wailing and crying in the small brick house where I have found sanctuary. An old woman sobs inconsolably. An old man lies dead. A heavy hand picks up the box and I am borne away. Then, weeks, months, maybe years later, the lid of the box is opened. Voices surround me, the voices of a man and a young woman. Then the lid closes and I am moved again.

Steamy humid air seeps in and reminds me of rainy days in my village. It feels familiar. I am back near the river, I'm sure of it. At night I ease myself out of the box and roam around. I stretch around corners and slither here and there. I cry out.

At times I hear one of the two women in my new home call to the other. It sounds like Ma singing out to big sister "Ai-ling, Ai-ling, come, come—where are you?"

17: Poetry and boiled sweets

In the middle of another crazy busy week Frank rang.

"I have to come up for a doctor's appointment… no nothing serious, no, it's nothing. Check-up, it's just a check-up. … Anyway, is it OK if I stay Friday night?"

"Friday's good," I said.

We were working on an art catalogue for a major gallery, deadline Thursday. The graphic layout was all me, Will liaised with the clients, and the others filled in where needed. Most nights it was after eleven before I got home.

Thursday came and it was all over. We sent the final version off to the printers and celebrated with a team dinner at Stokehouse on the river. Will was his usual charming self. I'd known him for a long time before I joined the company, even before his close clipped beard prematurely turned a distinguished grey.

"Feel like a drink?" he said to me as the others were leaving. I did. We walked to the nearest bar, ordered two ice-cold Jägermeisters, and wound up comparing stories of growing up in regional Queensland, the south-east for me, and Esk for him.

"We're just a couple of rural bogans," he said with one of his lopsided grins.

"So you grew up in Esk? Did you know the Kransky sisters?" I said.

"Hilarious aren't they? Yes, they did put us on the map, but Esk is their fictional hometown. I wonder if they picked it because it sounds so funny when they say it. Eskthh."

I laughed, perhaps a little louder than I should have. I looked around but no one had noticed. We ordered a second round. I was mellow, replete with food and a tiny bit woozy. Sitting opposite me was someone I liked, and he was being nice to me. How could I resist? The solicitous arm around my shoulder as we left the bar was the last straw.

I woke alone, spread-eagled on the soft grey sheets of a massive bed in an apartment in Southbank that was decidedly not mine. My head ached. I flinched at the bright morning light as I lifted my head gingerly and looked around. Shafts of sunlight slanted through the slatted blind patterning the white walls with interesting stripes. In the corner was a burnt orange Arne Jacobsen swan chair, all soft sinuous curves; next to it was a small round chrome table holding a stack of books, and a floor lamp.

Above the chair and opposite the bed were three large, familiar, black and white photographic prints. They were mine. From the days of my passion for the sensuous shapes of arum lilies. My Imogen Cunningham period, or was it Robert Mapplethorpe, or both? I'd sold quite a few at that exhibition but I'd forgotten that Will was one of the buyers. I was flattered.

The noises coming from the other room signalled that breakfast was on the way and soon Will appeared with coffee and warmed-up croissants. I took a sip of coffee, "This could be awkward," I said.

"What?"

"Us."

"Only if you let it," he said. "Hey, we're friends."

And that was that. He left for work, and I rushed home. Celeste had fed herself from the automatic feeder, but showed her displeasure at my absence by pointedly ignoring me. Dee was nowhere to be seen; there was just a collection of crumbs and a coffee cup on the bench to show she'd been home.

Back at work after a lightning shower and a change of clothes,

I caught myself snatching a few sideways glances across the room, sizing up the situation. Yes, we were friends, and maybe he thought that was all it was, but damn it, I was lonely. I yearned for more than brief mutual comfort. Could this be the beginning of a relationship? We'd known each other since Uni, but Will was my boss. Advisable? No. Possible? Maybe.

I left work early, rushed to the supermarket, then home before Frank arrived. I hid the scholar's box way out of sight in the back of the hall cupboard. After our last encounter I didn't want to upset him.

But I needn't have bothered.

"Okay," Frank said after dinner. "What are we going to do about the stuff in the box."

"Has Ronnie been hassling you?"

" No … , yes," he said. "What do you want to know?"

"I wonder how such a valuable antique come to be in the family in the first place. Christian said it's a scholar's box and could be worth quite a bit," I said.

"And?"

"And if the box does belong to our family, are we related to a scholar, or to a murderer, or to both?"

Frank cupped his head in his hands, elbows on the table, his eyes stared off into the distance. I shut up and waited. Frank wasn't Ronnie, who always knew what she thought, or what she should do, straight away, no ifs, and no buts.

"Look, I really have no idea," he finally said. "But let's find out."

"I think we should."

He smiled. "I'll ask the Darwin lot. They might know something, they're all older than me."

"OK. Good," I said.

Frank left the next morning. Dee briefly made an appearance then announced she would be away for the weekend. The silence of an empty apartment surrounded me.

The phone rang.

It was Christian.

"I've done a bit of research on the box. If you're home I could call in and tell you about it."

"OK," I said before my brain caught up. I muttered silently 'I vant to be alone', Greta Garbo fashion. First Will, then Frank. I needed to regain my equilibrium.

Still, no need to be churlish,"Give me half an hour." I said.

"Is ten too early?"

"No, that's fine. See you then," I said.

"Coffee?" I asked when he arrived.

"No, just water thanks. It's hot out there."

"Why are you still chasing this up? You've already done the translations."

"It's an interesting story. It always amazes me how wide spread the Chinese diaspora is, in time as well as geographically."

"What did you find out then? About the box."

"Most likely it's from the 17th century. That'd be the early Qing Dynasty."

"Qing, Ming, I never know the difference," I said, then cringed inwardly because I knew he was going to tell me.

"Qing is the Manchus, 1644 to 1912. 1912 that was when Puyi, the last emperor, was forced to abdicate. And Ming, was just before Qing, more or less. For nearly 300 years."

"Okay."

"I discovered a few other travelling boxes on-line, but yours seems unusual. It's bigger for a start, and I only found one other with a cut out front. Most were just plain, but some were covered all over with lovely hand painted scenes. Others were vanity boxes, money boxes, and even travelling opium boxes, but yours is an official's seal and document box."

"Well, thanks for that. But I don't think I'll ever want to sell it, even if it's valuable."

"No, of course not," he said putting his cup down on the table with a decisiveness that signalled he'd finished.

"By the way," I said, "Frank is going to see if he can find a family connection. Said he'd ask his brothers and sisters in Darwin."

"Great. Let me know if you find out anything."

I gathered up the cups and walked them into the kitchen.

"Ronnie said you live not far from here?" I said over my shoulder, hoping he'd take the hint and go.

"Yes, not far. I'm just off James Street on the Valley side. It was my grandparent's house. My parents gave the house to me when they moved to The Gap a year ago."

"The Gap … lots of trees?" I said.

"Sure. Every window of their house is a framed view of tree trunks and the bush. It's all white polished tile floors, light and bright. You'd like it," he said.

"Your parents, what do they do?" Why am I prolonging this, I wondered.

"Ma is a lecturer in law at UQ and my father, Chen, is a doctor."

"Nice. Living the dream," I said, and then caught myself. "Sorry, that sounds a bit rude."

He grinned, "Don't worry, I'm not that sensitive, I know what you mean."

"Your work sounds interesting," I said, then winced inwardly. Again? What was that about wanting him to go. Remember?

"It is. I travel a lot, sometimes with other journalists as their interpreter. And sometimes they let me loose on my own."

Then.

"I'm curious," he said. "Why aren't you interested in your background."

"I am … what background?"

"Your Chinese heritage."

"Half-Chinese. Not Chinese-Chinese. And anyway I'm

Australian."

"Yes, I know that. But you don't seem to want to learn anything about Chinese culture."

"What makes you think that?"

"You said, I'm not interested in all that Chinese stuff."

"I did?"

He was probably right. But did I have to explain myself? It seemed I did.

"Well, if I said that, it's because I find it especially irritating when others expect me to know the answers to any question about Chinese culture. When is the moon festival? How do you say Happy New Year in Chinese? When is the year of the rat? Et cetera."

"They're just being curious."

"Yes, I know, but what I usually say is—'I dunno, ask a proper Chinese.' And if I'm feeling really cranky I say, 'How would I know, I'm Australian,' and slink off."

"It's part of your heritage."

"Do I detect a critical note?" I said, and I'm sure I flared my nostrils at this point. It was a touchy subject.

"I'm sure you learnt all about your European cultural heritage— the poets, the artists, the kings, Shakespeare, Leonardo da Vinci, the Virgin Queen Elizabeth, and all that."

"I did."

"But what about the other side of you, what about Confucius, Laotze, Li Bai, Wang Wei, and Lin Yutang? What about the Spring Festival, Tomb Sweeping Day, ancestor worship and hungry ghosts?"

I smoothed my hair back and sighed … what to say?

"And then what about Chinese poetry?" he said.

"What about it?"

"The Tang dynasty gave us some wonderful poetry. Tang poetry 'fills the heart with blissful joy.' Someone once said that, can't remember who. Do you want to know what my favourite poem is?"

"No… yes… maybe. What is it?" I asked, feigning interest.

"It's called 'The Roads of Luoyang' by Chu Guang-xi from the mid eighth-century."

And then, shit, shit, he started reciting:

> *"The roads are straight as strands of hair*
> *And full of the glories of spring*
> *The noble young lords from the Wuling Hills*
> *Ride by in pairs with their bridles ringing*

"Can't you just picture it?" he said. His dark eyes burrowed into mine, intense and passionate. "The rich young bucks are racing along the road full of their own importance. And I love that 'roads straight as strands of hair.' Perfect. Translation by Red Pine, not me."

"I have my own interests," I said, looking towards the window, and straightening the pile of books on the table. I wanted out.

He took no notice.

"Here's another favourite by Li Bai about homesickness. From about the same time." He looked up at the ceiling, tapped his finger on the table, closed his eyes and recited:

> *"The moonlight shines bright beyond my bed*
> *And looks like frost on the ground*
> *I lift my head to gaze at the moon*
> *I lay my head down and yearn for home.*

"It's called 'Night Thoughts'," he said. "And there are hundreds more like that."

My face felt hot.

"I don't suppose you know what Dylan Thomas thought about poetry?" I said.

"No."

"He said poetry is not the most important thing in life, and that he'd much rather lie in a hot bath sucking boiled sweets and reading Agatha Christie."

Christian shook his head slightly, but it was his faint sigh that incensed me the most.

"And Dylan wrote some of the most magnificent verse, as you know very well," I added.

"Yes, sure, but," he smiled—a wry smile, "maybe you're descended from one of those Chinese poets, and that's where the scholar's box came from. It could be a romantic story. He was a disgraced official exiled to far flung Amoy, fell into love with a local girl, married her, and all that remained of his former glory was the scholar's box."

It was a tempting thought; I gave him that.

"I think you're missing out on a rich, vibrant, and diverse culture. Even today—"

But I'd had enough.

"I'm not interested in Chinese culture because it has nothing to do with me," I snapped. "I don't want anything to do with being an Asian." I air-waved my fingers in quotation marks around the word Asian. Could I have been any more childish? It was a vain wish, unlikely to ever be achieved, except by being reincarnated as a pure white Anglo-Saxon. Or having a head transplant.

"Can you obliterate your cultural heritage just like that?" he asked.

I was beyond the point of no return.

"It doesn't have anything to do with me!" I said sharply, almost shouting. "It doesn't. It's not part of who I am. It's an alien world to me. I might be part Chinese, but I don't even remotely feel Chinese. I have this face which says Asian to everyone, but inside I'm just a girl from country Queensland."

I should have stopped there, but I didn't.

"What about my other grandparents? Nan and Pop have Anglo-Celtic ancestry and were born in New Zealand. Does that mean I should be totally immersed in Welsh, Irish, or Maori culture, as well as Chinese?"

Christian shot a pitying look in my direction; he wasn't going to answer.

"But, you know, none of that matters—to everyone I am always that Chinese girl. I hate it."

A silence fell between us. I'd gone too far.

I was fuming and Christian looked perplexed. How could things go wrong so quickly? And why were we arguing? We were standing on opposite sides of the table, me glaring, he looking down. His arms dropped loosely by his side, his eyes turned away towards the window, and then back to me. The expression on his face was tinged with concern. But I was in no mood for that. I stared back angrily.

The phone rang and I grabbed it; I didn't care who it was, anything to get me away from Christian's criticisms. It was Ronnie. She came straight out with it, the tests were positive.

"Frank has cancer."

18: Kate

Dulbydilla: 1886

A few months before Hok arrived in Dulbydilla a ragbag assortment of tents had sprung up almost overnight, like mushrooms in a paddock. There were two camps, the railway camp and the boring camp. In the railway camp hundreds of navvies, plate layers, fettlers, and the foremen who lorded over them, the gangers, each one of them claimed a patch of dirt to call home, however temporary it was to be. In their wake came the businesses, moving along the train line in lockstep: the butchers, bakers, publicans, clergymen and even school teachers.

When Kate and her husband arrived the town had already begun to take shape. Kate thought it seemed like a good move at the time, but that was then. Now she cursed that man, her husband, every day of her life.

"Left me in this dump at the end of the line, didn't he," she told anyone who'd listen. "That Irish charmer left me high and dry, with these two wee 'uns to look after. Who would have thought he could be such an inconsiderate brute?"

"At first it was an adventure," she said to Moll, while scanning the vegetables on sale for anything slightly wilted that she might be able to bargain down. "You know what he said? 'Six months and we'll be on our feet again,' that's what he promised. 'It'll see us right, there's good money to be made—it's a government job,' he says. Then he roots us all up to live in a tent in this hellhole. And now look at me, can I sink any lower?"

"Once at the bottom you can only go up. Isn't that so?" Moll said, always the optimist.

Kate was lonely, but life in Dulbydilla wasn't without its upsides. She made friends. There was kindly Moll, who always bundled a few extra carrots or whatnot into her basket, Jess, who was always good for a laugh, and Nellie, the youngest of them all.

Taking the road of least resistance Kate managed to survive by taking in washing. There was plenty of work, the town was swelling by the day. The children were happy playing at her feet while she scrubbed her fingers raw, and when they got tired and scratchy a few jelly babies from Louis Carlsson's store did the trick.

After work, in the dark silence of the night, she entertained. At first it had been just one of the South Australians, a handsome bloke with a wicked grin. He charmed her. His mocking blue-green eyes, the colour of a fathomless sea, beguiled her from under a sweeping lock of coal-black hair. He brought supplies, goodies to entice her. And who can blame a girl for wanting a bit of satisfaction, not to mention the odd gift? You could scour your hands bloody and still not earn enough to buy a new pair of leather boots, or even a treat for the children. He was heaven-sent. Her dreams of finding a good man re-surfaced. Because then … *then* she could write to Mam without lying her head off.

"Watch out Kate," Moll warned her. "Don't be too free and easy. You don't want to wind up like Jess and Nellie. You're a respectable married woman." But she wasn't going to worry about any consequences. She had a yearning for the comfort of flesh on flesh. And that was what he gave her.

Until one day he just wasn't there. Mr Blue Eyes had disappeared. He'd always said he was too good for such a rough-as-bags camp, full of brawling, boorish louts. Sydney was the place for him he'd said—not in the middle of nowhere at the end of the line. Kate was more disappointed than anything else. Despite her fantasies she hadn't expected much, he was far too good-looking.

Moll wasn't surprised.

"I knew it! He's not the sort of fellow to stay by your side, thick and thin that kind of thing. Stands to reason," she said.

Moll was twenty-five, only three years older than Kate, but that didn't stop her dishing out motherly advice.

"You need to be careful, find a good man and stick to him."

"Easier said than done!"

"I'm lucky to have Ah Sue, he treats me right," said Moll. She'd been living with Ah Sue for just over a year—almost married, so she told Kate.

"How did you meet?'

"I was in a bad way," she said ruefully. "I was shacked up in a dirty hovel in the back streets of Roma. I'd sunk so low that I was tempted to give opium a try. It didn't take long, and I was hooked. Some days I could barely walk as I staggered in and out of that tumbledown cottage. Then I noticed a Chinaman watching me from a market garden across the road. Once he waved, but I turned away and hurried on, ignoring him."

"That was Ah Sue?"

"It was. He kept waving, and then, 'You good?' he'd say tipping his battered hat back from his sweaty, shiny, brow. His smile melted my heart, even if he was Chinese."

"And then?"

"I staggered out one day … I needed a fix, bad. It was a boiler, and I must have fainted because next thing I knew I was lying on a bunk with a wet cloth on my head. Ah Sue's worried face broke into a smile when he saw me open my eyes. I can't tell you how that felt. Someone cared about me. So I stayed."

"You moved in with him?"

"More or less. I was desperate, and he was my lifeline. It took a few weeks to get the opium out of my system, and they were a miserable few weeks too. He fed me and held my hand when I had it bad. After that we were a couple."

"Lucky you."

Moll repeated her advice, "You need to find a good man and stick to him."

Kate snorted. Her sun-streaked curls bounced as she shook her head.

"Ah Sue is alright, but I don't fancy shacking up with a Chinaman."

"I'd rather be with Ah Sue than be forced to bootlick a succession of trash from the camp," Moll said sharply.

There were many kinds of trash in the camp, they all agreed on that. Some were toffee-nosed, roughing it for the time being, and some were born to be navvies for life.

But Kate took no notice of Moll's advice. Soon there was a fresh pair of dusty boots parked at the end of her bed … and then another. She enjoyed being cocooned in arms that loved her, even if only for a few hours. She could feed her children well and spend less time with her red, cracked hands sunk deep in sudsy water. But with each new pair of boots there was less chance of finding a good man and keeping him.

A travelling photographer set up his tent not far from hers. How grand! she thought. A professional gentleman. Could he be the one?

The respectable wives of the town flocked to the photographer's tent to be preserved for posterity with their children. They posed against a painted ferny backdrop, standing statue still next to a pedestal of Greek origins on top of which was a real fern in a pot. Kate laughed to see them all line up in their Sunday best, and full of their own importance—scrubbed up and smart, if a little dusty around the hems.

But then the stories started. The children talked, first one, then two, then three. The photographer was arrested for molesting those same children. He had charmed the little girls into his tent as they walked past, entertained them with his photographs, and then ….

Kate was horrified, "Who would have believed it? Little Maggie was only five years old too. Good riddance, I say."

Jess agreed.

"I saw the Mitchell police drag the bugger off. You got enough to worry about without that sort hanging around," she said.

That night Kate gave Babby and little Joey an extra hug. "I'll not let that happen to you," she whispered into the air above their downy heads. Then she tucked them in, dragging in the scent of their youthful skin before dimming the lamp and lowering the tattered sheet that divided the tent into two rooms.

Christmas came, and Kate tied lollies to a broken off branch propped up in the corner of the tent. On Christmas Eve she wrapped their presents in paper she'd saved from here and there, smoothing out the wrinkles as best she could. They ate bright yellow oranges and roast chicken and potatoes. Kate's face glowed from lifting the lid of the camp oven too often, she so wanted it to be the best chicken they had ever tasted.

Not long after Christmas there were two new faces in town.

"Did'ya hear? We've got a police force now. Here in Dulbydilla." A breathless Jess announced.

Kate turned to her, "It's a bit of a laugh, eh? All they got for a station house is that old icebox car parked on the siding."

Disappointed that she wasn't the first to spread the news, Jess added, "I saw'em get here. A tall young streak and one a bit older, looked like the boss."

"Two against hundreds of those buggers? Some chance they'll keep the peace!" Kate said. And it wasn't long before she had to call in to the new police station for that very reason, her peace had been disturbed.

One of the boot owners had become quarrelsome after indulging in more liquor than he should have. "The children," she'd breathed, trying not to shriek or yell. It made no difference.

Afterwards he lurched out of the tent muttering darkly, and she lifted a pillow to her face rocking from side to side, pressing down to ease the pain and stifle her cries. It must have been her fault. But what had she said to deserve a black eye … and the rest?

"Oh, Kate," Moll said, when she saw her face, "You need to tell the coppers."

Kate banged her fist on the side of her head.

"I can't."

"You must," said Moll. " No-one has the right to do that to you."

So Kate crossed the railway line and climbed the steps to the old icebox car that served as the police station. The young one was sitting behind a desk of sorts. As she came in he stood up, his head near grazing the roof.

"Constable Kelly," he said , shaking her hand. "And you are?"

He sat down again and listened to her story, jotting down a few notes as she spoke. But Kate knew she'd get nowhere, there would be no justice. This earnest looking copper might listen, he might lock his pale blue eyes on hers, ruffle his hair and look concerned, but nothing would happen to the animal who beat her. It burnt her up to think that when he went berserk, her kids were there, asleep she hoped, on the other side of the flimsy fake wall.

"I won't do it no more," she vowed. Jess and Nellie took fright too. They got hold of a few bottles of gin and the three of them spent a few good rousing nights together, commiserating their lot, and taking the mickey out of every Tom, Dick and Fred that had crossed their path. But needs must. Jess and Nellie soon returned to their calling. For what else were they to do? There were no jobs for the likes of them. Who wants even a skivvy with a reputation? And who hires maids-of-work in a dump like this anyway?

Kate noticed the young Constable Kelly walking past her tent a few times.

"You want to watch out," said Jess when she dropped in on Kate for a chat. She hitched up her crumpled skirts and flung herself down flat on the camp bed. Folding her arms behind her head, she looked up at Kate and asked, "What's he up to? What does he want?"

Nell, who always looked for doom and gloom, had her own take on it. "I hope those coppers don't look our way; I don't want to be banged up for vagrancy. My sister Ann got six months with hard labour in Brisbane Gaol. Just for doing nuthin'. Those coppers had it in for her."

At first Kate didn't pay no mind. Sure enough, the policeman was just looking out for her. She'd reported an assault, he was only doing his job. A week went by and one night she caught a glimpse of him hovering in the shadows near her tent. And then, by day, it seemed like every time she straightened up, stretching her stiff back, there he was, walking past. It made her uncomfortable.

"A bit beyond the call of duty, d'you think?" she asked Moll.

"Maybe he fancies you?"

"Bugger off."

She curbed her night-time entertaining. The bruises that she tried to hide from the children changed from black to yellow. And who wants a repeat of that? No, thank you very much. Her hoard of rations dwindled. By day she took in more work, up to her elbows in suds at the back of Moll's shop; at night her back hurt and her hands ached. She stuffed her fat, red, cracked fingers under the pillow and pressed her head down on them. It helped. But the loneliness returned.

This time she vowed to be more sensible. No more of that railway riffraff. No more navvies. There must be others in the town, nicer types, who needed a bit of cheering up. That guy who owned the cordial factory, Edwin, he fancied her, she could tell. He was a bit of a drunk now that his wife had left him but at least he was a businessman. She flirted outrageously whenever he dropped his bundle of washing off, and before long he was under her spell.

But Edwin was an infrequent night visitor. Infrequent because his lunch time business dealings often left him unable to function after eight o'clock at night. She wasn't even sure if she liked him, so no skin off her nose if he didn't come. Another was that good looking Irishman, Finbar, one of the well-borers. The two of them, a tipsy toff and a charming mick, were a bit more respectable than the navvies.

Then a newcomer caught Kate's eye, the new cook at Mr Falconer's bore. She had spied him first at the Sunday cricket match. He wasn't half bad looking, he had a sparkle in his eye, and he looked different from the other John Chinamen. He was often at Moll's stall picking up stores for the camp. Once she was minding the stall for Moll and started chatting with him. He made her laugh. Somehow his stories seemed even funnier told in that quaint broken English of his. Kate caught Moll's approving look one day and snorted. She had no intention of jacking up with a Chinaman, despite what Moll thought.

He started giving her a few rations, left-overs and suchlike. She was wary. Though it didn't seem there were any strings attached.

"There's no harm in it," Moll said, "Hok's lonely and you treat him like a human being. Don't worry about it."

But how could she forget the beating she'd got? It didn't matter how respectable they were, they were all still men, and men could sometimes act like animals.

When that swine of a husband left, he'd just walked out in the clothes he was wearing. The drink had got to him, that's what she put it down to. There was nothing to do in this place but work, and drink, and fight—and the other navvies were just as bored as he was. Fists often flew in drunken furies. Her man was a big bloke though, and he usually came out of it untouched until, two months after they arrived, a six-foot-tall ganger threw down the gauntlet.

It was Queensland versus South Australia, forty-five minutes of bloody bare fist fighting. The whole town had been there that Sunday—every man, woman, and child in the godforsaken place. Kate watched in horror as they fought, and the longer they fought, the louder and drunker the crowd became. The crow-eater won, and that's what did it. That man of hers couldn't stand the humiliation. He slunk off, with not even a goodbye, and she never saw him again.

After the fight Kate returned to the tent and found their savings tin thrown down on the bunk, empty. Later she came across his gun as she rummaged under the bed for some new clothes for Babby.

Why did he leave the gun behind? It troubled her. Had that crow-eater addled his brains more than she thought? Maybe he forgot to take the gun? Or maybe in a last-minute act of decency he'd decided she might need some protection.

Before they came to the camp, he'd been away a lot on horse trading business, and he'd taught her how to use the gun. She was a good shot, but just looking at it gave her the shivers. At first she had wrapped it up in an old shirt quick-smart and pushed it back under the bed as far as she could.

But times had changed … there was no way she was going to put up with a beating again without a fight. Now she slept with the gun close to hand.

19: Family reunion

Brisbane: November, 2019

What goes for winter in Queensland turned into a blazing spring and then a fiery summer. Bushfires threatened up and down the country.

Frank finished his treatment, and we waited in limbo, wondering what the outcome would be.

"It wasn't that bad. I'm not ready to go yet," he said. "We're going up to Darwin next week to visit the family."

Despite his reassurances, this sounded worryingly ominous to me. As if he thought it would be his last visit.

They arrived to stay the night, and early next morning I drove them to Brisbane airport. Frank looked pale and frail and Ronnie fussed over him. He seemed to like the attention—Ronnie was not usually solicitous, however sick you were. He gave me an amused look as she insisted on man-handling the bags all by herself.

I watched the plane to Darwin take off. When we were kids, we'd twice made the long trip north to Darwin. The first was hellish. I was constantly car sick while Dee sulked from being told more than once to *please* sit down, stop poking your sister, and shut up. The next time we flew, and the wonder of that, my first flight, has never left me. That magical feeling of floating above the clouds, and then stepping into that warm fug of tropical air.

Meeting the cousins was fun but the cultural difference was obvious. We were all Aussie kids screaming around on the lawn playing but, inside their houses, things were different. They ate differently, they behaved differently, their furniture was different, and they spoke fluent Chinese with their parents. Unreal, we thought. They were the exotic. Forever after Darwin seemed quite remote from our normal life, an idyllic steaming foreign paradise, and not even a part of Australia.

After another frantic day at work I drove home like an automaton, I slumped down on the couch and closed my eyes. Celeste jumped up next to me and began to purr, and then my phone rang. I scrambled for my bag.

"Yes."

" Hi. It's me, Christian. I wondered how Frank is doing. Well, I hope."

"Fine, so far so good," I told him.

"Good to hear. Keep in touch," he said.

"Sure," I said, but didn't mean it.

Dee bounced out to spend the night with Patrick, Will was in the country visiting his parents, and I was alone—again. I scrambled something together out of the fridge and poured myself a glass of wine. Some completely forgettable comedy was on the TV so I soon switched it off and settled into bed to read a few chapters before turning out the light. I'm nothing if not loyal, it was the latest Stephanie Plum, twenty six and still going.

With a jerk I surfaced through a thick fog. The room was pitch black. I tossed from side to side. I peered out through thick black bars. My heart pounded. I yelled, again and again, but no sound came out. A man in a crumpled uniform appeared rattling a huge bunch of outsized keys. Strands of greasy hair surrounded his fat face and poked out from under his cap. He opened the barred gate. Another man was behind him. 'I didn't do it, I didn't. I'm innocent,' I screamed into a silent void. The men grabbed my hands, shackled them behind me and placed a rough canvas hood over my head. I shut my eyes. And that's when I woke to hear myself screaming.

It was so dark that I couldn't see a thing. Did I still have a shroud over my head? Where was I? A startled Celeste dug her claws into my calf muscle, and then jumped off the bed and padded out of the room. I sensed a strong presence, and clutched at the amulet around my neck. My first instinct was to rip it off, and get rid of it, but as soon as my hands closed over it I felt calmer. I switched on all the lights and staggered off to the bathroom. Come on Eirene, it's just your subconscious re-creating the horrible story in the box, I told myself. Somehow I got back to sleep.

The morning was a chasm of emptiness. I flopped on the couch staring into space. I missed Will. I enjoyed our carefree relationship. He was funny and warm. When we were together it was all about work, and art, and having fun. There hadn't been any repeats of breakfast in bed, but I liked the idea of being Will's partner rather than being *that* Chinese girl. Still, even if he hadn't gone away, no way would I have told him anything about my nightmare.

I shuddered and tried to shake the ghastly scene from my head. The weight of the baggage in that battered red box was suffocating. Who were those people, Tee Hok Siong and Tee Ai-ling? Surely nothing to do with our family. I leapt up, dammit, there must be some clues in the box—I turfed out all the papers and started to go through them again, methodically, one by one.

"What the hell are you up to?"

I looked up, dazed, to see Dee had arrived home. She glanced around at the mess strewn across the table and pulled a wry face as she took in my uncombed hair and my eleven o'clock in the morning pyjamas. "What *are* you doing, Sis?"

Dee was the vivacious one. The one who flounced around in stilettos and chintzy dresses imprinted with overblown red roses or huge Marimekko poppies. Even when she was at work in her lawyerly black, her streaked hair cut fashionably short and that slash of bright red lipstick defined her as less than conventional. She was always busy, and often the only time our paths crossed was late at night or, on rare occasions, early in the morning—she on her way home, and me on my way out for a jog along the river.

Naturally I hadn't got around to telling her anything about the contents of the box. But now I had to tell her. I started to explain.

"What? That's odd," Dee said, looking bemused. Then,"Tea, I need tea."

She pottered around in the kitchen while I told her the rest, about the murder, the letters, Christian.

When I got up to the ghost part she was even more incredulous. I left out the latest creepy happening—I was still freaked out by that nightmare and the story was weird enough without it.

"So, you think you're being haunted by a ghost, and it's related to that musty old box Frank gave you? Are you crazy?" she said. "I always thought you were the sensible one of the two of us. Yet here you are, off on this wild goose chase. ... Is there more? You'd better tell me everything."

"There are even these trial reports," I said, waving several sheets of yellowing newspaper at her.

She looked up from dunking her tea bag.

"I can't believe that the newspapers would report the trial in such detail," I said. "There are columns of it. And he was just a simple illiterate Chinese from the back of beyond."

She plonked down next to me and peered at the newspaper clippings.

"Maybe because the prosecuting lawyer was Mr A. Rutledge, the Attorney-General of Queensland," she offered.

She read some more. "I wonder if he really was guilty," she said.

"You think? But even if he was innocent does *any* of it have to do with us?" I said.

"Dunno." She shuffled the pages back together and handed them back to me. "Let's wait and see if Frank remembers to ask the clan in Darwin."

I bundled everything back in the box.

Frank and Ronnie arrived back a few days later but we were both too busy at work to meet them at the airport. They got a taxi to our place, picked up their car and drove home. That weekend we had a family reunion down in Tallebudgera Valley. Frank was in a festive mood. He'd set up a table outside with a red tablecloth, wine glasses, candles, and the all-important mosquito coils under the table. It was almost summer, and the doors were flung wide open onto the timber deck which meandered around the sturdy tree trunks of the remnant bush. Ronnie waved hello from the kitchen.

A silence fell as we sat over the remains of a dinner of fresh pasta with asparagus, lemon, and spring herbs. Frank cleared his throat.

"Well," he said, "I asked the family about the box."

"You did? What did they say?" We turned to look at him.

"They said Dad's family originally came from Xiamen—or Amoy as it was called then."

"So Christian was right," I said. "He thought they must have."

"But does that mean we could be related to a murderer?" Dee asked.

"It seems so," Frank said. "Jimmy's grandmother's name was Ai-ling, Tee Ai-ling. She must be the one in the letters. Ai-ling married Lau Ming, which is where our surname Law comes from. Lau became Law when we moved to Australia. Easier to pronounce in English."

We sat around the table, silent. A twig dropped down beside me. Possums? Faint sounds came from the kitchen where Ronnie was loading the dishwasher.

I broke the silence. "Ai-ling would be our… great-great grandmother then. She must have stored her brother's letters, and the clippings that Mr John Holland sent, in the box."

"Sounds like it," Frank answered

"So, where did the box come from originally then?" I asked.

"We don't know," he said. "But they think Hong went back home when his mother, Ai-ling, died, and brought the box back to

Saigon with him."

"Hong?" Dee asked.

"Ai-ling and Ming had six kids and the eldest was Jimmy's father, Hong, your great-grandfather. He jumped on a ship when he was nineteen and landed up in Saigon."

"So Jimmy inherited the box from his father Hong?"

"And it arrived in Australia when we moved here. Quite a story, don't you think?" Frank looked pleased to have solved the mystery. Although he hadn't really.

Dee and I said nothing, trying to process the new information. A blanket of balmy night air wrapped itself around us. It was warm, but not warm enough to dissipate the cold feeling settling in the pit of my stomach.

Ronnie returned with a peach pie and cream.

"One more thing, I remembered this," Frank said, possibly making an effort to cheer us up. "Jimmy always said he liked the name Eirene, but he never seemed to say it properly. I just put it down to his accent but now I really think that all the time he was calling you Ai-ling, after his grandmother. They sound almost the same, don't you think."

Ronnie tilted her head to one side, like a curious magpie.

"You know I think you're right," she said, looking across to Frank. "I remember that. I always wanted to correct him, but I didn't say anything ... I didn't want to offend. Eirene, Ai-ling, they do sound the same."

I tried to take it all in. "So, Hok-Siong was Ai-ling's brother, and your great-great-uncle? I'm not sure if I want a murderer in the family," I said. Truth was, I definitely didn't.

Dee, always pragmatic, said, "We'd better keep on sleuthing then, and see if we can slay that ghost of yours!"

"What ghost?" Frank and Ronnie's heads turned in unison to look first at Dee and then at me. Naturally, my super rational parents didn't believe in ghosts—and neither did I ... well I didn't up until a few weeks earlier.

"Just some stupid things that happened. Christian has been teasing me about some kind of Chinese ghost, a *Yuan Gui* he called it."

"Frank?" Ronnie was on the case.

"Well, I don't know much, but that's one of the hungry ghosts. The *Yuan Gui* are spirits of those who died a violent or wrongful death. They roam the world of the living, restless and trapped. They can't find peace or be reincarnated until their names are cleared or justice is served."

"Christian talked about a ghost month," I said, throwing a questioning look at Frank.

"Ghost month, yes. That's when the gates of hell open, and the ghosts are temporarily set free. In the middle of the month, on the night of the full moon, people burn offerings and lay out food to appease them."

"I didn't think you believed in that kind of thing?" said Ronnie.

"Part of my childhood. Jimmy and Mei used to do it. And at the end of the month they floated lanterns on water barrels to help the ghosts find their way back to hell."

"When is it, ghost month?" Dee asked.

"Around August, September. It varies according to the Chinese lunar calendar."

"Sounds like you know a lot," Ronnie said. "You've never mentioned it before."

"I'd almost forgotten about it," Frank said. "When I was a kid every time we passed the lion statues on either side of the front door Jimmy would rest his big paw on the top of my head to stop me running away, and warn me about ghosts with enormous stomachs, tiny mouths, and long thin necks. They were always hungry because it was so hard to swallow anything. He said the lions would protect us but it still scared the hell out of me."

"Frank! You mean those stone lions in the garden?" Ronnie

could get a bit irritated when she felt left out.

"The same. I like them, and I know Jimmy and Mei believed they would keep their house safe."

"What else do you know?" said Ronnie.

Frank raised his eyebrows ever so slightly but refused to be intimidated.

"The *Yuan Gui* sometimes try to communicate with the living, to help them clear their honour. They are trapped in a transitional state, the *Bardo*, to borrow a Tibetan phrase, until their soul can find peace."

"So that means that Eirene's ghost could be our long-lost uncle trying to get her to clear his name?" Dee piped up.

"Don't worry honey, I'm sure it's all nonsense." Ronnie had caught the expression on my face, and quickly wrapped up the conversation.

They chatted on, and I made an effort to return to being sensible Eirene, level-headed Eirene, she who didn't have a supernatural bone in her body. But on the way out, with my recent nightmare in mind, I made sure to give those leonine guardians of the peace a pat on the head.

20: Hearts laid bare

Dulbydilla: 1886

Day after day, Ah Sue weeded, dug, hoed, and planted. Every morning Moll laid out the vegetables, big round cabbages to the left, potatoes to the right, and in the middle herbs and greens, fresh and sparkling with what went for dew in those parts. Sometimes piles of crisp carrots and fat juicy tomatoes added a touch of colour.

Ah Sue was a frugal type; he'd finally saved enough money to rent the land on the slopes of the creek in Dulbydilla. The railway line construction had been pushing on out west from Roma towards Charleville and the next staging post was Dulbydilla. They had seen the possibilities. The town was growing fast and likely to have hundreds in the camp before long.

Ah Sue tacked up a framework of rough-cut logs while Moll hammered every flattened kerosine tin, plank of wood, or flotsam she could scrounge onto the sturdy structure. It was only one room, but it did for them, it was their home. They added a lean-to on the side of the cabin. And that became the shop. Moll was happier than she'd been in a long time. She was a shopkeeper! How la-di-dah! If only her Da could see her now—said she'd come to nothing, hadn't he?

About a month after Moll finished setting up the shop Kate had turned up. Her man had led the way, a tall bloke with a bit of a swagger striding into the camp with a large, battered cabin trunk humped up on his shoulder. Kate trailed along behind, a bundle on her back, a baby on one hip and yanking a toddler along by the hand. You could tell she was a looker even if her clothes were bedraggled and her face peaky. They were down on their luck, and why would you come here otherwise, Moll thought—especially with two young ones in tow. Times were tough.

Later, Moll would tell anyone who asked how she met Kate, "She paid me no mind at first, Kate did," she would say. "Then her husband shot through, he just up and left. I took over some boiled sultana cake, and a big bowl of stew. There was a good lump of mutton in there too. 'For the little ones,' I said to her."

Here Moll usually paused mid-story, keen to see if her generosity was being recognised. All being well, she carried on. "Kate said thanks, but that's all she said. She stood there; her eyes fixed firmly down at the ground. I asked her—anything else you need? 'No, no—no, I'm grand, ta very much,' that's what she said. Anyone could tell she wasn't grand, but what can you do? Pride, that's what it was, stubborn pride. I knew it would pass."

And pass it did. Moll kept on visiting, and before long they were friends.

"Why don't you take in washing," Moll had suggested. "You can set up here, in the new lean-to at the back, you can't be lugging water all the way back to that tent of yours. And I can help you with the childers during the day."

So Kate started her business. And Moll minded the children on and off during the day until the little family went back to the camp at night. Moll enjoyed having the children near, almost as good as having your own. Most girls get with child at the drop of a hat or whatever—but not Moll, not so far anyways. She was only young though, plenty of time. Ah Sue kept saving the best morsels of food for her. Eat, eat, get strong, he said. She knew why, but they never talked about it.

Ah Sue had rigged up the most ingenious irrigation system and as long as there was water, the plants flourished. But the drought hit them hard. Moll was out of her mind. No water meant no vegetables, and no vegetables meant no money coming in. She arranged for oranges to be delivered from Toowoomba. At least then they would have something to sell. People complained about the price but what could she do? The freight cost an arm and a leg. Finally, a few weeks after Christmas, it rained—thank the lord! The creek ran, the dam filled and Moll heaved a sigh of relief.

Early in February, a new cook for Mr Falconer's boring camp had arrived. He was Chinese, but Moll noticed that the rest of his countrymen weren't exactly welcoming.

"He's from Amoy," Ah Sue explained, "and as good as a foreigner to them." Unlike the others Ah Sue greeted Hok with a warm smile and a nod, he was much too busy making ends meet to be bothered about such things. He was a good man, as Moll always said—he liked to see the best in everyone, whoever they were.

After serving breakfast to Mr Falconer's crew, Hok would hustle down to Molly's stall and buy up the choicest vegetables to cook for their main mid-day meal. He was always joking, and though his clothes were shabby, he wore them with a jaunty style.

Once, Kate was standing there by the side of the counter when he came in. He made a few jokes as usual, and Kate bantered back. He threw his head back and laughed out loud. Moll was pleased to see him loosening up. Though she did notice that his face fell as soon as he turned away, and he looked lonely and sad again. Not surprising, she thought, in a place like Dulbydilla. Most hated the Chinese, Mongolian hordes was the usual description, but some went so far as to call the Chinese debauched yellow savages. Even so, the hoi polloi appreciated leavening their usual diet of mutton with some potatoes, onions, and fresh greens. Buggers the lot of them, Moll always said.

Moll noticed that Hok wasn't the only one paying attention to Kate. There was that handsome fellow from the boring camp, Finbar Murphy, for one.

Finbar had fled Sydney the day after his twenty-first birthday. He joined a trail of young men looking for work and adventure, preferably both, but maybe adventure first, and work second. He thought himself lucky to find a job with Mr Falconer, an entrepreneurial mining engineer and boring contractor.

It was interesting work to begin with, drilling for the foundations of the Maranoa Bridge, and then boring for water in the railway yard in Mitchell, using Mr Falconer's soon to be patented auger. Steam trains needed water, a lot of water, and water was in short supply on the route of the new railway line out west. The only hope was the great artesian basin and for that you had to drill down deep.

After Mitchell they moved on to Dulbydilla but they were plagued with stoppages and breakdowns, and it all took much longer than anticipated. Mr Falconer's enthusiasm for his invention waned.

Even so, Finbar enjoyed the camaraderie of the outback, and the freedom, away from the narrow streets and stinking backyards of Surry Hills—and away from his parents. Bog Irish was what he used to call them, only partly in affection. *He* could call them that, but heaven help anyone else who said the same.

Despite his name, Finbar the fair headed, he had a mop of curly black hair—his Mam had mistakenly thought he would take after her. He had the habit of jauntily tossing his hair back from his forehead, laying bare his roguish hazel eyes. He was handsome alright. If you hadn't heard his name, you might have thought he was a gypsy, judging by his suntanned skin, the red bandana he always wore around his neck, and the faint scar on his left cheekbone.

Plenty of girls in Mitchell had fancied the dashing Irishman. In Dulbydilla there was no shortage of married women, publican's wives, shopkeeper's wives, and businesswomen, but as for young ones looking for a bit of fun—next to none. Then he'd spied Kate flouncing down the main street, a basket of washing on her hip. She had a sassy look about her that he liked. She had two young ones, but that didn't deter him. She had a husband though, and that did.

Finbar was there in the crowd watching when her husband took on that navvy from South Australia. He saw the humiliation in the man's eyes, as he flailed his arms uselessly, exhausted after nearly an hour, blood streaming from a cut above one bloodshot eye, and the other swollen and closed. It was a debacle. Then the vanquished warrior disappeared, unable to face the shame of defeat.

Kate was on her own, and after a decent interval, Finbar started seeing her. She was a fine thing, but no way was he going to get shackled with two wains and a wife. He tried to stay indifferent to her charms and keep his emotions in check. But before long he found himself wanting the comfort of her arms more and more. It was galling when she put him off, dipping her head and making excuses with a wry smile. He was lonely—not a feeling he'd experienced before—he hungered for her touch. The more she put him off the more he wanted her. She had relented at last, and his visits became more frequent. He delighted in the delicate hollow of her neck, the soft down on her arms and the determined tilt of her chin. She stroked his hair as he lay beside her, and he was captivated.

Finbar wasn't alone in burning with a desire for Dulbydilla's washerwoman. Edwin had fancied Kate—such a splendid-looking young woman—for quite a while before he succeeded in getting even a 'morning' from her. Things looked up from then on. She did have children though. Perhaps she was still married—he didn't know. All she said was that the scum had buggered off, and that was it. He didn't dare ask for any more details. It was probably none of his business—he wasn't going to marry her, in fact technically speaking he was still married himself.

Edwin Mallard was well known in the town—though he was not thought well of. Almost every day he visited the shops, hotels, bars, and billiard rooms in Dulbydilla. Most of them stocked his aerated waters and cordials and he was always keen to sell them more. He bought a drink at every bar and hotel he visited. That's what it takes to be a good salesman he used to tell himself—be sociable Edwin. As a result, he was frequently inebriated by mid-afternoon and had to retire to his factory to sleep it off, sneaking in past Ned who was slaving away as usual bottling and labelling. It was a lot quieter since George, his partner, had run off with his wife Ellen. They had both complained about having to do all the work. Bloody rubbish, Edwin told everyone. Repeatedly.

All the while Hok was becoming more comfortable in Dulbydilla. He enjoyed his daily chats with Moll and Kate, and the men in the camp were appreciative of his cooking. Problem was, Charlie had not paid him back and was showing no signs of doing so. Hok had dropped a few hints but the days were going by and he was losing patience.

One morning, early, Hok was in Yung Kee's shop, stocking up on salt, when Charlie walked in, glanced around, and threw a sour look in Hok's direction.

Maybe Yung Kee would shame Charlie into paying him back, Hok thought. Now was his chance. Worth a try. He seized the opportunity and confronted Charlie, "You have my money, Charlie?"

"No," said Charlie. He shrugged and looked over at Yung Kee, "I no owe him money," he said.

Hok's face flushed. He stepped closer. Charlie didn't move. They glared at each other. Yung Kee planted his hands on his hips and shouted at them both, "You! Out! I don't want any row in my shop. Go on, get out."

Once outside Ah Fook pleaded with Hok.

"Just one more day," he said.

"One more day, Charlie…one!" Hok shook his head at the slight smirk lingering on Charlie's face and walked away without another word. What could he do? Ah Fook had lied to save face in front of

Yung Kee, he was liar and a cheat, and not to be trusted.

That night Hok headed up to Kate's tent. Hok cradled a cloth bundle in his arms, saved leftovers from the midday dinner, cold now, but still delicious. Packed up with the leftovers were some rations, and a few toys from Mr Kreibke's store for the children. Worth every precious penny, he thought—just to put a smile on her face.

The shadows darkened as he neared her tent. There wasn't any lamplight showing. Was it too late? He struck a match, "Are you there Kate," he called softly. And then he froze.

A man was sitting on Kate's bed pulling on his socks. The match went out just as the man lifted his head towards the sound. Hok stepped back into the shadow of a tree, shocked. The man pulled on his boots, grabbed his coat, and strode away.

Another match strike came from inside the tent followed by the glow of a lantern. Kate pushed aside the sheet hanging across the back part of the tent and hung the lamp up on a hook. She gave a gasp as she caught sight of Hok.

"You! What are you doing here?"

"Who that man?" he asked.

"None of your business," she said.

He felt a chill in his heart, she didn't sound friendly. The talk could be true then. He hadn't wanted to believe what the others said, but now?

"Not good," he said. His chest tightened; his mouth was dry. He didn't know what to say.

She stared back at him, "Yes, well it's none of your business. Just go away! I don't need presents from a dirty little Chinaman!"

He took one look at her angry face and ran off so fast he nearly crowned himself on a wayward tree trunk. What did she call him? A dirty little Chinaman! That hurt. She had bewitched him, flashing her white teeth, and flicking her hair back as she laughed at his jokes. She accepted his bundles of food. And all the while she despised him. He ran to the dam and threw the bundle as far as he could into the water.

Moll was out the back as usual that night, getting the vegetables sorted for the next day. Carrots, parsnips, and potatoes were heaped up at the back of the shop, waiting to be scrubbed. A big pile of onions needed to be bagged into the six hessian sacks on her workbench—ready for delivery to the general store in Mitchell. Ah Sue was dead asleep after another long day in the garden, and all was quiet.

In the deathly stillness she heard the crack of twigs breaking underfoot and then a splash. She looked up, and on the other side of the garden near the creek she saw a figure standing, arms loose by his sides, and his head sunk low on his chest. The figure stood there motionless for a minute or so, as though in deep thought, and then turned and plodded off into the dark. She knew very well who it was, that hat… and the way he walked… it was Hok. It was him, no doubt about it. But what on earth was he doing. She had a heap of work to do before she could join Ah Sue in a well-earned rest, but curiosity got the better of her. She grabbed her lantern and clutching her skirts tight to clear the raised beds on either side she followed one of the deep furrows running across the garden towards the dam. She looked out over the dark water and at first nothing could be seen. Then, lodged up against a fallen branch, she could see a bundle half poking out of the water. The cloth was unmistakable, she had seen Hok passing bundles to Kate, wrapped in the very same worn blue and white patterned cotton fabric. No-one else in the town had anything like it. She tried to fish the bundle out with a stick but couldn't reach it.

Could Hok have had a row with Kate? Strange, she thought, and confusing. But those onions won't pack themselves, better get back to it or I'll never get to bed.

On the other side of the railway tracks Kate had calmed down enough to feel guilty about her outburst. But why did he have to come snooping around like that? It was really none of his business if she had a few visitors.

As Kate lowered her tent flap Edwin made his stumbling way back through the silent town feeling more content than he had in a while. You've still got it Edwin, he thought. Take that you bitch, and he shook his fist at his long gone wife.

And Finbar? Finbar smiled in his sleep and lazily rolled over dreaming of his last encounter with Kate.

Meanwhile Hok trudged back to the camp in a daze, Kate's words echoing in his head, over and over again. He crawled into his swag and wrapped his arms tight around his miserable body. Each heartbeat brought another wave of humiliation. How could he even look her in the face again? He would leave, get away from this horrible place. Right away. But first he needed his money back. He tossed to one side and then the other in an agony of despair before he fell into a fitful sleep.

FIVE

21: Hok

Brisbane, Australia: 2019

A hand stretches out. A woman's hand. One of the voices. Her fingers stroke along the top of the box, she empties the papers out, and studies them. I feel hope. I wait. I want to join my ancestors. Maybe she can help me? I have been too long waiting.

I am alone, trapped, abandoned, and lost. I have no life and no future. Charlie wasn't a good man but I'm sorry he died. Now he's in his own hell, and me, I am in mine.

Angry, I float out of the box and around the room. A whirlwind—all that remains of my physical presence—flutters the pages scattered across the table. I want revenge on those liars at the trial. I want justice. It wasn't me shot Charlie. Which one of them did?

22: Sleuthing

Brisbane: November, 2019

It was Saturday again, a week since we'd seen Frank and Ronnie down in the valley. I shuffled out of my bedroom still half asleep to find a dishevelled Dee in the middle of a paper chaos. Her hair had taken on an even more punk look than usual, and stuff was strewn everywhere. "What *are* you doing?"

"I've been studying those newspaper reports of the trial," she said.

"You mean our criminal great-great-great-uncle's trial? Is that the right number of greats?"

"You could be right about the greats," Dee said. "But maybe not about the criminal bit. He was a simple soul, but a murderer? I'm not convinced. There's something fishy about what happened. Look." And she rifled through the bundle of papers on the table pointing to sections she'd highlighted with a yellow marker.

"And then there's this." She pointed to her screen. "I've found the police file with his photo on it."

"You've been busy."

"It's disturbing, he looks a bit like Frank," she said.

I sat down next to her. Hok looked straight out of the photo at me. His hair was standing up on end like a messy echidna and he had a bewildered look in his eyes. He did look a lot like a younger Frank.

"He was short. Five foot two and a half inches—that'd be around my height," I calculated.

"God, read this." Dee had scrolled to a handwritten note below the photo, not quite in copperplate but with a few flourishes nevertheless. The underlined heading read 'Executed 5 April 1886.'

We stared at the report of his last days in silence.

"Adhered to his denial up to the day of his death," said Dee.

"Was apparently buoyed up with the belief that he would be able to return after death and wreak his vengeance on those who had given evidence against him," I read.

"After being pinioned he asked for a cigarette … when informed that the moment had arrived for execution he threw it down and walked onto the scaffold."

"Death was instantaneous!" I said, not sure whether that was good or bad.

Buzz! We both jumped. It was the door intercom.

Dee looked at me. "You expecting someone?"

"Damn, that must be Christian. I forgot."

"I thought you said he was an arrogant fuckwit and you weren't going to see him again."

"Yeah well, he called. Said he'd like to come over to discuss a few things. What could I say?"

"Could have said no."

"Could have," I said.

I'd agreed to see him, but reluctantly. He'd sounded so contrite, and after all, I'd told myself, I *was* a grown woman—I should at least try to be civil.

I keyed him in, and his eyebrows lifted when he saw the two of us in the middle of the paper chaos. Dee, still in her pyjamas, looked up at him with a mischievous smile.

"We have to do something to help Eirene slay her hungry ghost."

"Don't tell me she believes in that ghost stuff now."

"She doesn't," said Dee emphatically. "And neither do I. But I do believe in justice. Especially when it's one of the family."

"So … there is a family connection?"

"Tee Ai-ling was Jimmy's grandmother," I said.

"Oh."

"She was our great-great-grandmother and Hok Siong was our distant uncle."

"So it's personal then."

"Unfortunately," said Dee.

Everything had become more real now that we knew who Tee Ai-ling was. Was her brother really a murderer? Was there any escape out of this horrible legacy?

"Thing is, we're not sure if he was guilty. Have a look at this," Dee said to Christian.

She pointed out the crucial points in the evidence given at the trial. They bent their heads together studying the papers spread out all over the table.

"The prosecution had a field day. I could have put forward a better defence."

"Thank you Miss Law, but I put it to you that he was guilty, beyond question," Christian said, hamming it up.

Dee grinned at him, ready for the challenge. I'm not the jealous type, but sometimes you just can't help yourself. It was *my* ghost and Christian was *my* find. Inconsistent I know, because I hadn't forgiven him for what he said. *And* he wasn't my type. So why did it upset me?

Christian stabbed his finger on the page and said, "See what is says here. The police found a gun cap and some grains of shot in his pockets. And he virtually confessed to them in the watch-house."

"It was one grain of shot according to Constable Kelly's evidence," Dee said for the defence. "And Hok said he didn't have a gun."

"If he had leftover shot in his pocket then that means he lied about not having a gun."

"Wouldn't he have cleared out his pockets if he was guilty?" I said but they took no notice.

"And what about the confession," Christian said.

"Yes, that must have been the next morning," said Dee, pushing up her glasses with one finger and shuffling the papers in front of her. "Listen to it, the so-called confession: *If me knew you were after me, I would have cleared out when I done it.*"

"That seems pretty conclusive," said Christian. "Guilty as charged."

Dee shook her head, "Not so fast. To me it sounds more like an attempt to explain that his behaviour was not that of a guilty man. Don't you think he meant, *If I did it, I would have run away?* I don't think it's conclusive."

"Exactly," I said loudly, refusing to be left out. They both looked at me. "That's pretty much what John Holland said."

I grabbed a sheet off the table.

"… Here it is. From the Toowoomba Chronicle. Holland, well I think it has to be him, said: *The prisoner's statement that had he known the police were after him he would have cleared out, must be viewed in the light of his imperfect knowledge of English.*"

"Too true," Dee said. "I don't see how it could be considered a confession, when at the same time he continually said he was innocent right to the end."

"You could be right," Christian said, abandoning his role as prosecutor. "He could have been misunderstood or even misrepresented. He could have been framed. There was a heap of prejudice against Chinese at the time. And who's to say the police weren't biased."

We agreed. It was a possibility. But how to prove it?

"Well the trial was hopeless," Dee said flinging the papers in her hand back on the table. "He had no-one to represent him until the second day, and it was only then that they found a translator for him, or at least one that could speak Hokkien. No one saw him do it; no one saw him in the vicinity; no one saw him with a gun, and there was no testimony that he even knew how to load and shoot a gun."

"And no witnesses for the defence," said Christian.

"What's strange," I said, "is that he doesn't seem to have put up much of a fight to save himself. Did he just abandon himself to fate? Or, if someone else did it, was he covering up for them?"

"And how about a motive?" asked Dee. "Did he have one? He'd only been there for two weeks, could he have formed such an animosity towards the baker in such a short time?"

"There was talk that the dead guy, Charlie Ah Fook, owed him money," Christian said. "Here, Louis Carlsson asked Charlie why did Hok shoot him, and the answer was, *He want him money.*"

"Yes, money could be a motive," I said. "But the other motive sounds like rubbish. That woman Kate was most likely a prostitute, how could she be his missus?

"What woman?" Christian asked. "I missed that bit."

"Here," I said picking up the newspaper report of the trial. "The storekeeper Thomas Levy said:

> *On the 25th of February last, the prisoner was in the store. I had a conversation with him. I said, 'I heard you had a row last night Hok.' He replied 'Yes, I had a row with my missis, I told her I was not coming up to the tent that night, I did not feel tired, and took a walk up, and when I went to the tent, I struck a match and said, are you in Kate? I saw a man sitting in the tent pulling on his socks.' "*

"Who was the sock-man?" Christian asked.

"It doesn't say. But that's not all from Thomas. He said:

> *I asked Hok Siong whether he hit the man, and he said, 'No, I no hit him, I kick up a row and throw all the rations out. I no buy rations to keep another man.' Then he said, 'Chinaman baker been there too, all the same, dead now.' I*

said, 'Dead, where?' The prisoner said, 'To-night.' "

Christian looked puzzled. "Tonight?" he said.

"Yes," said Dee. "Thomas asked, 'Dead where?' and Hok answered 'Tonight.'"

"Weird," said Christian.

"Yes, weird,' I agreed. "The whole conversation doesn't sound quite right to me. Did you notice that the first part, up to the sock-man, is in almost perfect English. But the second part sounds more like the same person who said, 'Me no shoot,' in his defence."

"I think you're right," Christian said. "The first part could be Thomas putting words in Hok's mouth, a bit of an embellishment to make the story more interesting."

"And the second part, though it's very confusing, sounds more like the real Hok talking," I said.

"Can you believe it," said Dee, "after all that, the defence lawyer only asked one thing. He asked Thomas if he thought Hok meant the baker was dead, or that the sock guy was dead. It's ridiculous! What sort of defence is that?"

"And actually," I pointed out, "no one died that night. Because the conversation took place a whole day before the shooting."

"True," said Dee.

"There is another aspect to all that," Christian said, "I don't think Missus would mean a wife, or even a girlfriend to someone like Hok. It usually meant the station manager's wife or the boss's wife. Someone of importance, a white woman, a 'Mrs' in other words. I doubt very much that he would have called her *my* Missus, but he could have called Kate *the* Missus, or Missus Kate. He'd only been there two weeks; how could they have an amorous relationship already? And also … *if* she was his girlfriend, why were they sleeping in separate tents?"

"You're so right," I said. "I wonder what the jury made of that. No word from the defence lawyer though."

"The talk about the rations and throwing them out is a bit odd," said Christian.

"Okay," I said. "Let's assume Thomas Levy's statement is correct and Hok was on visiting terms with the woman, Kate, or he knew her from before … he could have just been friends with her. Unlikely but maybe. Two nights before the murder he told Kate that he wasn't coming to visit her that night, and then he changed his mind. He saw the sock-man, he was angry, kicked up a row, and threw out the rations, or whatever it was that he'd brought to give to Kate."

"But what about the rest of it?" said Christian. "That strange, bit about the Chinaman baker. Being dead, except that he wasn't. Not then anyway. Not till two nights later."

We sat in quiet contemplation.

"I have to go," Christian said. "It's all interesting, though I'm not sure we can get anywhere with it."

Yes, go, I thought, as my angst at him came thumping back. But then my mouth took on a life of its own. Horrified, I heard myself say in a perfectly reasonable tone, "Okay, I'll walk you to your car."

"What was it you wanted to say?" I asked to break the awkward silence as we stood side by side in the lift.

"What?"

"You said you wanted to discuss a few things."

"Oh, that," he said. "How about a walk along the river?"

"Sure."

A shaft of late afternoon sun pierced the clouds and slanted across to the opposite bank of the river where a row of white two story houses sat gleaming like a mouth full of gappy teeth.

"I wanted to say I'm sorry," he said. "I overstepped the mark. You have every right to be who you want to be. Whatever culture you identify with is up to you."

The grey clouds shuffled back over the sun turning the river waters a drab brown. We walked on.

"Yes, well, I might have been a bit sensitive," I admitted and the knot in my stomach started to loosen.

"I should explain my thoughts rather than criticise yours," he said stepping to one side as a cyclist wearing iridescent purple glasses and bright blue polyester outfit whooshed by—a pop of colour against the dullness of the day.

"You see I don't belong anywhere either. Everyone slots me into the Chinese box too, but my family left China more than a hundred years ago, just as yours did. I identify more as Malaysian because that's where I was born, but even there we will always be Malaysian Chinese—another box."

Feeling mollified I kept quiet and listened.

"Most of my formative years were spent here in Australia, and I'm an Australian citizen. But like you I am classified by my appearance. The answer to the question, 'Where do you come from?' is always complicated, yet the short answer, 'Australia,' is too blunt, and usually comes across as a bit smart arse."

I knew what he meant.

"I no more identify with the mainland Chinese who come here to study or for business than you do. I grew up speaking not just Hokkien, but Malaysian Hokkien. I had to learn Mandarin because it's part of my job, but it's not my first language. And it was even harder than learning to speak English."

He looked across at me with a smile.

"The thing is, I rather like the feeling of not-belonging. There's a certain freedom in being released from any ideas of patriotism. I can feed off the best of any of those cultures without being hidebound to be loyal to any of them."

It seemed to make sense.

"Let's face it," he added, "no country is perfect, no peoples are all good, or all bad. Take racism, it's everywhere, even among those who can claim to be the most victimised. But that doesn't mean I can't do my utmost to fight it. I choose to identify with, and to promote, the best of the human condition, of whatever culture."

I couldn't think of anything to say, apart from nodding my head at the right moments. I probably looked like one of those old rear window car mascots—the nodding dog.

"You can decide to be whoever you want to be," he said. "I had no right to criticise you."

We walked on. The evening quiet was broken by the wake of a ferry splashing up against the riverbank.

"Better get back," he said.

"Best wishes to Frank," he said opening his car door.

"See you round," I said.

I let myself go and gave a smile—just a little one.

"Yep," he said, and drove off.

23: Threats and resolutions

Dulbydilla: Thursday, February 24, 1886

In the morning Moll had another look for the parcel she'd seen Hok throw into the creek, but it had sunk down deep into the muddy depths. She hurried back to the shop and found her first customer waiting—Mary, Louis Carlsson's wife. Always keen for a chat, Mary had saved up some intriguing gossip especially for Moll.

Moll feigned an interest. "Well I never…really…who would have thought?" she said, her hand poised in the process of selecting the choicest carrots for Mary. She had the right words ready, but every woman knows the rules of the game, it's tit for tat, one revelation has to be balanced by another.

Moll cast around for a suitable divulgence. All she could think of was Hok throwing the parcel of food into the dam, and the thought that he might have had a row with Kate. It wasn't much, but it was all she could think of. Mary mustered a suitable response. Although, Moll thought, she probably wasn't very interested in the emotional life of one of the town's here-today-gone-tomorrow cooks—and a Chinaman at that. Moll added a complimentary orange on top of the vegetables and watched Mary walk off down the road towards Mr Kreibke's store.

That afternoon Hok finished clearing the remnants of the midday meal in a flurry of activity. Then he stopped, motionless, cloth in hand, staring into the bush. He had to get his money back. He had to confront Charlie Ah Fook. Now! He threw down the cloth, rammed his hat on his head, and marched off down the well worn track of red dust towards the town.

He found Charlie collapsed on his bed at the back of the shop. Some afternoons the baker liked to have a drink or two once all the bread had been sold, and this was one of them. Later, after his evening meal, he would get his dough ready for the dawn bake before collapsing again for a few hours. Dust motes floated lazily in the shafts of light coming through the open door of the shop. Hok shook Charlie by the shoulder.

"I need my money, Charlie."

Charlie grunted and shrugged his shoulder. The camp bed creaked and swayed as he turned his body over to look at Hok. "One more day," he said, "one more day. That fellow he pay me back next day…"

"That's what you said yesterday—one more day."

Charlie propped himself up on his elbow, and finally looked Hok in the face. "But what the matter, boy? Something wrong?"

Hok could smell the pungent scent of liquor on his breath. "I can't wait no more," he said.

"Thomas say you have a row with that pretty missus." Charlie was eager to change the subject. Maybe he suspected that there was more to Hok's dejected look than money.

"Thomas? Who is Thomas?"

"Thomas? You know. The manager at Kreibke's store," said Charlie.

Much as Hok didn't trust Ah Fook it was a relief to find someone he could talk to about the events of the night before.

"I find man there, in tent. He sit on bed, pull his socks on. Me think she good girl but no."

"I been see that too. I been there, walk past, go see my friend in railway camp. She no good that one." Charlie breathed in through his teeth, and spat on the floor. "Come here tomorrow boy, me sleep now," he said as he rolled over.

Before a confused and troubled Hok reached the door, Charlie's chest was rising and falling rhythmically, and his drunken snores had returned.

How did Thomas know about the row with Kate, Hok wondered. He decided to call into Mr Kreibke's store on the pretence of needing some more supplies. Thomas was behind the counter as usual and looked pleased to see the subject of his latest round of gossip walk through the door.

"Hey Hok, I hear you had a row with Missus Kate last night," he said. Hok struggled with a response.

"Yes, I see strange man in tent."

"What you do, you hit him?"

"No, I no hit him. I bring rations for the Missus, but I throw them out. I no buy rations to keep another man."

"So, you think she's no good?" Thomas asked.

"Chinaman baker seen that too, all the same … . Him dead now."

"Dead…?" said Thomas, looking up sharply. "Who? Where?"

"Not right," Hok said, ignoring Thomas's questions. Nothing would ever be right where that cheat was concerned. Was it right that the baker was lying in a drunken stupor in the middle of the afternoon, dead to the world, and had no intention of paying back the money he owed? He walked out shaking his head and hurried back to prepare the evening meal for the hungry well-borers.

Edwin Mallard's first call of the morning had been at the Black Waterhole Hotel. It was just before lunch and he had indulged himself in a gin and tonic—Mallard's best tonic water, of course. MacKenzie, the publican, was a good fellow in Edwin's estimation. He always served a tasty meal and usually ordered plenty of Edwin's stock. After a substantial lunch, and not a few glasses of the excellent 1882 vintage wine from Mt Abundance, Edwin wandered off down the road towards the town. "Not a cloud …," he observed looking up at the sky as he stepped out of the hotel on his way to the next victim of his sales technique. Although, in Edwin's case, who's to say who was the victim. He paid for all his own drinks—he insisted on paying. He was an honourable man, as he always said. Frequently. But the more he drank the less profit he made. So, honourable, but maybe not sensible.

His last call on that fine afternoon was Mr Kreibke's store. Colourful bottles of Mallard's Famous Cordial were stacked up on the shelves in tidy rows, like soldiers on a parade ground. Thomas, the manager, was a very obliging chap, a friendly fellow but a hopeless gossip.

Edwin strode into the store, his head full of the sight of Kate. He'd just seen her striding along the street, a bundle of washing under her arm, her blue skirt swishing around her ankles, and her golden red curls bouncing around the nape of her neck, escapees from all effort to tame them. Such a delicious neck, he was overwhelmed thinking about it. And with those thoughts running around in his brain it's no wonder that he was shocked by what Thomas had to tell him.

He ordered a glass of his own lime cordial to cool himself down and listened to Thomas repeat a conversation he'd had with the Chinese cook from the boring camp. "It seems," Thomas said, "that the new cook fancies that pretty one, her that takes in washing. Kate, isn't it?"

Edwin neither agreed nor disagreed, he took out his handkerchief and mopped his face. "It's hot, no?"

Thomas continued with barely a glance at Edwin's flushed face, "Hok came in here not an hour ago and said he'd gone up to see Kate last night for a chat, and he saw a man sitting on the bed in her tent pulling on his socks. He was shocked, I guess he didn't think she was that sort of a girl. I asked him what he did when he saw the man. 'Me angry but me no hit him,' he said."

"Mmm," was all that Edwin could trust himself to say. He hadn't known he was being observed.

"But there was more," Thomas said. "He told me, 'That Chinaman baker been there too, all the same the other one.' He said, 'Me very angry. Me lend him money and he no pay back. Him dead now.' Dead where? I said. 'Tonight,' he said." Thomas picked up a duster and swiped the counter before looking up at Edwin to gauge his reaction. "Sounds a bit strange doesn't it? As far as I know the baker is still alive and kicking."

Edwin mopped his face again. "It really is a stifling hot day," he said. He mumbled a few indistinct words that could have been in agreement with Thomas or not, said goodbye, and made it out the door.

By the time he got to Cavanagh's Hotel, Edwin could no longer ignore the import of Thomas's revelations. Suspicions were thrashing around in his head like eels in a trap. He had a whiskey to calm himself down.

It didn't work.

He left Cavanagh's bar in a rage. How dare those conniving Chinese make a move on Kate, his Kate. And there was not just one, but two of the little pig-tailed heathens hanging around her. And another thing, what did the cook mean by *him dead now*? For all his bluster Edwin was not a brave man. That the cook might be after him too was a disturbing thought, but it was swamped by his absolute rage at the fact that he might be sharing Kate with another man, and not just any man, but one of those dirty celestials.

He would ask Kate—straight up, he would ask her. Are you fooling around with those yellow chinky devils? I'm a respectable man, what about my reputation? He strode off to accost Kate. He barely noticed Moll serving a customer in the front as he rushed past to the back of the shop, trailing a miasma of alcoholic fumes behind him.

"What's up?" Kate noticed his agitated jumping from foot to foot, not to mention his red face.

"You've been seeing other men?"

"What men?"

"Those chinkys," his lips stretched back in a snarl as he spat out the words.

"What chinkys?"

"That cook from the boring camp, and the bloody baker."

"Hok's a friend."

"Hok? You mean that wretched little cook. A friend? What kind of a friend?"

"Just a friend, a normal friend. One you pass the time of day with." Kate picked a shirt up out of the sudsy water in the tub and gave it a vigorous rub on the washboard. She looked up at him, "You know what … if you don't like it, don't come up to my tent no more."

"Well, what about that damn baker. What then?"

Kate looked him up and down. She rested her hands on the edge of the tub, looked straight up to him, tilted her head to one side, and laughed. A scornful laugh, a take that and stick it up your pipe laugh, the kind that said I don't care what you think.

Edwin stepped back. His eyes widened.

"The baker? You've been consorting with the baker? How could you?"

He noticed nothing, and nobody, as he stomped back to his factory.

"Thanks Ned, you can go now. No, don't finish that, just go. See you tomorrow," he said to his assistant through tightly clenched teeth. He waited, rubbing his fist in his hand, while Ned lifted his paddle from one of the vats of sweet-smelling liquids, took off his heavy brown apron, rolled down his shirt sleeves, and walked out.

Edwin's mind was firmly fixed on the emergency bottle of whiskey in his bottom drawer. He marched past the piles of wooden crates full of bottles into the boxed off clearing which was his office and reached into the drawer.

Hok couldn't stop churning things over in his mind. What to do? There was Charlie, who had borrowed his precious hard earned money, and then there was Kate. He had set himself up for disappointment; he had been swept away by his feelings. Every time Kate gave him one of her golden smiles he'd felt a surge of happiness. But now he knew. She was no better than the rest of them.

He needed to get far away and out of the place. That baker better have the money ready as promised. Did Charlie take him for a pushover? Ten gold sovereigns is a lot of money. How stupid, to think he could buy friendship. He would have to tackle Charlie again, and the best chance of finding Charlie sober and awake was in the evening.

After serving a supper of leftovers Hok laid out what was needed for breakfast. A whiff of kerosine escaped into the air as he doused the cookhouse lantern and he set off alone to the waterhole through the encroaching dusk. A walk would calm him down before confronting Charlie, he'd thought. But it didn't—the more he walked the more annoyed and upset he became. Loneliness overwhelmed him as he gazed into the black depths of the waterhole.

He stumbled back through the moonless dark. It was so still he could hear the dead leaves crunching underfoot. He found Charlie in the bakehouse at the back of his shop. Charlie lifted a steaming pot off the stove and carried it over to his stool by the doorway.

"Charlie I need my money now," Hok said for the second time that day.

Charlie looked up, a disconcerting half-grin on his face, "Again? I told you before me got no money," he said. "Me can't give you any. One more day—one more day, boy." A twig snapped in the alleyway, but neither Charlie nor Hok noticed a dark shape hiding in the shadows.

Hok's fists tightened and he stared at the baker in despair. What a fool he was? He was so mad he could have strangled Charlie there and then. He was exasperated, but he didn't know what to do. Should he hit him? Would that help? He thought not. The baker was not a big man, but he was strong—Hok had seen him throw around those heavy sacks of flour.

He didn't want to look at that lying cheating face for one more second. "Charlie, me want my money, give me my money … or else." He shot a black look at the baker, and stalked off into the night, back to the camp.

His mind was a jumble. He lay on his swag and struggled to sleep. He was a double fool, he had trusted that Charlie Ah Fook, who still hadn't paid back the money he borrowed—and maybe never would—and he had fallen for Kate, who thought he was a dirty little Chinaman. How could he forget what had happened? He never wanted to see either of them again. He just wanted his money back and then he could clear off.

Meanwhile, after one or two, or was it three, whiskeys Edwin had slapped his hand down on the desktop and jumped up, decision made. I'm going to have it out with those wretched heathen Chinee, he'd thought.

He'd slammed the door of the factory shut behind him and marched off into the night towards the bakery. The front door was closed so he walked towards a glow of light in the side alley but pulled back when he saw two figures near the back door. The baker was sitting on a stool mixing something in a bucket. A single lantern hung on a hook just behind him and illuminated the face of the cook standing in front of him. The two culprits together!

The baker was talking. "Me got no money," he said. He stirred the steaming bucket then lifted his head again and shouted at the cook, "Me can't give you any." The cook yelled even louder. "Charlie, me want my money, you better give me my money … or else." He stood there glaring at the baker his fists clenched by his sides. He drew himself up to his full five foot nothing, and then threw his head to one side with a look of disgust on his face and turned to leave.

Edwin stayed hidden in the shadow of the wall and watched the cook stomp off towards the back lane. The baker continued stirring the contents of the bucket, and the unmistakable smell of boiled potatoes wafted into the air. But Edwin's whiskey courage had by now deserted him, and he felt ill.

He staggered back to the office, had a consolatory slug, and fumbled his way through to his living quarters at the back, and to bed.

The next morning Edwin woke with a raging thirst and a feeling of disappointment at his lack of courage the night before. Then Kate's mocking laugh rang in his ears over and over, and as the day went on his courage grew. He would go back and have it out with the baker. I'll just warn him off and then get out of there, he thought.

Night fell and after a quick supper he lurched down the road towards the bakery. Just like the night before he found Charlie down the side alley, sitting on a stool mixing dough. Edwin prepared himself to stride into the lamplight. Look fierce he told himself, but just as he was about to step forward, he saw another figure creeping through the shadows.

Edwin drew back. Sliding his shoulders along the wall he edged back around the corner into the street. There was a clanging noise and a muffled shout. Then a shot rang out, loud and unmistakably near, stopping him in his tracks. It came from the alley. He peered back around the corner. In the glow of the lamplight he saw Charlie stagger and fall backwards clutching his stomach. He stepped forward, acting on his first instinct to help, but then … he might get shot too. He pulled back into the shadows. No one stirred in the dark. Charlie groaned loudly. Edwin took one more peek; an indistinct shape moved towards the back lane. It wasn't the Chinaman cook. Who was it then? No, Edwin decided, he didn't want to find out, he might put himself in danger. He shrunk back, turned, and retraced his steps.

24: Who's lying?

Brisbane: December, 2019

In Brisbane's King George Square the official Christmas tree materialises even before the first days of December, and this year was no exception. Tall, green, conical, and synthetic, it was festooned with big brightly coloured plastic stars, balls, bows, and candy canes. Ronnie always joked that it's resolutely conic shape reminded her of those ridiculous pointy bullet bras seen thrusting forward from every starlet's chest in old movies from the 1950s. Tawdry dross was everywhere.

I buried myself in work. Will was taking off for a long-planned trip, and we had lots to do before he left. A few frantic days later, Will and I had a farewell dinner, just the two of us.

"Back before you know it," he'd said afterwards as he bundled me into an Uber.

"Six weeks … seems like an eternity to me," I said.

We kissed goodbye and I was surprised at how tender and passionate it felt, almost as though we were never going to see each other again.

On Sunday morning there was another goodbye. Dee was jetting off to Italy.

"It'll be great," she'd said when she booked the trip. "Cooking classes, and all that lovely wine."

I drove her to the airport.

"Don't worry Sis," Dee said as she unloaded her suitcase, "I'll be back for Christmas."

"Get off," I said, wiping the forlorn look off my face with a forced smile. "I'm going to enjoy the peace and quiet. Have a great time."

I returned home to an empty apartment.

Can't sit around moping all day, I told myself. I opened my laptop and started ploughing through my photos. If I ever wanted to have an exhibition, I needed to prepare a portfolio. The sun dropped and I sat down to a lonely dinner before heading to bed to watch the latest streaming sensation on-line.

Days went by. I buried myself in work, but at home the apartment was so empty even the silence echoed.

From the other side of the room the scholar's box taunted me. Dee and I had conveniently managed to forget all about our great-great uncle. But now the thought kept banging away in my head, what if Hok really was innocent as Dee had suggested? Nothing would change the gruesome outcome, but maybe, maybe, he didn't do it. I decided to read the trial reports again, from beginning to end, and see if we'd missed anything.

I pulled out all the papers from the drawer we'd shoved them in and started reading. Nothing jumped out. But the first witness was Constable Kelly, and he was the one who reported Hok's so-called confession. If the case was fabricated—if it was more a persecution than a prosecution as the defence lawyer said—then Kelly had to be at the centre of it. I needed to find out more about him. I went back to trawling the internet.

Aha. The constable had moved up the ranks, and had an illustrious career in the police force—he'd even written a book. That afternoon after work I hunted it down in the State Library and skimmed through. One of the chapters dealt with a murder in Dulbydilla. The names had been changed, but it was obviously our murder. The dates, the place, it had to be.

I couldn't borrow the book, but the obliging librarian said I could photograph the relevant pages on my phone. Back home I printed it out and read it more carefully. Dejection hit me. Kelly described our distant uncle as the vilest, most vicious, and godless criminal that ever came under his notice, and said that the world was well rid of him.

My mood was low, Will was on a once in a lifetime trip to South America, Dee was gallivanting around Italy, Christmas was coming—in all its guilt-ridden glory—and by now I had been alone for three weeks.

I rang Ronnie.

"Maybe I should accept the inevitable—we have a disreputable murderer in our family."

I downloaded all I'd unearthed onto Ronnie.

"Hey, don't take it personally," Ronnie said, "even if he was a murderer, it's not something you or Frank are responsible for."

"I know. I want to forget all about it, but in the back of my mind something is bothering me. Contradictions. And I keep hoping that he was innocent."

"I can see the effects of your namesake appearing," Ronnie said.

"My namesake? What's she got to do with it?"

"I must have told you. Eirene represented peace. She was one of the three Horae, the goddesses of order, justice, and peace."

I rolled my eyes towards the heavens, glad that Ronnie couldn't see. Although who knows, she might have thought that I was looking for confirmation from the goddess herself.

"And her mother, Themis, was the goddess of divine law and justice."

"I know Ma. What's your point."

"Seems to me," Ronnie said, "that it's unfinished business, a puzzle to solve and a mess that needs ordering. Only then will peace be restored."

"Anything to get rid of this nagging feeling," I agreed. I would resolve the questions raised by Kelly's book and that would be the end of it. Order restored.

The next morning was Saturday.

I woke with a sense of purpose and turfed all the stuff out of the drawer again. Last time, I told myself.

Dee had said she thought that the trial was a farce, a possible mistrial. And the jury took ten minutes, ten minutes! The jury, and even the witnesses, wouldn't have been immune to the strong anti–Chinese bias of the time. In 1886 Australia was becoming ever more hostile to the Chinese. Every newspaper was full of caricatures with buck teeth, slanted eyes, and flying pigtails—it fed the cartoon industry for years. I needed to find the truth. But all I had to go on was what was reported in the newspapers, and that policeman's damned book.

I laid the trial reports and the extract from the policeman's book side by side. This time I would read them with a critic's eye. I would take nothing at face value. Before long I was fuming. Without thinking too much, I rang Christian. I needed to talk to someone.

"You wouldn't believe what lies that man told. Either he lied, or he was in his dotage when he wrote the book and couldn't remember what really happened. The book was published nearly fifty years after the trial, and on almost every point he contradicts the evidence given at the trial, even his own evidence. It's like he was desperate to tell a good story. It's full of salacious details as if written for a crime obsessed audience … "

My verbal onslaught lasted almost fifteen minutes. Christian was so quiet I thought he'd dropped out. "Are you still there?"

"Yes."

"I think he's full of shit. I can't believe a word he wrote! … And then there's the story about the ghostly lantern."

But Christian had had enough.

"Stop. No more—I can't take it in," he said. "What if I come over and have a read of it myself."

I rushed around scrambling up some lunch and barely thirty minutes later there he was on my doorstep. I'd managed to raid the fridge and concoct a meal of stir fry eggplant with chilli, ginger, and choy sum.

"You don't mind cooking Chinese then?" Christian chanced his luck, as he helped himself to rice. I gave him a withering look and handed him a beer.

"How's the family," he said.

"Dee's been away, on some kind of foodie wank in Italy. Coming back later today. She's getting a taxi from the airport."

"And Frank."

"We think he's over the worst. He seems OK now."

"That's great. So what was that about a ghostly lantern?" he said in between mouthfuls.

"Kelly was on his way to Roma in the train with the dying man and the prisoner."

"Charlie Ah Fook and Hok?"

"Yes. The train left Dulbydilla in the middle of the night and Kelly says that when Charlie died the lamp hanging from the roof of the carriage went out. Four more lamps were brought in before daybreak, and each of them went out immediately."

"Hmm," Christian raised his eyebrows.

"At daybreak they stopped at Mitchell, halfway to Roma, and the news of a supernatural event spread up and down the train— the guard thought it was a Chinese devil.

"Well, that story probably helped to sell some books. A murder and a ghostly lamp-snuffing Chinese devil."

"I think it's all nonsense," I said.

I handed him the print out of chapter from Kelly's book.

Christian took a pair of reading glasses out of his top pocket, those narrow ones from the chemist that people wear when they're in denial about needing them. They didn't suit him, but for the first time he looked like a normal person instead of a cool, aloof, and supercilious cat.

"This woman who lived in a hut and took in washing. Could that be the Kate that Thomas was talked about?" he asked.

"He doesn't give her a name but yes. They are both washerwomen. Except Kelly's woman lived in a hut and Thomas's *Missus Kate*, lived in a tent. But it's obvious they would have to be the same person."

"Kelly says that the woman was unfairly subject to many insults. Could he have been sweet on her?" Christian offered.

"Maybe. He also *gathered* that the two Chinamen were fighting over the woman, but said she didn't fancy either of them, that they were mistaken."

"Gathered? But didn't know? And didn't introduce it in evidence? If it was common knowledge surely someone else apart from Thomas would have mentioned it at the trial? You know what small towns are like, nothing's a secret," he said. "And then how did he know she didn't fancy either of them?"

"And why mention it fifty years later? In a book," I added.

"Maybe the insults and innuendos towards Kate carried on well after the trial, and he wanted to redress them," Christian said.

He was trying a bit too hard to be understanding, but that policeman wasn't going to get such an easy ride from me.

"Even if she was a good woman, or, more than likely, even if she was a prostitute handing out sexual favours, *or* anywhere in between, she would have been an old woman when the book was published. It doesn't make sense."

"Still," Christian said, "Kelly and Thomas do seem to agree on one thing, that Hok shot Charlie in a jealous rage over Kate."

"I don't know that I can believe anything Kelly said. Either at the trial or in the book. If he thought the motive was jealousy over a woman, why didn't he mention it at the trial?"

"Why indeed?" Christian's glasses had shuffled down his nose till he was peering over them. "Could what Thomas said at the trial have been a surprise to Kelly? For all those years after, he'd been stewing about Kate being implicated, for whatever reason. He had to let people know that she was a good woman."

"No, I don't agree. It was unlikely to be a surprise. Kelly must have known what Thomas was going to say, he was the key policeman on the case, he would have taken notes of all the evidence."

"Although," said Christian, "if no one else corroborated it, maybe Thomas made all or part of it up. We've already noticed how disjointed his account of what Hok said was."

I made a pot of tea while Christian continued to pore over the mess of papers strewn up and down the table.

"Hey, have a break," I said to him as I delivered the tea. "I know why I'm obsessed with this stuff, but why are you? It's great ... but you must have other things to do."

"It's intriguing," he said. "I like a good puzzle. And you called me, remember." He looked up, took his awful glasses off, and smiled, "You sounded a bit alone."

I nearly launched into an explanation of how bereft I felt now that Will had deserted me for six weeks, but didn't. I just gave a weak smile.

"OK," Christian said, setting his empty cup down. "Let's say it's possible that Hok shot Charlie in a jealous rage. But two, no three, witnesses mentioned money as a motive. Even Charlie did according to Louis Carlsson, the shopkeeper. And that seems more likely. Although why shoot someone to get your money back? It was never going to work. Unless Hok only meant to threaten Charlie and it all went horribly wrong."

"Could be."

"Both motives have problems, so let's say Hok *didn't* do it. Then who could have?" Christian tapped the table slowly.

I hauled out one of my lists.

"I made a list of the people we know were involved. But really it could have been anyone. Most likely lots of them had a gun, and if not, they could have used the gun from the boring camp."

Christian ran his eyes down the list.

"How about that guy Edwin Mallard, the cordial manufacturer," he said. "How does he fit in."

"He was one of the witnesses. He said he got to the baker's shop about half past ten, and Charlie told him what happened. Charlie said he was sitting in one of the buildings at the back of the baker's shop at about 9 o'clock mixing something in a bucket—Edwin thought he said potatoes—to set a batch of bread. He told Edwin that Hok came to the side door with a gun in his hand and said, *You give me money; suppose you no give me money me shoot you.* Charlie replied, *Me got no money; me won't give you any.* Hok then said, *All right, me shoot 'um you,* and then shot Charlie and ran away.

"Pretty damning evidence even if it does sound melodramatic."

"No! It's suspect! All of it. The baker had been lying there in pain for an hour and a half saying that he was going to die. Then Edwin appears and the dying man tells him that whole story. And he, Edwin, is the only one who hears it."

"I see what you mean. So that's two lots of dubious evidence, first Thomas and now Edwin. We'll leave him on the list then."

"Could it have been that guy from the boring camp? Here …" I stabbed my finger at a name on the list "… Finbar Murphy. He is the one that owned the gun that they say Hok used to shoot Charlie. He left it lying around on a table outside, anyone could have used it."

"Maybe that's what he wanted people to think."

"Could be. And then he disappeared with it before handing it in to the constable in Mitchell two days later, saying he'd found shot in it."

"Suspicious," said Christian.

"I wonder if Finbar knew that Charlie had died when he handed the gun in at Mitchell. He'd gone there on Saturday morning but didn't hand it in till the next day."

"Pity they didn't have fingerprints in those days," Christian said.

"Yes, well, that might have made things easier. Or DNA. But why were none of these contradictions challenged? How could they convict someone on such inconclusive evidence?"

My head raced from one proposition to another. Edwin did it, and concocted the story about what Charlie told him. Thomas did it, and deliberately altered the conversation with Hok to sound as though he intended to kill the 'Chinaman baker'.

Or Finbar did it and two days after shooting Charlie, he handed the gun in to the Mitchell police with some concocted story about being surprised to find shot and residue in one barrel. Each of the theories sounded plausible but there seemed to be no way we could pin anyone down.

"I have to go," Christian said.

"Oh sure. This must be incredibly boring for you."

No. It's not. But I've got something on tonight. I could come back tomorrow and pick up where we left off. If you like."

He looked genuinely interested. How could I resist?

25: Let me die

Dulbydilla: Friday, February 26, 1886
The day had been an especially busy one for Louis, but since sunset a delicious quiet had fallen on the town. From behind the shop counter of the largest store in Dulbydilla, Louis Berliner Carlsson was king of his domain—each and every parcel was handed over to the customer as though it was a gift bestowed to a worthy subject, and not a monetary transaction.

Louis enjoyed his work but it had been a long day. At last it was closing time. He unwound the apron strings from his portly stomach and took one last look out into the empty street. It was dark—the moon had been full and round exactly a week before, but now it was waning and wouldn't rise till after midnight. Apron in hand, Louis locked the shop front door at nine o'clock precisely. No sooner had he walked through to the back of the shop when he heard what sounded like a gunshot. He stopped dead, his hand poised on the handle of the door, and turned his head in the direction of the sound. It definitely was a gunshot. And it wasn't someone doing a bit of night shooting in the bush, no, the shot came from nearby. He threw the connecting door open and rushed into the kitchen.

"Stay here!" he said to his wife Mary. "Don't come out."

Almost the whole town stirred. As if one their heads turned in the direction of the sound.

James Hill, the labourer at the bore site, was still at work when he heard the loud report of a gun. He'd looked up, listened, but hearing nothing else went back to work.

Moll had been almost asleep when she heard the shot echoing through the stillness. She sat up in bed, stark upright. It definitely was a gunshot, and it came from the township. Probably nothing, she thought, although it did sound close. She looked across at Ah Sue but, bless him, he was fast asleep, it had been another long day for both of them. Exhausted, she pulled the blanket closer around her, rolled over, and was soon asleep.

Harley had been sitting at the big table behind his tent rifling through some papers by the light of the lamp. No one was around—payday was coming up and the men were resting up in anticipation of once again having some money to spend. Then through the stillness came the crack of a rifle. He thought nothing of it, though—just another possum hunter. He tidied up his papers and retired to the tent. Lionel was already rhythmically snoring away and Harley's snores soon added a counterpoint.

Hok was on his way back from his customary walk to the water hole when the shot rang out, loud in the night air. Wasn't it a bit dark to be shooting brush-tails out of the trees? It wasn't unusual though, lots of them liked a bit of night shooting—and Hok had other things on his mind. Would he ever get his money back? Probably not. Too bad, he thought. He still had enough money to get himself back home, and more. Another week in this place would kill him. He would just clear out anyway. Tomorrow.

Louis was unnerved, the shot had sounded so near. He grabbed a lantern and ran out the side door. Could be nothing he thought—best to make sure. But it was to be no ordinary night. Not for Louis, not for Hok, and not for Charlie Ah Fook.

Pausing in the middle of the road Louis held his lantern aloft, looking one way and then the other for any signs of a disturbance. Two shadowy figures were running towards Charlie Ah Fook's shop and he could hear loud agonised groans coming from that direction.

He hurried across the road. The weak light from his lantern lit the worried faces of Jimmy Ah Gow and Yung Kee. On the floor in front of them Charlie lay spread-eagled near the doorway of his shop, clutching his stomach, and moaning, "Me die, me die."

Louis put his lantern down on the dusty road, lifted Charlie's tattered bloodstained shirt, and sucked in his breath between pursed lips. The wounds were horrible. Fear in his eyes, Charlie reached out and clasped Louis's hand. His eyes pleaded, "Save me!"

Louis was friends with everyone who came into the store, everyone in the town in fact—no matter how grand or how lowly— and he had always given Charlie a smile and a nod.

The crowd grew, everyone jostling to see what had happened— he knew them all, even that new young constable pushing his way through the throng.

"Stand back," Louis said. "Give us some space." He patted Charlie's hand, "Stay still, stay still."

"Charlie's been shot," he explained to Constable Kelly.

"How? Who did it?" said the constable.

"Me die, me die," Charlie moaned.

"Who did this to you Charlie?" Louis asked gently.

Kelly put his head down close to the injured man as Charlie mumbled a name. The constable nodded at Louis, looked around, asked a few questions from some in the crowd, and left.

Putting his arms around the baker, Louis dragged Charlie from the centre of the door and laid him down next to the shop counter. Charlie shut his eyes, winced, and cried out, "Let me alone, me die, let me die."

Louis shook his head and looked up at Yung Kee's anxious face. Why was there no doctor in the town? With the potential for injury, both on the railway line and at Mr Falconer's bore, it was surprising. But there wasn't. There wasn't even a doctor in Mitchell. Dr Salter had been transferred to Thursday Island a few months earlier, and Dr Comyn was as good as six hours away by train, in

Roma. Dulbydilla had a chemist though, surely he could help?

Louis made haste to send someone to fetch him. A message came back, the chemist refused to attend—he did not feel inclined to come.

Meanwhile walking back through the dark night, Hok had decided. Tomorrow night, after Saturday's supper, he would tidy up, wait till the train arrived from Roma, and jump on before anyone saw him. They'd all be sleeping anyhow. He strode back to the camp. Decision made.

Heading towards him through the darkness a dim figure strode into view. It was Mr Hill, one of the bore workers.

"Did you see Kelly?" Hill said. "He's looking for you."

Hok hadn't. He walked towards his swag, yawning. Out of the shadows the lanky figure of Constable Kelly materialised, blocking his path.

"Are you Tee Hok Siong?" Kelly asked.

"Yes."

"Where is your gun?" Kelly pushed his face up close, his pale skin damp and luminous, his moustache bristling.

"Gun? Me no have gun," Hok said.

Kelly grabbed his arm in a grip so fierce it felt like an iron band. "Come with me."

Hok's mind raced to find an explanation. That gunshot earlier, could that be it?

Kelly dragged a stumbling Hok towards the main street. A bunch of people were shuffling around outside Charlie's shop. The dim light from the lantern in the shop doorway lit up some familiar faces. Kelly pushed him through the crowd and there was Charlie, just laying there, his face screwed in pain. He was in a bad way.

Kneeling by Charlie's side was Louis Carlsson, the shop keeper.

"Lift his head up, Louis…can you?" said Kelly.

Louis eased Charlie into a sitting position, trying not to exacerbate the pain.

"Charlie, look up, open your eyes," said Kelly, ignoring Charlie's groans. "Do you know this man?" He pulled on Hok's arm thrusting him forward, but Hok threw himself back, trying to wrench free. Kelly tightened his grip and jerked him forward.

"Get down man, let him see your face." A heavy hand clapped down onto the back of Hok's neck as Kelly forced his head down into the light from the lantern.

"You know this man?" he repeated.

"Yes," whispered Charlie.

"What is his name."

"His name Tee Hok Siong."

"Is that the man who shot you?" said Kelly.

"Yes."

What? Hok couldn't believe it. How could Charlie say it was him? He didn't even have a gun. How could he shoot the man?

"What for?" asked Louis.

"Him want him money," Charlie said laying back with a half groan, half sigh.

"Charlie, you see me here tonight?" Hok asked. The answer would have to be 'no,' because he hadn't been near the bakehouse since the night before. Charlie must know it can't have been him. Charlie twisted to one side as though to shift the pain, and closed his eyes—Hok couldn't hear whether he answered or not. Kelly tightened his grip on Hok's arm and jerked him away before he could say anything else.

"I arrest you for shooting Charlie Ah Fook," Kelly said. One of the constable's strong hands tightened on the back of his neck, the other firmly gripped his arm.

Hok was paralysed with surprise and fear but managed to push some words out of his dried-up mouth.

"Me no shoot," he said, "Me no shoot." But it was futile. Kelly was in no mood to listen.

Sitting by Charlie's bedside, Louis felt helpless. He held the injured man's hand and mopped his brow. What else could he do? He looked up at the faces clustered around the bed. He knew most of them, the water carrier James, the butcher Lester, Charlie the publican. Ah Gow and Yung Kee were still there, and some others he knew from the railway camp. Then he saw that old windbag, Edwin Mallard, shoving his way in.

Back at his office Edwin had been relieved to see that he hadn't polished off the remains of the whiskey the night before. He'd sat there, hands clutching his head, staring at the same spot on the wall, wondering what he should do. Report what he saw to the police, admit that he was there … but what if they thought it was him, Edwin, who shot Charlie? Or thought that he should have done something immediately. Been a hero … or a dead man.

Edwin had never been very good at making decisions; people were always saying to him, 'make up your mind, Edwin!' — his wife, his ex-business partner, and now he was saying it to himself. Should he go and have look at what was happening? Others would have heard the shot and investigated, surely. At last he'd made up his mind. He would see how bad Charlie was, and then he'd know what to do.

He was surprised to see Charlie lying inside beside the shop counter. How did he get from the bakehouse door in the side alley then? By himself? Or had someone shifted him?

"Did anyone call for the chemist?" Edwin asked. For, as everyone knew, the nearest doctor was in Roma, nearly a day's ride away.

"Yes," a voice replied, "Louis sent me to get him but the swine said he didn't want to get involved. Give us a hand there to move him onto his bed."

Charlie's groans grew more intense as four of them lifted him up and over to his bed.

"Does anyone know who did it?" asked Edwin.

"Him over there, that new cook at Mr Falconer's camp."

Edwin looked over and saw the slight figure of the Chinese cook being handcuffed by Constable Kelly.

"Charlie said it was him who did it."

Did the cook shoot Charlie? But no—it couldn't have been. Just an hour or so before Edwin had watched a figure moving in the shadows, and then heard the shot. He didn't know who the person hiding in the shadows was, but he felt sure it wasn't the cook. It was a dark night, but, even so, judging by the height and gait, it wasn't the Chinaman who shot Charlie. The cook was short, maybe not much more than five feet tall, and had a quick and dapper way of walking. The person Edwin saw in the shadows was much taller and moved in a fluid motion.

Edwin milled about with the others, all watching as Kelly dragged the cook off in the direction of the lock-up at the railway station.

Should he say something? His mind raced with contradictions. If? Then? But? At last the jumble in his head settled on a conclusion. Don't say anything, Edwin, don't rock the boat. No one needs to know you were there. A state of euphoria flooded over him. He'd been scared out of his wits and now he was safe. Enough was enough. He walked away just as he saw Kelly come back, swinging his truncheon.

"Me die, me die," Charlie whispered.

"Give the man some air," Louis said, but no-one moved. Life and death entertainment like this didn't happen every day in Dulbydilla. The crowd were going nowhere.

If only there was a doctor in the town, thought Louis. He muttered some soothing words, and Charlie's eyelids fluttered but did not open. Louis shook his head, and patted Charlie's hand. He could do no more. Overwhelmed, he left Charlie in the care of Ah Gow and Yung Kee and returned home.

"Poor Charlie is done for," he said to Mary. "He's shot up bad and he's in agony. Says he's going to die … and there's no-one can help him. The chemist couldn't even come look at him."

"Couldn't or wouldn't?"

"Wouldn't. I sent for him. He said he didn't feel inclined to come."

"Couldn't one of the coppers have forced the chemist to come and help Charlie? Charlie could have got some pain relief at the very least."

"At the very least …," Louis said nodding his head, exhausted after the nights events. "At the very least … ." He sighed and settled the lantern on the side table next to the bed. "The senior constable is away in Mitchell, but that young one Kelly could have forced the chemist come. They're friendly after all. But he seemed more interested in securing a conviction than in helping Charlie. He was jumping in, boots and all, desperate to arrest someone."

"So they know who did it?" Mary asked.

"We don't know for sure. But Kelly thinks he does. I reckon that young constable is mad keen to prove himself. He's arrested that new Chinese cook from Mr Falconer's camp."

"Hok. He's arrested Hok?"

"You know him?"

"I do. I've seen him often at Molly's stall. Seems a nice sort but doesn't speak much English. Why him? Did anyone see him do it."

"No, it appears not. But Charlie named him. I heard it myself. Though he was in such a bad way, Charlie was, that it was not much more than a whisper. … It's such a dark night, I wonder that he could see anyone clearly, let alone the person who shot him."

"If he did do it, Hok I mean, what do you think the motive could be?" Mary looked up at Louis as she turned down the coverlet on the bed. "No one goes and does something like that without a reason."

"I believe that Charlie borrowed some money from the cook. That's what the chatter is amongst the other Chinese, and Charlie said Hok wanted his money back."

"I've heard talk about that young red head at the railway camp. Takes in washing."

"Is gossip worth repeating?" Louis liked to see the good side of everyone, and that involved not repeating the never-ending stories that raged around a town fed by boredom.

"I'm only telling *you*, dear."

"What then?"

"I heard," Mary said pulling her nightgown over her head, "…I *heard* that the washerwoman, Kate, was friendly with Hok … and the rest of them. They say she's no better than she should be. Could that have something to do with it? A jealous feud over a woman?"

Louis Carlsson was a keen observer of human nature. Barely three weeks ago, at one of the Sunday cricket matches, he'd noticed the young woman eyeing up the new Chinese cook. He knew that she already had quite a following, a few midnight visitors to her tent, so to speak. Louis had warned the cook to stay away when he saw the effect she was having on the newcomer. To no effect it seemed. He turned to his wife.

"Who knows? It seems more likely, a fight over a woman, than to shoot someone to get your money back. You can't get money out of a dead man," he said.

"I also heard …"

"Ye … s."

"There's a rumour about the washerwoman and Hok having a row."

"Is there? I hope you didn't repeat it. People make up all sorts of things."

"No … well … yes. Only once mind you! I happened to mention it to Thomas, in passing."

"Thomas? From Kreibke's store?" Louis shook his head. It couldn't be worse; Thomas always had his ear out for a bit of gossip and wasted no time to repeat it. "You should be more careful dear. Rumour is a terrible thing."

And with that he turned the wick down on the lantern and they retired for the night.

SIX

26: Hok

Brisbane, Australia: 2019

At night I radiate my presence to one of the sleeping women. Don't be afraid I say to her, but she jumps up in fright. I follow her around the room and beam my hopes and memories into her mind.

Please, I am not a bad man, I just want to go home. I don't belong here.

27: Saturday

Dulbydilla: Saturday, February 27, 1886

At almost two in the morning, Constable Kelly waited impatiently by Ah Fook's side for the night train to arrive. He couldn't leave the injured baker in that state. There was no other option, he would have to get him to the doctor in Roma.

Senior Constable Doyle had been in Mitchell giving evidence at a trial, and Kelly hoped to hell that he would return on the night train. But, he reassured himself, everything was under control. He might be a rookie but he was in complete charge—no worries there.

A faint sound from an easterly direction heralded the train's arrival and Kelly sprang into action. All this time Charlie had been lying groaning in agony, for more than four hours.

"Here," Kelly said to the nearest person, Jimmy Ah Gow, who hadn't left Charlie's side all night. "Give us a hand."

Together they lifted Charlie off his bed onto a stretcher and carried him up to the railway platform ready for the trip to Roma. Kelly dragged Hok from the lockup a few minutes before the train arrived and as the few passengers stepped down, their faces froze mid-yawn, mouths open wide and amazed at the unusual sight. A policemen, a Chinaman in chains, and what looked like a dead man on a stretcher.

Kelly chained Hok to a steel lamppost, left the injured man in the care of Jimmy Ah Gow, and went to look for Doyle. Thank god—he was on the train. Kelly nabbed the sleepy policeman.

"I'm afraid you're no longer off-duty, sir. There's been an

incident. A Chinamen has been shot."

"Who?"

"That baker, Charlie Ah Fook. One of the other Chinamen did it. I've arrested him. He's over there, and we've got to get Charlie to a doctor. I need you to help me get them both on the train before it leaves."

A bewildered and sleepy Senior Constable Doyle helped Ah Gow manoeuvre the wounded man up the steps and into the last carriage. Kelly hauled the prisoner on board, and half an hour later the engine began its slow chug out of the station. There was only one train a day on the run from Brisbane to the end of the line in Dulbydilla, and then back again—and this was it.

Constable Kelly sat in the corner of the carriage keeping a watchful eye on his prisoner, who was now chained by both his hands and his feet. Every now and then the policeman glanced across to Charlie who lay motionless on a makeshift stretcher in the aisle. It would be a long trip to Roma.

The train had barely steamed off into the distance before Doyle's bunk creaked with the ponderous weight of his body. There was an investigation to conduct but he needed sleep. Kelly's last words before the train pulled away were, "Find that damn gun." Doyle had smarted at the insult. Who did Kelly think he was? He, Doyle, was the superior officer. Still it made sense, they would need to find the weapon and he'd spotted a gun at the well-boring camp a few days before. He grabbed a fitful two hours sleep and, still groggy, he headed over to the camp at Mr Falconer's bore.

It was after four o'clock in the morning and the sky had just begun to lighten. Finbar, too, had roused himself early, he planned to get in a few hours work before riding to Mitchell to catch up with his mate Robby. He would ride back late on Sunday. He sluiced his face and hair at the trough. Shirt sleeves rolled up, hair slicked back with water and with his towel slung around his neck, he walked back towards his tent.

Doyle was standing by Mr Falconer's table. A gun lay there in the midst of a pile of teacups, and dust, and canisters.

"This your gun?" said Doyle.

Finbar's face was a stony blank slate as he answered the senior constable's question.

"Yes. What about it?"

"Mind if I look at it?"

"Help yourself."

Doyle was familiar with guns—it was part of a policeman's training. This was a double-barrelled muzzle loader, good for shooting birds and small game or even a roo, with the right ammunition. But he wasn't sure what he should be looking for. The gun could have been used by the cook—it could have been used by anyone—and it wasn't as though it was the only gun in town.

"What's this all about?" asked Finbar.

"Didn't you hear? There was a shooting last night. Charlie Ah Fook, the baker. "

"Shot? What? ... Who did it?"

"That fellow who cooks for your mob, Hok Siong. Kelly arrested him. "

"And you think it might have been my gun?"

"Just exploring all possibilities," said Doyle. "Kelly's taken them to Roma. On the train. ... Charlies in a bad way," he added.

Finbar's face was impassive, his eyes expressionless.

Doyle noticed a few of the other bore workers stirring in the shadows. "I'd advise you to put that gun somewhere safe. We might need to look at it again," Doyle said. And unsure of what to do next, he walked off back towards the police van. Time for breakfast. He'd had nothing to eat since he left Mitchell.

Inside his tent Francis Harley Griffith stirred, woken by the mumble of voices outside. Mr Falconer's right hand man cursed loudly when

Finbar told him the news.

"They've arrested Hok?" he queried.

"Fraid so. Kelly's taken him and the baker to Roma on the night train."

"'Struth! … Was that Doyle I heard outside."

"He came to look at the gun."

"Your gun? He thinks Hok used your gun?"

"Maybe."

"Where is it now?"

"It's inside my tent, for now."

"What do you mean, for now?"

"I'm heading off to Mitchell soon, it's my day off, remember? I'll just set the boys up first, then I'm off."

Harley—for that was the name his seven year old self had chosen to use—stomped over to the cold and silent cookhouse and grabbed some of the day before's leftover pot roast and potatoes. Not going to be a good day then. The crew stood silent behind him. He didn't know the victim, but he sure as hell did know the accused. His bloody cook!

Hok had only been there for two weeks, and now he, Harley, most likely had to find yet another one. Cooks come and cooks go— far too often for his liking—though he had hoped this one would settle in and stay a while. How many cooks had he employed in the few years he had worked for Mr Falconer? And which were the worst, John Chinamen or the Irish? Hard to say. The last was a man called Dinny who couldn't stop talking. He thought he had the gift of the gab; while everyone else just wished he'd shut up and get on with the job of feeding them. Harley was glad to see him go, but he'd needed a new cook, and fast. Now he cursed himself for not being more careful in his selection.

Of course he'd heard a gunshot the night before, but thought nothing of it—just another possum hunter—until he woke to hear the unwelcome news.

He turned and yelled at the crew standing around behind him.

"No damn cook! Grab what you can and get to work. Finbar, set them up. Trains don't run on coal alone, they need water, a lot of water. We have to find it. Get going!"

The drill had been running for a few hours when Harley saw Doyle coming back towards the bore. The policeman spoke to Finbar, then they both headed over towards Harley. Harley knew what it would be about, that bloody gun. Lionel had used the gun a few days before. But what had happened to it after that? And why did Finbar have to leave it there, on the table?

Harley walked with them over to the camp, and Finbar ducked inside his tent to retrieve the gun.

"When did you last use the gun," Doyle asked.

"I think Lionel used it last, not me. Lionel Hughes. A few days ago."

"Is the gun loaded?" Doyle asked.

"No. I checked it yesterday about noon, I snapped two caps on it. Both barrels were empty. Nothing."

"You're sure it wasn't loaded?" asked Doyle.

"Like I told you, no it wasn't." Finbar scowled.

Doyle held out his distinctly un-calloused hands for the gun, hefted it up and down a few times as though the weight of it would tell him something and then handed it back.

"Right oh," he said, and turned to Harley. "I'd like to see the cook's bunk."

They were both surprised to see Hok Siong's swag strewn with shot, lots of shot of different sizes, some wrapped in newspaper. Doyle looked excited, but Harley thought it all a bit strange. If Hok shot the baker, why leave incriminating evidence lying around on his bunk. Unless he didn't have time to clean it up afterwards, or he was too stupid, which was quite possible—or someone else planted it.

And another thing, thought Harley, wouldn't it have been

difficult to load the gun in the dark? A muzzle loader took some time to load, even for an experienced shooter. First one had to measure out the powder and pour it in, then ram down some wadding, then pour in the shot, ram down some more wadding, and then repeat the process for the other barrel before snapping on the caps. They found shot and a single cap on the bed, but no spilled powder. Odd.

Moll was kindling up the embers of the fire ready to cook breakfast when she heard a loud banging. She opened the door to an exhausted and worried looking Yung Kee. He wanted to be sure they'd heard the news.

"Charlie's been shot. Last night. That young constable took him off to Roma in the train."

"No!"

"Near dead," Yung Kee said. "The police took that Tee Hok Siong too, he's the one did it."

Moll was shocked. "No. Hok did it? What! ... How do you know?"

"No one see. But Charlie say he the one done it."

"Why?" asked Moll. "Why would Hok do such a thing?"

"Charlie say him want him money."

After Yung Kee left, Ah Sue had just one thing to say to Moll's enquiring face, "They didn't like him."

"Who? Who didn't like him?" Moll asked.

Ah Sue sighed, and said, "No one. Nobody likes Chinamen. And the Chinamen didn't like him."

"Why?"

"He's not one of them."

"What about you? What do you think?" Moll asked.

"I don't care where he come from, if he's a good man."

"He *is* a good man," Moll said, and Ah Sue nodded.

Through the open door, Moll saw Kate arrive with Saturday's bundle of washing. She had a bounce in her step these days, Kate did, something she didn't have when Moll first saw her.

"You heard the news?" Moll now asked Kate.

"I did."

Moll couldn't tell if Kate was surprised or not by the night's events.

"You were friendly with Hok, do you think he shot Charlie?"

"No. Dunno."

"It seems no one saw him do it. Why would they accuse him?" Moll, arms akimbo, gave Kate a sharp look.

"I heard the baker named him."

"Yes. But I still can't believe it."

"They didn't like him."

"Who?"

Kate rubbed the clothes hard on the washboard, a few foamy bubbles rose in the air as she shook her head, her lips set in a straight line. And that was all Moll was going to get out of her.

All along the main street clusters of people gathered in the steel grey morning light. Snatches of conversation drifted around like eddies of wind … I heard … he said … you should have seen … they say … did you hear? The town had never known such excitement.

It wasn't long before the gossip reached Moll. She knew straight away where the story had started. She'd watched Mary head for Kriebke's store a few days before and now she knew, Hok must have been the hot topic. Thomas was the store manager there, a permanent fixture behind the counter and ever ready to pass the time of day. He must have repeated the story, but by now it was second or third hand and seemed to have been embellished with each telling. Moll was horrified. Luckily Mary seemed to have kept to the gossipers' unspoken code of honour and had not mentioned her source. It was the only lucky thing about it. Moll asked Kate to mind out for any customers and marched over to Kriebke's store to get a first-hand account from Thomas.

"Mary told me Hok had a row with Kate," Thomas said, "So when he came into the store later that day, I asked him what happened. Hok said he went up to see her … Kate, and then he saw someone in her tent. A man was sitting on her bed and pulling his socks on."

"Who? Who was it?"

"He didn't say. He said he was bringing Kate some rations but he threw them away—said he wasn't going to provide for another man. And you know what else he said?"

"What?"

"He said 'Chinaman baker been there too.' "

"He did?"

"He did… . And that's why Hok shot him," Thomas said with conviction. "In a jealous rage."

A load of rubbish thought Moll. She saw Kate every day and would have known if anything was going on. Kate had never mentioned Charlie, and Moll had never, ever, seen Kate with Charlie. But she knew—only too well—there was *some* truth in Thomas's story, Kate *was* friendly with Hok, and Hok did throw something away. But as for the rest, two Chinamen fighting over Kate? No. Not even likely, Kate would never have encouraged a romantic attachment with either of them. It couldn't possibly be true. She'd often told Kate that living with a Chinaman wasn't as bad as one would think, and the unfailing reply was always the same—'not in a million years.'

28: Lateral thinking

Brisbane: December, 2019

Christian arrived back just after lunch on Sunday.

"Where were we?" he said.

I was beginning to feel less lonely, and that inclusive *we* helped.

"I've been trying to simplify things," I said. "According to the judge, there were three types of evidence: one, Hok's confession, two, Charlie's accusation, and three, circumstantial evidence.

"Circumstantial—I suppose that means all that stuff about the gun, and Thomas's story."

"I guess so."

"Number one, that confession, it was pretty dodgy," Christian proposed. "Although I think it must have been close to what he really said. If it was concocted, surely the police would have made it sound more convincing, more straight forward, and less open to mis-interpretation."

"You have a point." I read it out again slowly, "'If me knew you were after me … I would have cleared out when I done it.'"

"It sounds like a volunteered statement, not the answer to an interrogation," Christian said, and then added, "If that means anything."

"The watch-house keeper at Roma also reported Hok as saying, 'He didn't see me do it, you'll have to prove it.' Which again is open to interpretation."

"I bet Hok wished he'd not said anything—whatever it was that he meant. It sure came back to haunt him."

"If I was on the jury, I wouldn't have accepted either of those as a confession," I said.

"Yes. I still think it's more like a misunderstood protestation of innocence than an admission of guilt."

"And look here," I pointed to the summing up in the trial report, "even the judge said that the jury must 'regard with care' the confessions the prisoner had made. He said that the cross-statements of the prisoner were narrated in the witness box by men who 'might have mis-understood' what the prisoner really said."

"Exactly," Christian said, rapping his fingernails on the table in thought.

"Then there's number two of the Judge's three types of evidence, the accusation of the dying man. Charlie accused Hok and lots of the witnesses heard him. That seems pretty crucial."

"Yes, and hard to refute too." Christian said. "Why would Charlie name Hok if he didn't do it? He could have been being malicious, or perhaps ... "

"... perhaps he really *did* think it was Hok." I said trying to think outside the box. "It's quite possible that Charlie genuinely thought it was Hok, since that was the one who had a grievance against him. It was a dark night, maybe Charlie couldn't see clearly, he could have jumped to the wrong conclusion."

"Right. He had been arguing with Hok a few days before and could have assumed it was him."

"And if you're sitting in lamplight, it's hard to see anything in the surrounding shadows."

"If it was one of the other Chinese, they might have kept quiet when Charlie accused Hok. Self-preservation."

"Yes, and not just the Chinese, anyone else too. Perhaps Hok wasn't the only one Charlie owed money to. Possible ...," Christian said.

"But maybe Charlie didn't have a clue who shot him. There was only the light from the one lantern after all. Hok had been pestering him for money. Charlie didn't like it. As you said he could have been being malicious. Pay back. He thought he was going to die and wanted someone to suffer for it, especially that annoying Hok."

Christian nodded.

"The judge said … ," and I checked, " … that Hok repeatedly denied both the shooting and being at the place of the shooting, at once, and without hesitation, or deliberation."

"Hok could have been lying though."

"Whose side are you on?"

"Just trying to be impartial."

"And then we come to number three," I said. "Circumstantial evidence."

"Right."

"Why would Hok still have one cap and a grain of shot in his jacket in the lock-up? If he shot Charlie surely he would have cleared out his pockets before Kelly arrested him?"

"Of course."

"Kelly found Hok near the boring camp, quite a while after the shooting. He would have had plenty of opportunity to ditch anything that implicated him. So why hadn't he cleaned out his pockets."

I consulted the trial report again and compared it to Kelly's book.

"Listen to this," I said. "In the book Kelly says he found forty-three pellets of numbers two and four shot mixed in equal numbers in the right-hand pocket of Hok's coat. Yet at the trial he said: 'I found on the prisoner a gun cap and one grain of shot in his waistcoat pocket.' "

"Coat, waistcoat. Semantics? Could mean the same thing."

"Yes, but one shot turns into forty-three. A bit of difference there!"

"It's crazy." Christian said. "Still you'd have to take what Kelly said at the trial as being right."

"I don't agree. Why? It doesn't tie in with what he wrote fifty years later, and both could be false. Once a liar etcetera."

"But there was no reason for him to lie in court unless he found nothing at all and it was planted. If he found more, as he says in the book, then why not just say so."

"You're right, either he found one gun cap and one grain of shot in Hok's waistcoat pocket, or he found nothing, lied to the court and committed perjury. The book has to be a total exaggeration."

Christian picked up Dee's printout of the trial report. "They found shot strewn over Hok's bedding. Very convenient for the prosecution," he said.

"Sounds unlikely as well, as though it was planted."

"Surely if you were going to shoot someone, or you had shot someone, you wouldn't leave evidence lying around on your bed, or even in your pocket?"

"It certainly sounds like planted evidence, in both cases," I said. "The pocket and the bed."

"Probably the police in the case of the pocket." said Christian. "Were they corrupt? Determined to get a conviction? Pretty serious for a policeman, but not unknown."

"And the shot strewn over Hok's bed could have been planted by them too or by someone else. Maybe the one who actually did it."

Now we were getting somewhere.

The confusing evidence was settling into an either or.

"So," I said with increasing confidence," … just to recap where we're at. Number one, the so-called confession either really was a confession, *or* it was his exact words and was misunderstood to be a confession, when it was in fact a denial. Number two, Charlie was either right, or mistaken in his accusation, or being malicious."

"And," said Christian, "unless Hok was exceptionally stupid, the shots found in his pocket and on his bed were most likely planted … by person or persons unknown."

I grinned. "By person or persons unknown?" I repeated. "Have you been reading too many detective stories?"

He smiled.

I contemplated the pile of papers for a few minutes.

"Enough … . Thanks for your help," I said, and started packing it all back in the drawer. "There's more, but enough for now. I know what I think although there's probably no way we'll ever know if I'm right."

And that was when Dee arrived home. She looked surprised to see Christian but before long they were exchanging reminiscences. It seemed that Christian had once spent an idle summer in the same part of Italy. I listened with half an ear as I poured us all a glass of wine.

"What was that all about?" I said into the solid silence after I shut the door behind Christian.

"Good to see you too, Sis. What do you mean what about what?"

"Flirting with Christian."

"Was not… *was* not!" she protested. "And anyway, what do you care?"

"Just asking."

"What was he doing here anyway? I thought you were still pissed off with him."

"I was, I am. But … "

"But what."

"I had to talk to someone. I found this book written by Kelly the policeman that arrested Hok. It got me so mad that I called him."

She threw me a blank look, I'd say inscrutable, but that's obviously a no-no.

"How's Frank doing?" she said, changing the subject. "Are we heading down to the valley for Christmas?" And she rambled on— about Christmas and about her trip.

However annoying she was, I was happy to get my little sister back.

We drove down early on Christmas Eve in Dee's little red sports car. Ronnie was in full-swing classic Christmas mode. The tree was garnished with painted wooden angels, red ribbon, and gingerbread shapes. A light dusting of fake silver snow was a nostalgic touch from her stint in Germany as a junior foreign correspondent. On the sideboard in the hall were three small black pottery bowls each holding three golden mandarin oranges, complete with stalks and a leaf or two.

"Frank's decorations," Ronnie explained. "You'd have to ask him what that's all about. It does look festive though, doesn't it?"

I cocked an eyebrow at Frank.

"It's really for Chinese New Year," he said. "I'm a bit early. Symbolises good luck and prosperity. The mandarins are from our garden ... the last of the season."

Our parents had, as happily married people usually do, invited a few lame ducks to join us for Christmas lunch. A friend of Frank's from long ago university days and a friend of theirs from the valley, both single, he divorced and she a widow. Ronnie the matchmaker.

As we were driving back home, Dee turned to me, "About Christian," she said.

"What about him?"

"I'm not interested, you know."

"Why the flirting then?"

"I was just playing with you. He's far too serious for me."

"Mmm?"

"I like Patrick a lot. He's good fun. We're happy together."

I lapsed into silence, deep in thought.

"I don't think I'm interested either," I said at last. "I've been seeing Will."

"Will? From work? Why didn't you tell me? ... Is that wise?"

I gave her a don't-you-dare-say-another-word look and we drove on in silence.

Christmas Day over, we spent the next few days watching in horror as bushfires raged up and down the country. And then it became more personal. Nan and Pop had moved to a property down south a while back, and were now in the path of a colossal fire that was raging all the way up from Bateman's Bay northwards towards them. We loaded the Rural Fire Service app on our phones and watched as day by day the fire grew. Then the inferno jumped the Shoalhaven River. Ronnie rang them every day. Yes, they have a fire plan. No, they won't try to be heroic. We worried. They evacuated. Twice.

And then it was over. They were lucky, the fire came within a few metres of their house—but many others weren't so fortunate. And who could forget the scene of almost four thousand people trapped by smoke and flames on the beach at Mallacoota on New Year's Eve?

A few days later I woke with a terrible thirst. I needed water, and quick. To my surprise Patrick was standing in the kitchen, barefoot and stripped down to a tight-fitting pair of Armani boxer shorts. He was all bulging thighs and hairy chest.

"I'm nearly finished here, just fixing breakfast for your little sister," he said.

This was not what I wanted to see early on a Sunday morning. When we bought the apartment Dee and I agreed not to bring guys home. Apparently Dee had wavered.

I suppressed a snarl.

"You know," he said, "I heard you yelling out in the night. Bad dream?"

I filled my glass at the tap and managed a small non-committal, "Mmm?"

"You know what I think?"

No, I didn't want to know what he thought, but he was going to tell me anyway.

"You should give up all that stupid nonsense about the guy that got hanged. Even if he is vaguely related."

I'm not usually hot headed but this did it, my blood boiled. Blame it on the early morning or on finding an uninvited man in my kitchen, one who was asking awkward questions. I gulped the water down and banged the glass back on the bench. He didn't take the hint.

"You guys, you're not even real Chinese anyway."

"We are … I am. I'm half Chinese and proud of it too!" I said vehemently, surprising myself.

"And how can you believe in all that weird Asian ghost stuff?"

So Dee had told him everything. How could she? I was livid.

"Lots of people believe in the spiritual world," I said.

"You do?"

"Well, maybe I do and maybe I don't. And you know, it's none of your business."

I glared. He raised his eyebrows ever so slightly and looked back at me before lifting up the breakfast tray.

"Sorry," he said, as he edged past.

I caught the stale scent of last night's aftershave and took a despairing look at the mess he'd left in the kitchen. I poured another glass of water, icy cold from the fridge this time, and stomped off to my bedroom, slamming the door hard.

It was true, I'd had another bad dream. But that was the least of my worries. I was so angry I couldn't think of anything else. I pulled on some loose pants and my favourite black tee shirt, made my bed and tidied the room in a demented frenzy, my head exploding with conflicting thoughts. Buying the apartment was a good way to get out of the rent trap, and neither of us could have bought it on our own. But we'd agreed, no awkward sleepovers. And why did she have to tell him everything? How dare he interfere?

I grabbed my keys and was in my stride even before I hit the river path. By the time I got back Patrick was gone, and Dee was in the kitchen stacking the dishwasher.

"Sorry Sis," she said. "It was late. We just crashed."

"Okay," I said. I'd calmed down by then, I even felt a bit silly for overreacting, but still I couldn't help feeling betrayed. Was Dee in a serious relationship?

Of course we'd talked about the what-if scenario—and I knew, I really did, nothing lasts forever. One of us was bound to want to move out, rushing off into a promising future. But in spite of that passionate kiss from Will, I knew it was most likely not going to be me. I had hardly heard from him since he left.

Was I just jealous?

29: Questions

Dulbydilla: Sunday, February 28, 1886

At 1:35 am, early on Sunday morning the train arrived back in Dulbydilla. Kelly was on board, and with him came the news that this was now officially a murder investigation. Charlie Ah Fook had died, and Tee Hok Siong was safely locked up in the Roma watch house. And—Kelly gave himself an illusory pat on the back—the case was coming together nicely.

"It's all in hand, sir," he informed his superior. "We've got our man. I'll report in the morning. I'm shot, I couldn't sleep on that damned train."

After a quick nap Kelly was up and at his desk jotting down notes. He wasn't too happy when Doyle told him he'd found a gun in the boring camp, that he'd examined it twice, but hadn't confiscated it. What was Doyle thinking of? He might have seniority, but he had no idea how to run a case—too easy going by far. He was a bit happier when Doyle told him he'd found shot strewn all over the prisoner's bed.

"Good, good," he said. "But I think *I* should interview the witnesses." He was going to take charge. After all he was the one who'd made the collar. Doyle wasn't even in town when it happened. Charlie had repeatedly said that he was going to die, and when he did, Kelly couldn't help himself, he'd felt a sense of impending importance. This could be the making of him in the police force, and these pathetic little Chinamen were going to be the vehicle.

Now it was to be a murder trial, but first he had to assemble a watertight case. Kelly was convinced he'd arrested the right man, that snivelling little cook had as good as confessed in the watch house. And he had the direct testimony of the victim.

Now for the witness statements.

First Louis Carlsson, he said to himself, and then that Mallard fellow, and after that down to Falconer's boring camp. He would leave the Chinese witnesses till last, they would be more difficult, and less likely to be convincing in court.

Notebook at the ready, he walked into Carlsson's store. Louis glanced up over the shoulder of his customer but didn't seem surprised to see Kelly. He finished wrapping a half pound of cheddar cheese first in greaseproof paper, then in brown paper. He tied the parcel up neatly with string, handed it over, and escorted his customer to the door before attending to the policeman.

"What can I do for you, constable?"

"You heard Charlie Ah Fook name the person who shot him."

"Yes."

"Who did he name?"

"Tee Hok Siong."

"Thank you."

Kelly put his notebook flat on the counter, licked his pencil and laboriously wrote down the evidence, looking up periodically to ask a few more questions. He finished with Louis and was on his way to see Edwin Mallard when Thomas from Mr Kreibke's store jumped out at him.

"Bad job this, eh, constable?" he said. "You know that cook, Hok Siong, he was in my store a few days ago. Said he had a row with his missus, that Kate."

Kelly's ears picked up at the mention of Kate. What did he mean by his missus? There's no way Kate was in a relationship with that chinky. The cook had only been in Dulbydilla for two weeks. What was Thomas talking about?

"He told her he wasn't coming up to the tent that night. But then he changed his mind. When he got there, he found a man sitting on her bed pulling on his socks."

Kelly was feeling decidedly uncomfortable. Surely not? He knew Kate had got into trouble in the past, but he'd been keeping an eye on her, a professional eye of course. He thought she was back on the straight and narrow.

Thomas continued. "I asked him if he hit the fellow. He said no. He said, he'd kicked up a row and thrown away the rations he'd brought for her—said he wasn't going to buy rations to keep another man. And then he said, 'Chinaman baker been there too, all the same, dead now. ' I said, 'Dead where?' And he said, 'Tonight.' "

Kelly shuffled his boots in the dust and gave Thomas a piercing look.

"Tonight … when did he say that?"

"A few days ago."

"That's a bit strange. Look Thomas, I don't believe that story."

"It's true, that's what he said."

"He might have said it, but I don't believe it. Don't you go around spreading that story, Kate's a good woman," Kelly said. But he knew there was no way that Thomas would keep his mouth shut without some good reason.

"Let's just keep that quiet for now," he added. "We might need it for evidence at the trial. Especially that last part, it sounds like a death threat. Dead now … I wonder what that means? When exactly did he come into your store?"

"Must have been … let's see … it was the day before Charlie was shot. Thursday it was."

"Well, it's a murder trial now, and we'll have to go up in front of the circuit judge. Could be a crucial bit of evidence. I'll make a note of it and come back later to take down your evidence. Just keep it quiet for now."

Thomas bristled with importance and retired back into the store nodding as if in agreement, although it was unlikely that he would be able to resist spreading the story.

By the time Constable Kelly got to Mallard's Best Cordials it was mid-morning. Edwin's face already had the tell-tale flush of a morning drinker and he was a little too precise in his speech. He, too, had a long story to tell.

"I got there at the baker's shop about half past ten. Just before you dragged that bloody celestial off to the lock up."

"Oh yes, I do remember," said Kelly.

"I helped a few of them to move the baker onto his bed and that was when Ah Fook told me what happened."

"What happened? What did he tell you?"

"Charlie said he was sitting in one of the buildings at the back of the shop at about nine o'clock, when Hok came to the side door with a gun in his hand and said, 'You give me money; suppose you no give me money me shoot you.' Charlie told him, 'Me got no money; me won't give you any.' Hok then said, 'All right, me shoot 'um you,' and then shot him and ran away. Charlie ran to the front of the shop and fell down."

Kelly thought that the dying man must have revived considerably to have added so much detail to his earlier remarks, which had been spat out through clenched teeth, interspersed with groans and moans. He was pleased that Edwin had corroborated that the dying man had named the prisoner. And the money? Could be a motive—money. Thank the lord, Edwin had said nothing about Kate—what had that idiot Thomas been talking about?

"Well, Edwin, looks like you might be a key witness. I'll let you know what happens."

Kelly walked off towards the boring camp. He sighed. A hopeless gossip with a made-up story, and a daytime drunk. How am I to build up this case? But it's my chance to show the world what I can do, he thought. I have to get it sorted. Next on the list was the Welshman, Harley Griffith, foreman of the boring camp. Sunday's cricket match had been a bit subdued, and Harley was back at the camp finishing his scrabbled together lunch. He looked up mid-mouthful, to see Kelly striding towards him, chest puffed with importance. Harley wasn't too pleased. That bloody gun again. He should have told Finbar not to leave it out there on the table. It had been there for so long he hadn't even noticed if it was there or not.

"Harley, how are you?" said Kelly.

He got a grunt in reply, could have meant anything.

"About that gun. Can I see it?"

"It's not here. Finbar's gone to Mitchell, he took the gun with him."

"When?"

"He left after breakfast yesterday. He worked early and took a half day off. Doyle came back to have another look at the gun and Finbar left not long after that."

"He's not back yet?"

"No, he's not, his horse isn't here. Should be back sometime tonight, Monday tomorrow."

Kelly didn't look too happy, "Where was it before that?"

"What? The gun, you mean? It was here, right here on this table."

They both looked at the table.

"Mr Falconer's table," said Harley in explanation. It was an ordinary table but imbued with a special significance. Mr Falconer didn't like to eat with the men, and Harley was the only one privileged enough to sit at the table with the boss. Mr Falconer hadn't been seen for a week or so and when he wasn't there the table was used for all sorts. But now the table was bare.

"What else was on the table?" asked Kelly.

"Well, I don't know. I don't pay too much attention to it. Got better things to worry about."

"When did you see the cook last … that night?"

"I suppose I saw him at about seven Friday night, just before I saw you playing billiards in the town. You remember?"

"What happened when you got home?"

"I mucked around for a bit finishing my paperwork, down there, by the big table."

"Did you see the cook in his bed."

"No, but I didn't look. I went to bed myself straight after. Sometime later, something, I don't know what, disturbed me. I opened my eyes and saw a shadow walking past the tent. Then I heard someone rattling things on Mr Falconer's table. I heard a match strike and looked out. It could have been Hok ..."

"You're not sure?"

"No."

"Anything else? You say you heard things rattling on the table. What things?"

"All sorts. I cleaned it up. Some lazy beggers can't clean up their own mess."

He reached into a ditty bag hanging off the tent pole, and handed a tin of shot and a leather gunpowder pouch to Kelly.

"It was on the table," he said in explanation.

"I need you to testify," Kelly said.

"What can I say?"

"Just tell them that the gun was on the table. And the powder and shot. And the caps, were they there too?"

"I think Doyle took the caps. I don't remember."

"Also tell them about when you saw the prisoner rattling around on the table."

"I said I *thought* it was him."

"Yes, but, look, you need to be more positive, if you thought it was him, it was him."

Harley was doubtful. Could it really have been Hok who struck the match outside the tent? It was a dark night and all he saw was a shadowy figure. Even if it was Hok, who's to say he was putting the gun back. It sounded like the clatter of teacups—and he'd assumed it was Hok looking for something. But ... it could have been anyone. Still, perhaps Kelly was right, it was better to sound positive … wasn't it? Seems like Charlie saw who shot him, so it must have been Hok.

Moll was confused.

That young Constable Kelly had been rushing around all day Sunday interviewing various people. There'd been talk about a gun—talk about Charlie being shot with a gun from the boring camp—left on a table in front of Harley Griffith's tent for at least a week, so they said.

"Why would anyone leave a gun and shot lying outside on a table?" Moll said to Ah Sue. "And with the railway camp not far away. Everyone knew the gun was there. Anyone could have used it."

But why focus on that gun? Moll wondered as she walked over the railway line towards Kate's tent that evening. It wasn't the only gun in the town. And had Charlie really been sure it was Hok who shot him?

She found Kate sitting on her bed, folding her washing.

"Is it true that you had a row with Hok?" Moll said perching herself on the camp stool next to the bed.

Kate looked out past the tent flap into the distance and dropped her swollen, red washer-woman's hands into her lap. "Yes."

"Why?"

"Oh, nothing," Kate said. She lifted her head sharply, as if to clear her thoughts, and patted the pile of folded clothes. Moll could see her blush a little and wondered what that meant.

"I told Hok not to bring anymore presents. He didn't like it. I told him …"

"What did you tell him?"

Kate pushed her palms together between her knees; she rocked forward, her shoulders hunched, and after a long pause, said, "Nothin'. I just told him … don't come up to the tent no more."

"Thomas says Charlie was mixed up with you. And that's why Hok shot him."

"He said that, did he?"

"It's not true, is it? Surely not," Moll gave Kate a sharp look. Kate shook her head and resumed folding the washing.

"Thomas made it all up then?"

"Some."

"What do you mean some?"

"I did have a row with Hok."

"Yes. But what is Thomas going on about, about you and Charlie?"

"Don't know. I never had anything to do with him."

"Well, what then? Yung Kee says that Charlie owed Hok money. Hok wanted his money back, and that's why he did it. … Well, he didn't get his money back, did he? You can't get money from a dead man. It just doesn't make sense … . Could Hok have done it?"

Kate's eyes, not quite blue and not quite green, like the deep ocean on a summer's day, swivelled slowly towards Moll.

"Dunno," she said.

There was more to this than Kate was willing to say, thought Moll. She couldn't think of a plausible reason why Hok would shoot Charlie. He didn't run away, and he didn't resist arrest. Didn't that point to being innocent? And if Hok didn't shoot Ah Fook, then who did?

Edwin didn't feel the least bit remorseful about the story he'd told Constable Kelly. You're not a bad fellow, Edwin, he told himself, it's just those annoying celestials. Everywhere you look there's one of them. That's the reason you've got yourself entangled in all this. You're not to blame. If anything it's the fault of those pig-tailed heathens, for being there at all.

It's true he'd had a rare pang of wrongdoing the night before. Should he have reported that he saw Charlie being shot? But by

Sunday morning any sense of the right thing to do had been wiped away as he busied himself. Better to say nothing, he'd decided. But first he had to get rid of the empty whiskey bottles before Ned arrived for work on Monday morning.

When Constable Kelly arrived on his doorstep the temptation to be an important witness at a murder trial became too much. Edwin made up a story—he had bent his head down close to a groaning Charlie and heard him explain how Hok had threatened to shoot him, and the rest.

In the confusion around Charlie's bed that night, who would know what Charlie had or hadn't whispered to Edwin. And the story was true, wasn't it? Well, most of it.

Charlie had definitely said that it was Hok who shot him. And Hok really had threatened the baker. Except that the confrontation happened the night before the shooting, and Hok didn't threaten to shoot the baker, he had just said … *or else.*

Still it could very easily have been the cook who shot Charlie. Except that it wasn't.

And Edwin knew it.

30: Locked in

Brisbane: January - March, 2020

Late in January we woke to a world that was slowly asking itself what is a pandemic, and what will it mean? Every day we logged on to the Johns Hopkins Covid website and watched the numbers escalate, China, then Italy, then the rest of Europe, and then the virus was no longer on the other side of the world, but on our doorstep.

By the end of March, the closures started, the libraries, the art galleries, the coffee shops, almost everything. We worried about Frank and his immune system. We rang every day. They said they felt safe down in their valley and being in isolation was something they were used to. Ronnie could keep on working, though her world would now have to be a wholly virtual one.

"Don't go out. You've got enough food, haven't you? Just stay inside. Don't let Frank go out," we said.

We worried about Frank. And they worried about us.

"Don't go out," they said the same to us. "You can work from home, can't you? Just stay inside."

By the end of March we were officially in lockdown. Dee and I adjusted to the new reality, as did the rest of the country, and the world. We tried to stay out of each other's hair. I had the study and Dee set up a substitute office in her bedroom. Like almost everyone else in lockdown, I comforted myself by cooking. It was a strange time.

Feeling suffocated after barely a week of isolation, I leant through Dee's bedroom door.

"I'm going for a walk," I said to her bent back.

She grunted and barely lifted her head from her papers.

It was officially autumn, but here in Brisbane that signifies not much more than a small drop in temperature. Our world had contracted but I could still enjoy a night-time walk.

The riverwalk was crowded with bodies, all pretending to keep the regulation pandemic one-and-a-half metres apart. Almost impossible, by the way. But I was lucky, not too many joggers, and more importantly, not too many annoying lycra-clad bike riders. I walked past the empty Brisbane Powerhouse, scene of many an enjoyable night out, circled around the park and back along the river, relishing the thinning crowd of walkers and the break from the many claustrophobic days of screens and zoom.

The sky was a watercolour of mauve dissolving into pink. Little grey birds coasted past silently. On the opposite bank strings of purple clouds hovered like long thin spaceships. Lower down, alternating bands of mauve and pink were dotted with palm trees rising above the rooftops. I passed the empty dog walking area. Ancient fig trees murmured in the faint breeze; bats chittered as they flew away on silent wings. The river was like a sheet of dark glass gleaming in the night light.

Suddenly ripples raced across the surface towards me.

Leaves pattered down from the trees.

Not again?

Another strange happening?

Was the hungry ghost of Hok Siong trying to catch my attention?

The flurry of wind died, the river calmed.

The blue-black velvet sky was clear except for the occasional feathery white cloud lit by the rising moon. The ghost of a whisper hung in the air,

I want to go home

I shook my head. Imagining things again? Or was I going crazy? Then a feeling of empathy with our distant great uncle came over me. The threads connecting us were woven together like a strange embroidery. It was about belonging, yet not belonging. We were both *the other*, set apart by our physical appearance.

But, belonging? Did it matter? I'd always felt envy for the indigenous of our nation, surely they truly belong. But the convicts, the soldiers, the other immigrants, and their descendants, like us, do we belong too? Is two hundred odd years enough? Or are we all—all of us—just like flotsam strewn over an ancient land, superficially owning it, but deep down no more than a flea on a dog's back.

I gave Christian a call the next day. We couldn't meet up because of the coronavirus but we could talk.

"Another ghost?" he said when I told him about the weird ripples and the leaves dropping. I left out the disconcerting whisper I'd thought I heard. Too embarrassing.

"Yes, I'm getting used to it now," I said, "I'm starting to feel a bit of kinship."

"Who with? Your distant uncle?" he said.

"Yes."

I could swear that he was smiling.

"And I really believe that he was innocent," I added.

"Well, if he was innocent," Christian said, "the obvious question is, who did it? Who shot Ah Fook? Thing is, we'll probably never be able to answer that one. But that trial was grossly unfair."

"It sure was," I agreed.

"Have you thought about getting a … what's it called … a pardon?"

"A pardon? Can you do that?"

"I read about a journalist who managed to get a posthumous pardon for an aboriginal guy called Kipper Billy. Must have been a few years ago."

"Kipper Billy, memorable name. What happened?"

"It was a rape case, a white woman, in Ipswich. Around the 1860s, I think. Two of them were convicted, one was Kipper Billy. They were sent to the old Petrie Gaol here in Brisbane, to be hung. Kipper Billy, desperate I guess, scraped his leg irons on the stone floor till he wore through a link. He covered his legs with a blanket and said he was sick. Then when the turnkey wasn't looking, he jumped up, and ran. He made it over the first fence, but was shot dead leaping over the second."

"But he didn't do it? The rape?"

"No, they were both innocent. Evidence turned up later that meant neither of them could have done it. Ironically this happened just before the second guy was hanged, and he was released. If Kipper Billy hadn't tried to escape, he would have been released too."

"Sad."

"The journalist worked on the case for years. He was ninety by the time he managed to get the pardon. And it only took around 150 years for Kipper Billy's name to be cleared."

"Amazing," I said. "Give the man a medal."

"Just goes to show that pure bloody mindedness can work— eventually. A small step and all that."

Christian had a point. But …

"Even if we could do it, would it be any use?" I asked.

"It might get rid of your hungry ghost."

I ignored his facetious remark and conceded that, yes, it *might* be a good idea.

"Dee would know how to go about it, wouldn't she?" he said.

"I'll ask," I said. And that night I did.

Dee and I occasionally met at the open refrigerator door around lunchtime, but there wasn't much to talk about. We were still in lockdown. Time slowed down to a crawl. Our rare dinners together had morphed into every-night dinners. We cooked, ate, and then disappeared back into our rooms, Dee for endless phone conversations with Patrick, and me to watch the longest series of Nordic noir I could find.

It was my turn to cook when Dee walked into the kitchen waving a few sheets of paper at me.

"It's not a pardon as such. It's a royal prerogative of mercy," she said.

I stopped slicing onions, glad of the break, wiping the tears from my stinging eyes.

"You hadn't forgotten about it then?"

"No," she said. "I've been working on it. That Kipper Billy story was interesting and from about the same period as Hok's trial. There are other precedents too. The Queen granted a posthumous pardon to World War Two codebreaker Alan Turing in 2013. And there have been a couple of cases in New Zealand. Posthumous."

"So, they were found to be innocent?"

"No. Not quite. The effect of a pardon, or royal prerogative of mercy, seems to be that it wipes out the criminality of the acts not the acts themselves. The applicant is given a complete discharge from criminal liability but there is not necessarily an inference as to factual innocence."

"What does that mean in normal lingo."

"It means it's an act of clemency but doesn't go so far as to declare innocence."

"But you must be able to find someone innocent," I said. "What if there was DNA that proved they couldn't have done it?"

"Yes. Well, there is a way. But it's difficult when it's posthumous and from a long time ago. In one of the New Zealand cases," Dee looked down at her notes, "… a Maori chief called Mokomoko, was convicted together with three others and they were all hung for the brutal murder of a clergyman at Opotiki in 1865. In 1992 Momomoko received a pardon. But his iwi, his tribe, his descendants, weren't satisfied, they were looking for an acquittal, a declaration of his innocence."

"And did they get it?"

"They did. In the end they got a statutory recognition of the pardon, which meant in effect that he was declared innocent, that he never committed the offence."

"OK. But how does that relate to our case?"

"Well, we can't prove innocence by producing new evidence."

"No."

"But, we can argue that it was a miscarriage of justice, just as they did with Mokomoko. Their claim was that the way the trial went there was no chance of true justice."

"Can we say the same?"

"Maybe. There are similarities. First, insufficient representation. In the New Zealand case one solicitor acted for all four accused, including Mokomoko.

"Hok had no one to represent him until the second day."

"Yes. And the defence lawyer had no time to prepare a case."

"Exactly," I agreed.

"Secondly, no evidence was called in defence of Mokomoko."

"Same." Things were looking more hopeful.

"Mokomoko's supporters argued that the Crown's case was inconsistent and the evidence that was given was not fully tested under cross-examination. And that is definitely the case with Hok's trial. There were obvious inconsistencies between the witnesses, and they weren't challenged.

"Finally neither jury spent any time considering the case properly. With Mokomoko they took just fifteen minutes to reach a verdict, and with Hok just ten minutes."

"So, we have a case?"

"Could do," she said. "But that was New Zealand. Australia might be a different story. Also, they were well known people, Alan Turing for his war service, and Mokomoko was chief of an iwi which today has over 12,000 members. Our case is just a simple illiterate Chinese cook that no one else is going to care about."

"We have to try. It all makes sense. We have a good case, and if anyone can do it you can. He wasn't guilty, I know it."

"Okay. I'll give it a go. Don't hold your breath, though."

We finished eating and threw the dishes in the dishwasher.

"Thanks for the dinner, Sis," Dee said. "Got an early start. G'night."

"Maybe we should discuss it with Frank first?" I said to her fast disappearing back, "The pardon thing I mean. He might not like the past being dragged up in public."

"Agreed. We should," she said, looking back at me before she firmly closed her bedroom door.

A thick silence fell over the room. I should go to bed too. I ran my hand over the box as I walked past.

"*Ai-ling!*" A voice sounded from behind, I turned to look, but no one was there. Was I going crazy? I shut my eyes. I rested my hand on the box. Disconnected words flowed past as though in some virtual reality head space. They drifted like snowflakes, fluttering down, lining themselves up, and making a sentence. I heard, felt, saw, a voice.

It's true I liked the girl.

You did? My answer tagged on as the words sailed out of view like a wavering sky banner, or a Times Square news flash. I smiled. And I was still smiling as I thumped my pillow and enjoyed the sensation of spread-eagling sensuously on cool clean sheets. It was kind of ridiculous, funny even—I must have unconsciously assimilated Hok Siong's presence and internalised it. Surely it was all in my mind, and not a ghost, or a spirit. I turned off the light. It was just too absurd.

SEVEN

If people do not fear death,

How can you threaten them with death?

*Tao Te Ching by Lao-zi**

31: The trial

Dulbydilla and Roma: Early in March, 1886
The good citizens of Dulbydilla were aroused from their normal torpidity—news of *their* murder had reached the metropolitan newspapers. But for them there was no question who was the murderer, their minds were not just a closed shop, but slammed shut and boarded up.

Molly was disturbed by the turn of events and horrified that the whole town had, as one, decided that Hok was the murderer. The day after the committal hearing she wasted no time in accosting Louis Carlssen in his shop.

"What happened at Mitchell?" she asked Louis. "You were there at the committal weren't you?"

"I was, and Edwin, and Harley, and the constables."

"What did you say?"

"Well, I had to tell them—I did hear Charlie name Hok as the one who shot him."

"He must have been mistaken." Molly felt indignant. "Hok's a good man. Why would he do such a thing?"

"I believe there was bad blood between the two of them. Charlie borrowed money off Hok and didn't pay it back."

"It was as dark as Hades that night, would Charlie have been able to see who shot him?" Moll asked.

Louis scratched his head. "According to Edwin, Charlie said that Hok confronted him that night and asked for his money back. He must have known it was Hok if they were having an argument, don't you think?"

"I suppose so. But did anyone else hear what Charlie said to Edwin? Or was it just his word?"

"Just Edwin. But, you know, Charlie was in such a bad way, I'm surprised he said that much—and to Edwin."

"What else happened at the committal, did they ask you any more questions?"

"They asked if Charlie thought he was on the point of dying when he named Hok? I had to tell them, yes he was. Over and over he'd said, *Me die, me die.*"

"And Hok, how did he look?"

"Not good. He looked bewildered. When the poor fellow was allowed to speak, he asked each witness, all of us, *Did you see me shoot?*"

"Did anyone say they did?"

"No, they didn't, but that wasn't enough to stay the magistrate. The fact that Charlie named Hok was pretty damning, I'm afraid. He's going to stand trial in Roma, on Tuesday next. In front of the circuit judge."

Molly resolved to show her support for Hok and attend the trial. It was the least she could do—Ah Sue said he didn't mind, and Kate said she would help out with the stall.

She caught the night train and arrived at the door of the School of Arts Hotel at a quarter past seven in the morning. Ellen Hogan, the owner, had been a good friend to Molly in the old days—before the curse of the 'tears' from those pretty opium poppies had taken hold of her! But now Molly was almost respectable, a shop keeper no less, and Ellen welcomed her to her new premises. Molly was in awe. The new hotel was a step up from the old Cornstalk Hotel, the furnishings glowed with newness. The bedrooms were spacious, light, and airy, but they were beyond Molly's meagre budget, and she settled for a vacant staff room.

The next morning—Tuesday, March 9, 1886—Molly put on her best hat and hustled up to the courthouse. Another case was to be heard first. The accused was a photographer named Richard Andrews. Molly knew very well who he was. That dirty sod was the one who had done God knows what to those two poor girls in Dulbydilla a few months before. Mary was ten years old and the other, poor Maggie, was only five. Molly hoped the girls weren't scarred for life. He got put down, convicted of indecent assault, and was sentenced to four years hard labour in Brisbane Gaol.

"I hope he rots," Molly said to the woman sitting next to her in the courthouse. "Four years is not enough for the likes of him."

After the photographer had been dealt with, Hok was led in, handcuffed. Molly was dismayed at his appearance and his demeanour. His head was sunk on his chest and he looked as though he didn't care one way or another what would happen to him.

Molly listened to that young copper Kelly give his version of events. Then the judge asked if Hok had any questions to ask. Hok muttered something.

"What's that?" the judge asked.

The court official bent his head down to Hok's then turned to the judge and said, "Yes, your honour, the prisoner has some questions but his English is not good, he would like to have an interpreter."

"Ah," said the judge and whispered with the court official who looked from one side of the courthouse to the other. The official's gaze finally settled on a short man in a crumpled jacket and he called out, "Mr Ben Sue, please come forward."

"I'm not the crown interpreter," the man said shifting uncomfortably from side to side, and he sat back down.

A whispered conference took place around the bench. "Mr Georgy Chung, please come forward," came the next call.

Georgy Chung agreed to interpret and was sworn in by blowing out a match. But he was of no use, he spoke Cantonese only, and he couldn't understand Hok at all.

There was another whispered conference, another call.

"Mr Mong Sing!"

A small Chinaman stood up not six places away from Molly. He was sworn in on the Bible, and Molly hoped, prayed even, that this one would be of some use. But it was a disaster, Hok could not understand what Mong Sing was saying, and Mong Sing could not explain the problem to the judge.

The judge clenched his right fist and banged it softly on the bench in thought. "Thank you, that will be all," he said to Mong Sing. He looked up at the clock. "It is now twenty past five, we will adjourn till tomorrow."

The jury were led out to be locked up for the night and the first day of the trial was over. Hungry to catch up with the latest fashion, Molly dawdled back to the hotel, greedily feasting her eyes on every shop window in the main street of Roma. She arrived just in time for dinner in the School of Arts' brand new dining room, the aroma of steak and kidney pie barely managing to rise above the smell of fresh plaster and wallpaper glue.

In another part of town Jimmy Sam sat ready to eat his evening meal, a big bowl of *pan mi.* Homemade flat noodles floated in a broth of mushrooms and sweet potato leaves surrounded by small dishes of fried dried anchovies, green onions, and chilli oil. Contented, he inhaled the delicious aromas wafting up from the food, and waited till the white of the egg his wife Lin had cracked over the top turned opaque before dipping his chopsticks in.

Full of comfort food, Jimmy Sam was about to wash himself ready for bed when he heard a knock at the door. Two policemen were on the doorstep. He had a moment of panic as he scrambled to find a reason why he would be in trouble. Finding his conscience was clear he relaxed, but not completely. In his experience no one in Chinatown was ever completely safe from the constabulary.

"You Jimmy Sam?" the tall one said.

"Yes."

"We have a Chinaman in the lock up. He's from Amoy. We need

a translator—can you speak his language?"

"Yes."

"Come to the courthouse in the morning," the policeman said. "You will be paid the usual. Eight o'clock at the courthouse, don't be late."

Jimmy Sam knew what it was about. All last week there was talk-talk everywhere, especially among his countrymen. Although only some of them knew the prisoner Tee Hok Siong personally, they all knew that he was to be tried for murder, and they all thought that the verdict was inevitable.

"That fellow come from Kang-thau, the village near Amoy, at the end of the inlet," Jimmy told Lin after the policemen had gone. "He been 10 years cook around here. Long Sing say he see him here in Roma a few weeks ago. The man say he going straight home, back to China. But he change his mind, he go to Dulbydilla. Two weeks he's there, and now look at the trouble he's in."

"Too late now," said Lin. "He should have gone home when he was ready. It's the end for him."

Jimmy Sam tried to shake the feeling of dread. He hoped that his wife was wrong. But all the time he knew that it would take a miracle, and—guilty or not—Tee Hok Siong was most likely bound for the hangman's noose.

He made sure to arrive early the next morning and was hustled into a room at the back of the courthouse. The prisoner stood propped up in the corner of the holding cell looking confused, ragged, and unkempt. He was a slight figure with a small moustache and looked around thirty years old. His forehead had not been shaved for some time, and his queue had been chopped off leaving him with an uneven thatch of black hair standing on end.

"Wait here," the official said. "Mr Forbes will be here soon. For the defence."

The prisoner lifted his head and peered at his visitors through the bars. His eyes had a glint of stoic determination, but underneath that he looked scared and wary. *What is going on in that head of his?* Jimmy wondered.

"I guess you know why you're here?" said the official to Jimmy. "Yesterday they swore in two interpreters. But they couldn't speak his language. And there was no defence lawyer. But now we have you … and Mr Forbes," he said, his voice sounding more hopeful.

A kindly man, thought Jimmy, observing the official's sympathetic look in Hok's direction.

Mr Forbes, when he arrived, knew nothing about the case, except that it was a murder trial.

"Ask him if he is guilty or not-guilty," said the lawyer.

Jimmy asked.

"I didn't shoot him. I no kill him," Hok said.

"Not guilty," said Jimmy.

The official came back and escorted Mr Forbes, Jimmy Sam and Hok into the courthouse. The benches were filled with a bustling crowd shuffling about chattering. Jimmy knew some of them. Most were Chinese although there were a few white women, dressed in their best, and the odd toff.

"Quiet," said the court official.

The chattering turned into a whisper as Hok was led into the dock.

"All stand," said the court official and the judge took his place at the bench.

The jury filed in and sat themselves down in the jury box to the left of the courthouse.

Mr Forbes stood up and cleared his throat.

"Your Honour, the Crown has but a few moments ago employed my assistance for the prisoner. I crave your indulgence if I should be in anyway lax as I have not even had time to read over the evidence."

Mr Justice Mein ranged his piercing blue eyes over the courtroom and said, "Indeed, Mr Forbes. I'm very glad to see that the prisoner now has legal assistance, it relieves me of a considerable amount of anxiety. I'm also very pleased that a more competent interpreter has been found. It appeared to me that the two interpreters sworn in yesterday had less English than the prisoner." The corners of the judges mouth twitched slightly.

Jimmy Sam had been called to translate before, so he knew the procedure. He stood up when he heard his name called. He blew out the match and swore to tell the truth. If he did not his soul would be gone forever after, like the flame of that match.

The judge read aloud the evidence that Constable Kelly, the arresting officer, had given the previous day.

"Does the prisoner understand all that was said?" he asked.

All eyes turned to the defence lawyer, whose head was bent low over a pile of papers. After a few minutes of silence bar the odd cough, Mr Forbes lifted his head and said, "The prisoner told me that he thoroughly understood the evidence and did not think an interpreter would be required yet."

Did he? Jimmy Sam asked himself. Not that I heard. He twisted around to face the prisoner. Hok looked confused. Jimmy had a bad feeling, he felt like running a mile from the sense of doom that hung over the courthouse.

Constable Kelly was called back. He answered a few questions from Mr Forbes.

"Yes, I asked him what his name was and told him to come with me."

"No, I did not tell him what it was for."

"Yes, he came with me voluntarily."

Then a trickier question.

Mr Forbes' eyes swept the room and settled on Constable Kelly, "At the watch house in Roma, you heard the prisoner say, *If me knew you were after me I would have cleared out when I done it. Is that right?"

"Yes."

"His English is not good. Do you think he meant, *Supposing I done that, I clear out?"

"No."

Yes, Jimmy thought, Mr Forbes ask the right question but got the wrong answer. He, Jimmy Sam, knew what Hok meant: If he was guilty, he would have run away before they could find him. But he did not shoot Ah Fook, so he didn't run away. It wasn't a confession. He was trying to explain why his actions were that of an innocent man.

But no-one asked Jimmy what he thought.

A few minutes later Doctor Comyn took the stand. He had examined the body. Lots of shots—a spray of about forty shots but very little external bleeding. The doctor thought they were number four shot. He considered that the seven shots that had penetrated the liver were the immediate cause of death.

Mr Forbes cross-examined.

"Would lifting him into a sitting position increase the internal haemorrhage?"

"Yes."

"Would moving him to the train and transporting him by train hasten his death?"

"Yes," answered Dr Comyn. " Most certainly."

Molly Dunn listened intently as the doctor described the wounds. Poor Charlie, how he must have suffered. She was sorry she hadn't gone to investigate what happened that night, at least she could have helped nurse the poor fellow. And not let them lump him round like a sack of potatoes.

Dr Comyn sat back down and they all waited for the next witness to be called.

Moll wondered again, if it wasn't Hok who shot Charlie, then who was it? It could be someone in the courtroom, right in front of her eyes. She looked around at the sea of faces surrounding her, trying to interpret each twitch of the mouth, each turn of the head.

"Mr Louis Berliner Carlsson," the official announced.

Louis next, then.

The prosecutor shuffled a few papers and stood. He was the Honourable Mr A. Rutledge, Molly noted—and Attorney-General of Queensland, no less.

"Mr Carlsson. Do you remember the evening of the 26th of February last?" he asked.

"Yes."

"Did you know the deceased, Charlie Ah Fook?"

"Yes. He was a baker and lived about two chains away from my store."

"Please tell the court what happened that night, the night of February 26."

"A little after 9 o'clock I heard a shot and what sounded like a man in great agony. I lit a lamp and followed the sounds to Charlie's shop," said Louis.

"What did you find," asked the prosecutor.

"I found Charlie Ah Fook stretched out in front of the store. I put the light to Charlie's face and he said *me die, me die* several times. I asked him what had happened. He said he'd been shot. I lifted his tattered shirt and found he was riddled with shot about the stomach."

"What did you do then."

"I asked him who shot him."

Mr Rutledge was silent for a moment then he asked, "Did you consider Mr Ah Fook to be in a dying condition?"

"From what I saw, yes."

"What was his state when he spoke to you, was he calm and collected?"

"He spoke every word intelligibly to me. I've always been his friend and he seemed relieved to see me. He clasped my hand in his."

"Did the deceased tell you who inflicted his injuries?"

The judge interrupted. "Mr Rutledge, I see no evidence yet that the deceased at the time was aware that the wounds he had received were mortal. I cannot allow that question. The circumstances described so far do not yet seem to rule out the possibility that the accusation was a fabrication."

Mr Rutledge nodded and continued.

"So Mr Carlsson, what did you do after you examined the deceased?"

"I moved Charlie from the centre of the door. While I was moving him he said, *Let me alone, me die, let me die.*"

"What was his state after you shifted him?"

"He was irritated and distressed. I came to the conclusion that he would soon die."

"You may put your question, Mr Rutledge," said the judge.

Mr Rutledge repeated his question, "Mr Carlsson, did the deceased tell you who inflicted his injuries?"

"Yes. He told me before I moved him."

The judge interrupted again. "Moving him may have caused a spasm that would cause him to first believe that he was going to die. But before that, no. I can only accept the statement the deceased made as to how he obtained his injuries when it is shown that at that very time he was aware that he was suffering from a mortal injury and about to die. So, after he was moved, but not before."

"Your Honor I put forward that the words *me die, let me die* were indicative of a feeling that death was coming on him," said Mr Rutledge.

The judge's face took on a stony look. "I'm not convinced on that point, and I cannot allow the statement to be given in evidence."

Mr Rutledge folded one arm over the other briefly and looked down at the floor, then looked up at Louis and moved on to the next question.

"What happened after you moved the deceased."

"I saw Constable Kelly bring the prisoner into the house."

"Was this before or after the deceased said *me die*?"

"It was about ten to fifteen minutes after."

"What time was that."

"After 10 o'clock I'd say."

"Where was the deceased that time."

"He was laying alongside the counter where I had placed him."

"Your Honour, I now wish to put in the statement that the deceased made to Mr Carlsson and Constable Kelly, after he was moved," said the Attorney-General.

The judge cleared his throat, looked down at his papers and nodded his head.

"Very well, Mr Rutledge," he said. "Under the circumstances I will allow you to put your question. I think I am justified in coming to the conclusion that the deceased was now in a settled hopeless state, expecting death."

"What did you do when Constable Kelly brought in the prisoner?" asked Mr Rutledge looking intently at Louis.

"I lifted Charlie into a sitting posture and told him to look at the prisoner. The prisoner would not look Charlie in the face, but threw himself back, and the constable put his hand on the back of prisoner's neck and made him stoop down. I asked the deceased *Was that the man who shot you?* He replied, *Yes*, very distinctly."

"Were any other words said?"

"I asked Charlie … the deceased, *What for, why did he shoot you?* and he replied, *He want him money.*"

"Did the accused say anything?"

"He said, *I wasn't here to-night. Charlie, did you see me here tonight?* and deceased replied, *Yes, you come and speak to me to-night.*"

Molly was puzzled. She was sure that yesterday Kelly had said that he was the one that lifted Charlie up, and he was the one who asked the question, *Was that the man who shot you?*. Bit confusing! And then hadn't Kelly said that Charlie didn't reply to Hok's question, *Did you see me here to-night?*. Whereas Louis said he heard the reply, *Yes, you come and speak to me to-night.* Maybe Louis was the only one to hear the answer, Molly thought. That must be it, Louis wouldn't lie. But then she wondered why Hok had asked that question. He was obviously expecting Charlie to say no. She looked over at him.

Hok was turning his head from side to side, as if he wanted to say something. He lifted his handcuffed hands and then let them flop down again into his lap. As Louis walked back to his seat he gave Hok a look. Almost apologetic, Molly thought. He was a good man, Louis was. He obviously felt for Charlie, and had done everything he could for the man. He wouldn't lie about what Charlie said, even though he knew the consequences for Hok.

By all accounts Hok had been hassling Charlie for the money he owed, but would he have shot Charlie over that? No. It had to be someone else, or some other reason. Could Charlie have been in such agony that he got mixed up? And why did they keep moving him, first back from the door, then onto his bed and then to the railway station. No wonder he died.

After Louis it was Edwin's turn as witness.

"Mr Mallard, did the deceased say anything to you when you arrived at the baker's shop?" asked Mr Rutledge.

"He said, *Me die to-night; me die soon*, two or three times," Edwin replied. "I heard someone in the crowd say, *You'll get over it Charlie*, and he contradicted them saying, *Me die; me die soon*."

"What happened then?" Mr Rutledge stroked his bushy beard and looked down at his notes.

"They shifted Ah Fook from the floor of his shop near the counter—and after, when he was on his bed, he told me how he came by his injuries."

"What did he say?"

"He said that he was sitting in one of the buildings at the back of the baker's shop at about 9 o'clock. Hok Siong came to the side door with a gun in his hand and said to him, *You give me money; suppose you no give me money, me shoot you.* Ah Fook said he replied, *Me got no money; me won't give you any,* to the prisoner who said, *All right, me shoot 'um you*. Charlie heard a loud bang and was knocked off his stool and the prisoner then ran away."

Edwin's face was expressionless. He looked out at the crowd, over at the jury—anywhere but at the prisoner. A truthful face? Molly thought. Or one that was trying to conceal something?

"Anything else, Mr Mallard?"

Molly watched the Honourable Mr Rutledge intently as he strutted up and down asking his questions. He had rather a nice face she observed. But since he was putting the case against Hok she wasn't prepared to give him any credit. He looked a bit bored— she told Ah Sue later—almost as though he knew what the outcome would be, and he just wanted to get it over with as quickly as possible.

Edwin straightened himself up, looked across at the jury and said, "Ah Fook... ah... the deceased said he was mixing something—I think he said potatoes—in a bucket, to set a batch of bread with, when Hok Siong came up."

Why would a dying man become so eloquent with insignificant details? Molly noticed Kelly shake his head ever so slightly. What did that mean?

"Did you see a light in the back premises when you were at the shop?" Mr Rutledge asked.

"No, I didn't see any lights in the back."

Mr Rutledge might have been expecting a different answer. He caressed his beard, and frowned slightly.

"Did the deceased have anything else to say?" he continued.

"He said that after he was shot, he ran to the front shop, and fell down just as he got there."

"How far is it from the shop to the bakehouse?"

"Standing at the side door you look into the bakehouse. It is about fourteen or fifteen feet from the door to the bake-house."

"Thank you, Mr Mallard."

Questioned by Mr Forbes, Edwin agreed that it was a dark night, and said that it was after ten o'clock when he arrived at the scene.

"Do you know where the prisoner comes from?"asked Mr Forbes.

"I have heard people say that the prisoner comes from Amoy."

"Thank you, Mr Mallard."

Next came another Chinese cook, Ah Gow. He was from Hong Kong, and Georgie Chung translated for him. He said that he helped the two constables carry Ah Fook to the railway station. Mr Forbes asked him if it was a dark night. He said yes, it was a very dark night.

The judge nodded at Mr Forbes and said, "We will take a break there, thank you gentlemen."

The crowd, released from a morning of sitting still and listening intently, filed out chattering away. Edwin Mallard's evidence sounded fishy, Molly thought as she followed them out. He had arrived at the bakery more than an hour after the shooting, at a time when Ah Fook must have been on the verge of dying. According to others the dying man had barely been able to say, *Let me alone, me die, let me die.* Yet, despite being in such a terrible state, the baker had told Edwin a long story about who shot him and why.

And then, all that Mr Forbes had asked Edwin was if it was a dark night, was it past 10 o'clock when he arrived at the bakehouse, and did he know that the prisoner came from Amoy? What use was that? Surely there should have been more questions. Was there no defence?

And why did Charlie tell Edwin, and only Edwin, about his deadly confrontation with the cook in such detail? Odd. Was Edwin lying? Why would he do that?

32: Love bird prawns

Brisbane and a visit to Tallebudgera: April, 2020
We couldn't visit Frank and Ronnie; travel was restricted in an effort to stop the rampaging coronavirus. So we zoomed. They were surviving, and Frank was returning to normal.

"Have you noticed," said Ronnie, "that the new catchphrase is an 'abundance of caution'. I wonder how often we'll hear that in the future?"

I brought up the subject of the pardon. It wasn't easy. Ronnie interjected, Frank ummed and ahhed, Dee gave the facts, and I tried not to overdo the persuasion.

Then, "No," Frank said.

We all fell silent.

"No," he said. "I don't want our family dragged through the mud. And for what?"

Dee took a deep breath. "The evidence supports the fact that Hok didn't get a fair trial," she said. "And there is reasonable doubt that he was guilty. Wouldn't we all feel more comfortable if we could get some kind of exoneration for him."

"It's the least we can do, don't you think?" I jumped in, shamelessly partisan. "Wouldn't your great-grandmother, Ai-ling, have wanted it. It was her brother after all."

"Okay," said Frank. "But if there's any chance of the press getting hold of it, we will need to cancel. The family wouldn't like it."

"Is that a yes then?"

Yes, he agreed, we could go ahead.

Dee and I went to work on a list of reasons why Hok should be pardoned. It took a while but we wound up with a twenty point argument.

I nodded at the box on the other side of the room. *Done!*

I didn't do it. Please help me.

Again? ... *I'm trying,* I channelled back.

I emailed the list to Christian. He called me back and apart from a few minor amendments he gave it the thumbs up.

"Any more ghosts?" he asked.

"No," I lied. I didn't want to tell him about the voice—the words—that kept springing into my mind.

"If it is Hok Siong who has been visiting you…or the ghost of Hok Siong, getting a pardon should help," he said.

"If I believed in ghosts," was my huffy reply.

Dee worked on the submission when she could, and we all thought that eventually, either way it went, that would be the end of it.

After thirty-three long days the lockdown was over, and the pandemic restrictions were gradually eased; we were getting let out of the cage, we could mingle again. Seems crazy now but that's how it was.

Christian rang and invited me to his parents' house for dinner. I had mixed feelings. I hoped he hadn't told them that my possibly murderous uncle was haunting me.

My next thought was what to wear? A mound of discards piled up on my bed and I hated myself for feeling so vulnerable. At last, I was ready. And would you believe it? I was wearing the first outfit I tried on.

Christian drove and twenty minutes later, we arrived. His parents, Chen and Li-ling rushed downstairs to greet us. They were warm, and funny, and…nice, and the house was lovely.

Before long the table was piled with steaming dishes. There were tofu dishes and vegetable dishes, but pride of place went to a platter piled high with prawns. Half on one side were covered with a spicy red sauce, in the middle were crisp snow peas, and on the other side the prawns were seasoned with spring onions and ginger.

"You said you eat seafood, didn't you?" Christian said with a worried look, noticing me eyeing the prawns.

"Yes, I do, occasionally. Looks delicious," I answered with a positive smile.

"It's called Mandarin Duck Prawns," Li-ling explained giving Chen a quick glance as she said it. Chen asked how I'd coped with the lockdown and then told us a few stories about his experiences as a doctor in the middle of a pandemic.

"We were very lucky," he said. "It could have been much worse."

We all nodded in agreement.

"And we might not have seen the end of it yet," Chen said.

"Enough of doom and gloom," said Li-ling. "What do you get up to when you're not at work, Eirene?"

What is it that I do? I didn't have a ready answer, but Christian came to the rescue.

"Eirene's a photographer and a bit of an art collector. She even has a Mabel Juli piece, from the East Kimberley," he said.

"Have you been there?" Li-ling asked. "The Kimberley?"

"Yes, David and I were there a few years ago."

"David?"

Without thinking I replied—"My husband."

There was a shocked silence. Christian's eyes locked on to mine. Li-ling lay down her napkin and excused herself to deal with something in the kitchen. Chen looked down at his plate, a confused look on his face.

"Ex-husband," I answered to the question beamed at me from the other side of the table. "We're divorced."

It was awkward; why hadn't I mentioned it earlier? No need to ask really. I knew why. I'd tried hard to forget that chapter in my life, to wipe it from memory. Yet there it was … I had blurted out the uncomfortable fact of my failed marriage on auto pilot. I gabbled on in embarrassment about where we, or I—as I quickly corrected myself to eliminate David—had been in the Kimberley, and my impressions. The moment passed but left me shaken. They had all looked so shocked.

Li-ling returned with a big square white platter of fresh fruit arranged like a star burst flower. The colours were carefully arranged, from the pale green of honeydew melon in the middle blended all the way to the intense purple of plums and black grapes on the outside. It wasn't just my shock announcement that had delayed her return then—it was a seriously beautiful plate of food.

Christian brought up the subject of the scholar's box, and how we met, although I felt sure his parents already knew. Reluctantly I explained the story of the box. But once started I couldn't stop. I rabbited on about the inconsistencies in the trial. All thought of my previous husband bombshell seemed to have disappeared as they became enmeshed in the story. They latched on to the Kate motive.

"Cherchez la femme," Chen said. Li-ling gave a nod.

"The thing is," I said, "where to go from here? We think the trial was a sham, and there is at least a possibility he didn't do it. We're trying to get a pardon. My sister Dee is a lawyer and she has submitted an application. Could take some time though."

"Yes, that's a tricky one. It's not something I'm familiar with," said Li-ling. She paused, then added, "Christian told us you've been experiencing some strange events. Do you think the ghost of Hok Siong is in the box?" She looked earnest and not in the least as though she was making fun of me.

So he'd told them. I cringed inside.

"Well, I like to think I'm a pragmatic person," I said, "but I have started to think that he's in there. Hok Siong. I hear voices now." There, it was out—I waited for the embarrassed laughter, for their eyes to swivel down to their plates, for a change of subject.

"Voices?" they said in unison.

"More like words floating in my head."

"You need to send that ghost packing," Chen declared. "You will get sick if you keep on going like this."

"Do you think it's a Yuan Gui, Ba?" said Christian.

"Could be. But whatever it is, what is the harm in following the old traditions and trying to send it on its way?"

"You believe me then?" I wasn't expecting that.

"Ghost month is coming up. I think you should do your utmost to appease the ghost and get rid of it." Chen's worried face turned to me. I nodded.

"I'll try," I said.

On the way home Christian turned to me. "David?" he said.

I scrambled for an explanation."We were young and stupid, and it didn't work out. It lasted two years, end of story. He lives in London now."

I hadn't told him because there was no reason to. I thought we were just friends and it hadn't come up in conversation—until now. I hadn't told him about Will either, and why should I? Christian was good company, but he wasn't my type. It was great to meet his parents, but I felt as though I'd been on some sort of job interview. Was he attracted to me? If that was it, how embarrassing was my revelation about David? What must his parents have thought? It was all too much.

I had a calming camomile tea when I got home and tried to forget the worst parts of the evening. On my way to the bedroom my hand smoothed the top of the box.

I want to go home—I didn't do it.
They lied.

I know, I said.

Threats of a resurgence of the pandemic surfaced, and my identity was given another shake up. Did they think I couldn't hear the whispers at the supermarket? Or see their faces turning away as they edged past me? I was frightened to cough in public or blow my nose. It hurt to feel ostracised. At work I couldn't help exploding and raving about some people.

"I guess they can't help associating anyone who's Chinese with the virus. You have to admit that it originated in China," Will said.

"But I'm not Chinese," I said. They all turned to look at me but not one of them was game enough to say anything. The heads turned back to their screens.

"Will, I'm not Chinese, I'm just as Australian as you are."

"Sure. Are those proofs ready yet?" he said glancing at his watch.

I got the message. I bit my tongue. I would stew later—back to work as the man said. But it hurt.

Barely hidden most of the time, the ironic go-back-to-where-you-came-from syndrome was re-surfacing in spades. Over the years the I-belong-but-you-don't message had been sent out to the latest wave of immigrants, Greeks, Italians, Asians, and a mixed bag of Muslims. But what about 'We are one, but we are many'? What happened to that?

In the back of my mind hovered the thought of what I'd said to Patrick when he accused me of not being a real Chinese—"I am," I'd yelled at him, "I'm half Chinese and proud of it too!" Now I'm saying the opposite. I am? I'm not? Would I ever be able to feel comfortable in my own skin?

I took the opportunity of a long weekend to visit the family again. Frank was subdued but he looked OK. I chattered away to avoid the usual questions about his health. Frank was never bored talking about food, so I just happened to mention the delicious prawn dish Li-ling made.

"She called it Mandarin Duck Prawns. Absolutely delicious."

"Love Bird Prawns," said Frank.

"What?"

"Mandarin ducks are called love birds because they are always seen together. The dish has two sides representing a pair of ducks and stands for love and happiness."

I tried to conceal the blush rising from my neck to my forehead. Oh, shit. Did that dish mean what I thought it meant? I felt embarrassed all over again. I was pretty sure I had failed to live up to their expectations, Christian's included. Had he set me up without any warning? How was I to know what he was thinking?

Frank gave me one of his quizzical looks laced with a smile. An unmistakably Frank look. The same one he used to give us when we, earnest young souls that we were, thought we were being terribly serious. We were usually puzzled by the reaction, but secretly pleased to have raised a laugh. I loved that look.

I immediately changed the subject away from love birds and prawns, and rambled on about the latest films I'd watched and exhibitions I'd seen. Frank always wanted to know all about what was going on in Brisbane.

"Any nightlife? Clubs, boyfriends?" he teased, knowing very well that I hated going to nightclubs.

I gave him a playful punch on the arm. "No, I'm good," I said.

At work a few days later we were near the end of a group brainstorming session. My phone rang. I took a surreptitious under-the-table look at the screen; it was Ronnie. Ronnie hardly ever rang me at work, she's not the chatty type. It had to be something urgent. I waved apologetically to Will and the rest of the team and slid out. The glass door of the boardroom closed with a whoosh behind me as I heard the words I had been dreading.

"Frank's had a relapse."

Ronnie's voice shook. My normal, calm, sensible mother had disappeared.

"They're taking him up to Brisbane. In the ambulance—now.

I'm driving. Be there in about an hour."

"I'll meet you. Where?"

"The Alex."

Ronnie had found Frank collapsed on the cold black tiles of the kitchen floor. He'd been cooking up one of his delicious dinners. It was lucky, Ronnie said, that she'd arrived before the place caught fire. The wok, with half a cup of oil in it, was sitting right next to the blue flames of the gas ring. And next to Frank's outstretched hand, lying flat on the ground and oozing a puddle of yellowy green oil, was the four litre can he'd been pouring from.

All the surgery, and radiotherapy, and chemo hadn't stopped Frank's brain tumour from spreading. On a beautiful sunny Sunday morning in June, Ronnie, Dee, and I, stood broken by his bedside as my precious father died. Dazed, we walked out of the hospital into the fresh winter air—the cheerful bright blue sky a slap in the face of our pain.

33: Finbar

Finbar wasn't too happy knowing he'd been nominated to testify for the prosecution. He'd never been in court before, and certainly had never been a witness. But it was his gun that was supposed to have killed Ah Fook. There was no way he could get out of it now. He fidgeted in his seat, sighed, and closed his eyes, trying to calm himself down.

He remembered everything with absolute clarity. It had been a Thursday, the day before Charlie was shot, and he'd been rummaging around the dusty shelves in the corner of Kreibke's Store. He was trying to avoid asking Thomas for help; he didn't like the man—bit of an old woman, always gossiping. Just then the tinkle of a bell signalled the shop door opening, and through a gap in the shelves he saw Edwin walk in. Thomas had leaned forward, hands spread wide on the counter, eager for a chat.

"It seems," Thomas said, handing a drink over the counter to Edwin, "… that the new cook fancies that pretty one, her that takes in washing. Kate, isn't it?"

Finbar noticed Edwin raise his eyebrows either in surprise or agreement, it could have been taken as either.

Thomas continued, "Hok came in here yesterday. Said he'd had a row with Kate. He'd gone up to see her, and he saw a man sitting on the bed in her tent pulling on his socks."

Kate? Finbar thought. And a row? What's the old gasbag talking about? He'd edged closer so that he could hear better, all the while pretending to look for something on the shelves.

"There was more," Thomas said. "He said—*that Chinaman baker been there too, all the same the other one. Me very angry. Me lend him money and he no pay back. Him dead now.* Dead where? I asked. *Tonight,* he replied. …Sounds a bit strange, doesn't it? As far as I know the baker is still alive and kicking."

Finbar heard—*Chinaman baker been there too, all the same*—and the words were like a knife in his heart. He felt a roaring in his ears, just like the times when his father threw him into the surf on one of the rare occasions they made the trip to Bondi Beach.

Finbar watched as Edwin mopped his brow, mumbled a few words to Thomas, and said goodbye. As soon as Edwin made it out the door, Finbar straightened up, stunned by the revelation. He emerged from behind the shelves, mumbled, "Can't find what I want," and rushed out the door.

It had been a slow all-night burn, but the implications of the overheard conversation had eventually sunk in. She was playing him along, and he was enraged beyond belief. He knew she flirted with everyone. But the Chinamen? And who was the fellow pulling on his socks?

He couldn't stop thinking about it, he felt stupid, and used. At lunch Finbar couldn't look at that little yellow shite, the cook. He shovelled his food down and walked back to the tent, just to get away from the others, who had surely noticed his foul mood. He stood by Mr Falconer's table, hands resting on the edge, his head low. His mind was a blur but eventually his eyes focused … and there was the gun. His gun.

To be honest he wasn't that keen on shooting, but it was what you did in the endless stretches of the Queensland interior. He'd bought the gun in Mitchell, egged on by his mate Robby. Whenever they had a day off, they rode away from the town, back into the scrub, and camped by a stream in the wet, or by a dry creek bed in the drought. They told yarns by the campfire and occasionally shot a possum or a roo, but the shoot was more of an excuse to get away than anything else, mates having fun together.

Lionel had borrowed the gun a day or so before to shoot some game, and left it on the table. Out of habit Finbar picked up a couple of caps, half cocked the gun and pushed the caps onto the nipples. He aimed away from the camp and heard a satisfying bang, one, then two. Both barrels were clear then. Time to go back to the never-ending slog at the bore. Pray to God they would strike a decent flow of water soon.

Just his luck though, the auger was playing up again. He tried to wrench the connecting bolts undone but his hand slipped and slammed down onto a sharp metal edge. He watched the blood well up out of the gash on his wrist—the icing on the cake! Could it get any worse?

Finbar liked a drop—Irish whiskey if he could get it—but he wasn't fussy, anything would do. So, when Lionel suggested a drink that night and a shot of billiards at Cavanagh's he didn't refuse.

"Are you okay?" asked Lionel when Finbar missed yet another easy shot. The cue ball almost jumped off the table then smashed onto the cushion and careened wildly, but ineffectually, towards the red. No, he wasn't okay, he was angry. The whiskey inflamed the feeling he'd had all afternoon. He felt like smashing the balls to kingdom come. He hadn't thought of Kate as anything more than a fling, but now the thought of sharing her sickened him. At eight o'clock they relinquished the table to Constable Kelly and the chemist. Finbar staggered back to the camp and Lionel disappeared into the tent he shared with the Welshman, Harley. The night was a fizzle, a damp squib like so many others.

Finbar pulled a half-empty bottle of whiskey out of his trunk, sat on his sagging camp bed and had another slug. He was ready for combat. Those yellow devils will get what's coming to them. How dare they hit on a white woman. And not just any woman, his woman, or so she had been promoted in his sodden mind. His head filled with the image of her, the golden wisps of her hair refusing to be tamed, that look of longing in her eyes, a temptation which he was ever ready to fulfil. When she stroked his hair, he felt like he was five years old again, and his mam was trying to soothe him to sleep.

He would frighten them off, he decided, he had to, for her sake. He picked the gun up from the table and grabbed the can of shot with the rest of the doings. He looked around. Lionel's snores could be heard coming from the tent behind, and Harley couldn't be seen. Back in his tent Finbar loaded the gun by lantern light, first one barrel then the other. His hands shook, and his eyes squinted as he tipped the black powder from the measure, rammed in the wadding, poured in the shot, and shoved the over-wadding down the barrel. He took another swig, threw a handful of caps in his pocket, and lurched out, grabbing the tent pole with one hand to steady himself. First that cook! But Hok was not in his bed and the glow from the embers in the hearth showed an empty galley. The baker then.

The camp was quiet, and no one was about, they were either in the town or asleep. He concealed the gun under his jacket as best he could and cut through between the back of the shops and the outhouses. The baker was sitting on a stool at the side door of the bakehouse preoccupied with mixing something in a bucket.

Finbar readied the gun and fitted a cap onto each nipple. He would warn that bastard baker off, fire a shot over his head to show that he meant business, and tell him he'd better stay away from Kate.

He launched himself forward, but—clang!—his foot hit something hidden in the dark. Sweet Jesus, a bucket full of God knows what! Charlie stood up peering towards the crash. Finbar floundered, flinging his arms wide trying to keep his balance, and the gun flew out of his hands. It bounced butt first on the dirt path compacted by a thousand footfalls. There was a loud explosion. Charlie keeled back and sunk to the ground clutching his stomach.

Finbar rolled away from the bucket as he fell and onto his hands and knees, instantly sober and fearing the consequences. Charlie groaned—loudly—and thrashed around. In a daze of disbelief Finbar stood, grabbed the gun, and slowly edged himself along the wall, past the back of the shop and into the dark alley behind.

His breath was heavy, he thought his heart had stopped. He hadn't even had the chance to say, *Stay away from Kate, you yellow devil*. He looked down at his hands still clutching that wretched gun. Got to get the gun back, he thought. It wasn't my fault ... I only meant to scare him off.

He hid behind one of the outhouses for a few minutes listening and looking. Had anyone seen him? Charlie's groans were becoming faint. Had anyone heard? But there was no-one about. He couldn't believe his luck. He crept forward, taking care to avoid crunching any twigs underfoot. Then the soft dried grass of the campsite muffled his footsteps as he gently placed the gun back on the table. A symphony of snores drifted out from the tent, Harvey's alternating with Lionel's. The steel band around Finbar's chest loosened just a little.

What should he do? Report it to the police ... it was an accident ... but then why did he have a loaded gun ... and it would all come out about Kate ... he would be a laughing stock.

He'd hoped like hell that Charlie had not seen him. He crept into his tent and lay back on his cot. A leaden tiredness overcame him. He imagined a soft hand stroking his hair and soon all thought of the night's events drifted away. It didn't happen. It was all a dream.

Early next morning, even before the first blush of dawn, Doyle came sniffing around asking about the gun. His gun.

"What's this all about?"asked Finbar.

"Didn't you hear? There was a shooting last night. Charlie Ah Fook, the baker."

"Shot? What? ... Who did it?" Finbar made an effort to sound normal.

"That fellow who cooks for your mob, Hok Siong. Kelly arrested him."

"And you think it might have been my gun?" asked Finbar.

"Just exploring all possibilities," said Doyle. "Kelly's taken them to Roma. On the train. ... Charlies in a bad way," he added.

Finbar's heart sunk. Jesus, Mary, and Joseph, no! The clang of the bucket, the sound of the shot, and Charlie's cry as he sank to the ground reverberated in his mind.

He contemplated his situation. Usually he was a slow thinker, but now, faced with the current predicament, his mind raced faster than the train still chugging its way to Roma. No one, he was sure, had seen him. They thought the cook had done it. Well, that could be true, anyone could have shot Charlie, the gun was just there lying on the table. Perfect. All he had to do was go along with it. He was off the hook.

Then a horrible thought surfaced, Charlie could die—what if he, Finbar, had killed Charlie? It wouldn't be murder surely, it was an accident. But who would believe him? No way was he going to confess. No. And anyway it wouldn't happen. The doc in Roma would patch Charlie up, Hok would get a few months in gaol, those sneaky fornicating devils would be punished, both of them, and Kate would be all his from then on.

He forgot how angry he was with Kate. Thomas's story had sounded believable when he'd first heard it, but it could be no more than gossip or innuendo. In that cold pre-dawn light, he acknowledged that it could all be made up. He could even have misheard what was said. Jumping to conclusions Finbar, he thought, got to watch that. Maybe she hadn't been deceiving him. He would give Kate the benefit of the doubt. Too bad about the Chinamen, they could both be in a bit of trouble.

He'd have to act normal though and go off to Mitchell to meet his friend Rob as planned. With the gun.

The sun had already begun its blistering march across the sky when he started packing up his things. He was busy tightening the girth on his horse when he had a thought. What if Charlie's head cleared and he remembered something that could be incriminating. He can't have seen who shot him or he wouldn't have accused the cook, but what if he remembered some small thing that gave a clue to what really happened. He tied his swag behind the saddle and strapped the gun next to it. They'd already arrested the cook, but if Charlie had second thoughts, the cook could be released and the police would turn their attention elsewhere. To him, Finbar. The owner of the gun.

His fully loaded horse snorted and tossed its head, as though impatient to get going, but Finbar was oblivious. If only there was some way of making sure that the cook could be proved guilty. He thrust his hands in his pockets, and his right hand touched on a small lump of cold metal, one of the caps from the night before. What if he threw some caps and shot around on Hok's swag? Just to be sure. He couldn't risk any suspicion landing on him. Finbar rummaged around in his swag and grabbed a canister of shot. No one was around, he made sure of that, as he sidled through the empty camp and scattered the shot and the cap from his pocket on the cook's bed.

"Let's go," he said to Sheba, and swung up into the saddle. The bay mare was part bred Arabian, and had the black points to prove it. She had the stamina and endurance of the breed, and from the first he'd thought she was the most devilishly handsome looking beast he'd ever seen. He stroked her neck, dug in his heels, and they set off. It was nine o'clock; they would make good time to Mitchell. Could be there by mid afternoon, in plenty of time for a night out with Robby.

Next morning Finbar woke in Mitchell with a blinding headache, not helped by the news that had arrived with the train's return trip to Dulbydilla, at around midnight. Charlie Ah Fook had died even before the train had reached Roma, and that pathetic little cook had copped a murder charge. It was all a nightmare. Too late to confess, he knew, because if he did, then he'd be the one up for murder or whatever. No one would believe it was an accident.

He panicked. That's all he could think of to explain what he did next. It was stupid really, his alcohol addled brain wasn't thinking straight. But he knew his gun would be at the centre of the case, and he wanted to remove any suspicion that he was the one that fired it. He bunged half a charge in one of the barrels, wrapped the rest in a piece of canvas, and reported in to the Mitchell police station.

"Could be the gun from the Dulbydilla shooting, you say?" said Sergeant Wright sounding a bit incredulous.

"That's what Doyle said."

"You heard? It's a murder charge now. The victim died."

"He did?" Finbar made an attempt to look surprised.

Sergeant Wright examined the gun. Finbar held his breath, finally doubting the wisdom of his actions.

"Looks like the right barrel has been recently discharged. Would you say that? And there's something blocking the left barrel."

"That's how I found it," Finbar said. "I started cleaning it and then realised I'd better report it. Both barrels were clear on Friday lunchtime when I checked them."

"You're sure?" the Sergeant had asked.

"Of course I'm damned sure. Someone's been using my gun and rammed in too much powder."

Yes, he remembered it all.

"Finbar Murphy," called the court official.

Finbar started, swallowed hard, and walked to the witness box, head held high. All he had to do was stick to his story and he'd be in the clear. Wouldn't he now?

34: Three hundred poems

Brisbane: August, 2020

It was August before I was ready to face the world again. Nearly three months had passed—easily the worst period of my life.

First there was the funeral to get over with. You could say that it was lucky that we were able to hold it at all—the threat of another Covid lockdown or border closure was always there. And thank the God, wherever she is, the restrictions on numbers attending had been lifted to one hundred. Two of the uncles, Ho and Sammy, travelled down from Darwin for the funeral together with Aunt Yanmei and Auntie Wei. In an unprecedented display of affection, I hugged them all. They seemed a little taken aback. Hugging in a pandemic is not de rigueur, nor sensible, nor is it embraced by Chinese culture, but I was beyond caring. It didn't make sense but seeing them made me feel that Frank hadn't gone completely.

I hardly saw Christian, though he was there. He exchanged a few quiet words with me at the door and then edged into the background. Much later I caught a glimpse of him in the distance, talking with the Darwin contingent. Will was there, and Kathy, and the rest of the guys from work.

I had been on leave since Frank was admitted to hospital. Will had rung a few times before Frank died, but our conversations had been short. His offhand remarks about the Chinese virus had stung. He'd voiced the everyday racism that I was experiencing—me and everyone else who looked the slightest bit Asian, and I wasn't ready to forgive him easily. But all that angst was dwarfed by the horror of Frank's death. Will's arm around my shoulders felt warm and comforting as he told me how sorry he was.

After the service, when everyone was leaving, I watched as Will walked away next to Kathy. With a shock I noticed the way he guided her with his hand under her elbow. That gently steering hand, I knew what it meant—it was proprietorial, it wasn't just two workmates looking after each other. A small thing, subtle but telling.

I couldn't have felt more miserable or lonely. In my wildest flights of fantasy, I had dared to imagine an all-Australian family life with Will and two curly haired little children, but that implausible dream had come to an abrupt end. I didn't need to be told. I knew. Stunned, I turned back to Ronnie who was struck dumb with grief, and not coping well at all.

At last, it was over. Dee and I took charge and helped Ronnie move into our spare room. She was in no state to cope by herself.

Every day, I brought her breakfast in bed before I went to work. Every day, I pulled the curtains back and hoped to see the old Ronnie, but it was always the same. She lay back on the pillows, her face pale, and her black hair a turbulent tangled mess, any semblance of elegance gone. My grief spread to both of them, I'd lost my father, and now my mother. My clever, capable, positive, mother.

We suggested interesting books to read, films to watch, and, eventually, Ronnie returned to normal. She started reading the newspapers again. She became incensed at the stupidity of the world's leaders, and, most importantly, she began writing again.

A few days later an official looking letter arrived addressed to Dee. She got back from work just as we were about to eat dinner, scooped the letter up from the sideboard, sat down, and ripped open the envelope. Her face looked confused, then surprised, and then angry.

"After all that bloody work. The application for the pardon has been refused. I'm so pissed."

"Why? Why can't we do it?" I asked.

"They don't give a reason, and they're not obliged to."

We finished our meal in a cloud of disappointment, cleaned up and went to bed.

The following morning I brought Ronnie's breakfast in as usual, but the room was empty, the bed was stripped and the sheets were in a pile on the floor. Ronnie emerged from the bathroom, hair done and fully dressed.

"I'm going back home," she said.

"Are you sure? Won't you be lonely?"

"No," she said. "Don't worry. My study is calling. And I'll have Frank's house to comfort me."

Breakfast was brief. Dee rushed out with half a slice of toast clenched between her teeth, and Ronnie went back home to Tallebudgera Valley. And me? I had an ache in my heart. I missed Frank dearly. Without him, what was I?

Unexpectedly, now I wanted to belong to Frank's world, I wanted that half of my ancestry back. But was it too late? And where would I start? The thread back to that part of my racial heritage was broken, Jimmy, Mei, and now Frank were all gone.

Next morning the spare room echoed with emptiness.

Christian rang.

"How are you?" he said.

"Fine. And you?"

"Good. Glad I caught you. … Sorry I haven't been in touch earlier. I thought I'd give you some space. And then this pandemic thing has kept me busy, checking all the stuff coming out of China, trying to separate the propaganda from the truth."

"No problem. I guess you've noticed that Ronnie is finally back at work," I said.

"Yes, I'm glad. I was wondering … would you like to come over for lunch on Sunday? Nothing special, just to catch up, and you can see where I live."

"Sure."

"Sunday at one? You know the address? It's number 23, the first street on the left past the school."

"Sure. See you then."

That Sunday not a breath of wind rustled the leaves of the trees. I sauntered down James Street under a beautiful clear blue sky and turned into Christian's street at close to one o'clock. Number 23 was a high-set Queenslander, with a generous verandah, and the usual central steps up to the front door. Recently painted, the house was white with a tasteful French-grey trim. Behind the picket fence was a dense hedge clipped slightly taller than the palings. A short gravel path led to the front steps between the two ubiquitous frangipani trees. I stepped onto the shuttered verandah and knocked. Through etched glass panels I saw a dark figure heading down the hall towards me.

"Welcome," he said. Then, "To hell with social distancing… ," and he gave me a quick hug. "Good to see you. How are you?"

"Good, good," I said, covering my surprise. He looked different. His hair was cut short at the back and sides with a hank of straight black hair on top loosely parted to one side.

"Come in," he said, smiling my reaction. "You like it?"

"Chic," I said, and meant it.

I followed him down a hallway of polished honey-coloured timber floorboards to a large open-plan living room. The all-white colour scheme followed through except for two of the walls which were painted in-your-face red. It was a red just slightly darker than scarlet—Chinese red if you like. On one of the red walls were two large scrolls covered with Chinese calligraphy. The inky black stokes were in a loose and nonchalant style and rendered with a fat brush, sometimes delicate and streaked, sometimes strong and confident.

"It's been a while," Christian said, ushering me in.

"It has. You know it's over a year since I first met you."

"That long? …Wine? Beer?" Christian asked. "Or what about a

gin and tonic?"

"Gin and tonic sounds good."

Christian headed for the kitchen, an expanse of charcoal and reflective glass sprawling along the other red wall. Fingers of soft light fell from a tall window thronged with tropical leafy greenness.

"The calligraphy, what does it mean?" I asked.

Christian smiled, looking pleased. "It's my grandfather's work, and he drummed its meaning into me from a young age. He used it to teach me my first lessons in simple Chinese characters. You read it from right to left, top to bottom. Here … see the two lines like a tent with a hole at the top, that means eight and after it is the character for a thousand. In the second scroll the three horizontal lines mean three, and after it is the character for a hundred."

"But what does it mean altogether?"

"Literally it says: 'Learning hold eight thousand books; culture broader three hundred works'. I think it roughly means: 'Your knowledge is as great as eight thousand books; you are more erudite than the Three Hundred Poems'. The poet Du Shenyan was praising a friend of his, but my grandfather applied it to me, as encouragement I guess, to keep on learning."

"That's a lot to live up to for a young kid."

"I survived. I like looking at them and remembering him…." He turned his head and looked back at the scrolls, a fond smile on his face. Then, "Let's eat on the verandah," he said, and palm up, gestured towards the open French doors.

We settled down into two comfy cushioned cane chairs washed over by the unusually warm winter sun. On the small table between us were the two icy gin and tonics complete with lime wedges, and a bowl of bhuja.

"Happy Birthday for whenever it was," he said and lifted his glass.

"You remembered. Last Wednesday actually. Thanks."

Whoosh, I ducked instinctively as a bird flew low over my head and sailed through the open doors into the living room.

"Did you see that?"

"Just one of my birds."

"You keep birds?"

"I don't really keep them. They keep me."

"What are you talking about?"

"OK. Bring your glass," he said and stood up.

I followed him back through the living room and down the hallway to a door on the left next to the front door. The room was light and bright, and filled with a cluster of dry tree boughs and branches stretching from the floor to the ceiling. A few brown speckled birds sat on the branches, and the windows were wide open. I followed him in stepping gingerly onto the butcher's paper laid over the floorboards, avoiding the black and white speckles of bird poop.

"They just fly in and out when they want. At night or when it's really cold I lock the door of the room and leave the windows open."

"Do you feed them?"

"Just water and a snack. I've planted a lot of native species in my garden for them to feed on."

"You're a strange one."

"You think I'm weird? You're not the first. But I like them."

"Looks like a lot of work to me. Cleaning up all this."

"Not really. But look, I promised you food, I need to get on to it."

Back on the verandah I sat swirling the ice cubes in my gin and tonic, savouring its bitter-sweet zesty tang. Faint noises came from the kitchen where Christian was weaving whatever food magic he could. I contemplated the garden. A swathe of small grey stones swirled out from one side of the garden, like the facsimile of a dry creek bed, ending in a flat stony circle about two meters in diameter surrounded by thickets of lush tall grasses. Inside the circle was a collection of oval shaped rough grey basins, of varying sizes and heights, filled with water. Beyond was a forest of trees and bushes. I recognised tall native frangipani trees amongst the unmistakeable bottlebrush, and red and orange of grevillea flowers. I felt sure that Ronnie would approve.

"Hope you like curry." Christian unloaded two large bowls of curry, some colourful side dishes, and a basket of paratha from a tray onto the table. "Roasted red pepper, chickpea and spinach curry, Goan style." He handed me a bowl.

We ate in a companionable silence.

Until—"How is your ghost?" Christian said.

I smiled. "I think the ghost is still there. After that horrible nightmare things calmed down."

"What nightmare?"

"It was a while ago." My skin crawled at the thought and I wished I hadn't mentioned it. "I guess I didn't tell you. I didn't tell anyone. … I dreamt I was in a gaol cell and the guards came and put a hood over my head. I woke up screaming. It was really frightening. One of those times when it's so real, so vivid, that it takes forever to snap out of it."

"It happened just once?"

"Well, twice. But that was before the voices started. I told you about them. It feels more of a friendly ghost now."

"It is?"

I blushed. It was embarrassing.

"We have conversations," I said.

"In Chinese?"

"Well, they're more like thought conversations. Thoughts and feelings are universal … generic even. Aren't they?"

Christian smiled.

I looked down at my feet, tossing up whether to say what I was thinking. Then I said it, "How can I release Hok's ghost? What do I have to do?"

He smiled again. His eyes took on a warm glow and an endearing crinkle appeared on each side of his face.

"I've heard that they must roam around until their soul finds peace," he said.

"And how do they get that?"

"In the case of the Yuan Gui or wronged ghost, until their names are cleared or justice is served."

"It seems we can't clear his name, Dee got a letter. The application for pardon was refused."

"Why?"

"No reason given. They don't have to justify the decision apparently."

"That's a pity."

"So we can't clear his name, and if we don't know who did it how can justice be served?"

"Maybe you just have to settle at appeasing Hok's ghost."

"When is it then? The hungry ghost thing."

"The seventh month. Of the Chinese calendar. I'd have to look it up again. But I do know that since this year was a leap year, there's a sneaky extra month in there, two Aprils in other words, and there are thirteen new moons in the year… "

I gave him a look. He stopped what I might have unkindly called his man-ologue and pulled out his phone.

"OK. Here it is. This year the seventh month starts on August nineteen … and the hungry ghost festival, the night of the full moon, is on September the second."

"Alright, I'll do it. Will you help me?"

"Of course."

"You don't think I'm deranged?"

"No. You have to do something. And I do believe in spirits, even if it is just a remembrance of things past. Like Scrooge's Ghost of Christmas Past, or the life forces embedded in old buildings."

"You feel those too? The old building thing. We're both a bit crazy then. What about ghosts?"

"If from antiquity to the present, and since the beginning of man, there are men who have seen the bodies of ghosts and spirits and heard their voices, how can we say that they do not exist?"

"Are you quoting someone?"

"Well, yes. I'm quoting Mo Zi a Chinese philosopher from around two thousand four hundred years ago. That's someone you could look into. His philosophy was universal love, meritocracy rather than autocracy, and a fair distribution of wealth. He was opposed to wars, violence, and inequality."

"And he believed in ghosts?"

"Yes, he saw them as either primal spirits of nature or souls of people who had died. He thought they would reward virtue and punish vice, and the world would be a better place for it. If people believed they would be punished by the spirits for wrong-doing, social order would prevail."

"Sounds like a cross between Communism and Christianity."

"Some say that."

I stood up to go.

"I'll walk you home," Christian said. Encouraged by a sympathetic listener and loosened up by several gin and tonics I raged on about the nasty, coronavirus-inspired backlash against anyone who looked Asian.

"I know that for some it can be much worse. But even in our well-heeled neck of the woods I can't help noticing the quick sideways glances in the supermarket. And then my neighbour shoots me disapproving looks as she drags her fluffy white dog pointedly away, all the while clutching her Jimmy Choo tote bag tightly under one arm. ... Don't you feel it too?" I asked.

"I do, but why worry about ignorant people."

"I guess you're right, but I'm fed up with being categorised. No matter that half of me is just as white as the rest of them. No ... to them I am Chinese, and always will be." My cheeks grew hot thinking about it. "But I'm not who they think I am, I don't belong in that box, I don't speak Chinese, I've never been there, I don't have any Chinese friends …." I stopped. "Except you," I said.

"Well thanks, … I think."

I smiled at Christian's efforts to lighten things up. But I had to unload my confusion onto someone. "I never valued my Chinese background, or felt any pride in it … and now, because of those fuckwits, I feel defensive. Now I want to reclaim it. But Frank is dead, and there's a break in the chain back to that part of my ancestry. Do I even deserve to belong there?"

"Of course you do. You belong where you want to belong. There are no restrictions."

"Yeah. Well, I have been making an effort. I've even read some of your Tang poetry."

"Good to hear."

"And I ploughed through all five hundred odd pages of Soul Mountain. I read Wild Swans; Balzac and the Little Chinese Seamstress; Jung Chan's take on the Empress Cixi. Oh, and The Man Who Loved China—by Simon Winchester."

"An eclectic collection. And?"

"Conclusion. I have a long way to go. Culturally I am Australian, and always will be … but I also come from English, Welsh and Chinese ancestry."

He laughed, "A bitser. A mongrel."

"Sure I am," I lifted my clenched fist in the air, "I'm all of those and I'm going to absolutely allow myself to take pride in every one of them. As you say, I can belong to all those worlds, it's up to me—"

"Good for you."

"—and I'm going to stop being so bloody precious. Unless I have a head transplant, or I'm re-incarnated, I'm stuck with being identified as Asian. I might as well embrace it. And as for the scholar's box," I add, "it's a link to the past. It may be haunted by the ghost of Hok Siong, but that's not the whole story."

"No?"

"No. It has another meaning altogether. It's a part of our family's history."

Christian looked impressed. I was grateful. At least someone took me seriously, and didn't think I was some deranged, obsessed, lunatic with a vivid imagination.

I opened the door to my apartment with a silly grin on my face. Lunch with Christian was a revelation. He could cook. And he had a bird room—how eccentric was that? The red box welcomed me from across the room. I picked it up, centred it on the long table, stood back, and contemplated its long journey from a humble house in a Chinese village to here, an inner-city aspirational ghetto in Brisbane. I prodded my fertile imagination and a scene mushroomed out of nowhere into an almost virtual reality.

A house stood under the shade of a spreading tree next to a dusty village road. Monsoon rains had pounded the beaten dirt yard and thrown a skirt of dust around its rough white walls. Moss patinated the rough, uneven roof tiles of the simple gable roof. A farmer passed by hauling his cart full of bouncing sugar cane. Birds flew overhead, swooping up from the estuary.

Through a window I saw a family gathered around a low table: a mother, a father, a falling chord of children, perhaps an aunt. My family—I dared to remind myself. The scent of steaming rice filled the air. On one side of the room was a shrine; ancestral tablets leaned against the back wall; at the front bowls of orange fruit and red incense sticks radiated colour in the dim light. A low table stood against the side wall and on it sat the scholar's box.

In a blink the scene changed. The house was the same, the shrine and the table, but the tree had grown even bigger. A man appeared at the gate. Children playing in the shade of the tree scattered and then attached themselves to the man. An old couple dressed in loose shabby blue clothes came to the door—his uncle and aunt. They handed him a box, filled with papers from his dead mother's house.

Together, the man and the box set off on a long train journey south, to another house, in another country—to a city thronged with people. The door of the new house opened directly onto a hard dirt road busy with hawkers and sweaty cyclo drivers peddling their eminent passengers through the crowd. Against a high wall on the far side an old woman sat at a low table fanning her fire and serving tea to thirsty passers-by.

In the dark interior of the house a woman in a long, yellow, high-necked dress looked provocatively out from a calendar on the wall. In one hand she flourished a cigarette and in the other she held a bright red parasol. On a black lacquer table, dulled by time, I saw a lush green jade plant in a fat-bellied iron pot. Next to the plant stood the red box. A man sat nearby listening to the static voice of his radio as the muddy waters of a river beyond the window streamed threats of war from the north.

The box travelled by boat, into the Java Sea, down the Flores Sea, between the Timor Sea and the Arafura Sea, to another country, to Darwin on the tip of Australia. A man, his wife, and a few pieces of furniture arrived at their new home where exuberant banana palms crowded the windows reflecting soft green sunlight onto the rough wooden floorboards inside. Not long afterwards the rooms echoed with children's footsteps as they toddled around. The box was put away and lay forgotten in a cupboard—an alien in the new country.

Then came another journey, to here in Brisbane.

The hungry ghost festival was only a few weeks away. I put the box back on the side table and gave it a pat. *Not long now*, I said.

I am ready.

35: The verdict

Roma Courthouse: March 10, 1886

In the hour and a half between court sessions Hok sat on a bench in the far corner of the holding cell, his hands resting on his knees, his head bent low.

He tortured himself wondering over and over, why, why did he go there to the end of the line, to Mr Falconer's bore? He was as welcome as a rat in a hen house. He'd spent ten nights in prison, and every night he'd dreamt the past would change. But no, when he woke the story was always the same. Why was he so greedy? Why didn't he go home when he had the chance?

He tried to buoy himself up with the thought that his destiny would be aligned with his name, rather than with the portents of doom from the last day and a half in the courthouse. Ma had often reminded him that his name meant lucky or good fortune.

A rectangle of striped sunlight burnt itself onto the dusty floor. He looked up at the patch of sky framed by the bars of the small square window opening and imagined, hope against hope, that the jury would see through the lies and confusion of the evidence. Then he would be free. He imagined his parents shouts of joy when he returned home. But ten years had passed since he left the village, and he had not heard from his sister Ai-ling for some time. Would all be well?

The gaoler thrust a meal of thin grey soup, bread, and dripping at him, but he couldn't stomach much of it. The forlorn remnants sat on a cracked enamel plate in the dust near the cell door. Fear had lodged in his chest and choked his throat dry.

He was innocent, surely they could see that! But Charlie had named him, and many had heard him say it. Did Charlie really think it was him? Did he jump to the conclusion that it was him, Hok, holding the gun? Maybe Charlie didn't see who it was, and named the first likely person he could think of. A mistaken assumption that could have a deadly consequence. There must be an explanation because he wasn't there, and he didn't shoot Charlie. Someone else must have done it. But who?

Mr John A Forbes took his place on the left side of the bar table. He sighed. How to defend someone with no defence witnesses, and no preparation. He'd drawn the short straw when the judge sent word that the crown needed a counsel to be assigned to the case. It would have been better if they'd asked earlier. He'd had no time to prepare, he'd missed the first day and was still trying to get his head around what was going on. Still, working out here in the backblocks of Queensland one had to be prepared for anything.

The accused was led back into the courtroom. Forbes turned to watch as the slight Chinese figure stepped up into the dock behind the bar table. The barrage of faces beyond looked eager for the excitement of a hanging verdict. Poor blighter, Mr John A Forbes thought, I can only do my best.

"All rise," called the court official. The room hushed and Justice Mein took his place on the bench. The jury shuffled in and the next witness for the prosecution was called.

Francis Harley Griffith was a tall man with dark hair and eyes, a well-borer from Mr Falconer's camp in Dulbydilla. Prompted by Mr Rutledge, he confirmed that he knew the prisoner. He had engaged him as a cook for the boring camp about a fortnight earlier. Yes, the gun produced as evidence had been kept for at least two or three days before the shooting, on the table in front of his tent. He'd been in the town that night and heard the shot immediately on his return to the camp sometime between half-past eight and half-past nine o'clock.

"Did you see the prisoner at the camp?" asked Mr Rutledge.

"No, I didn't see him. Although he might have been there in his bed. I didn't look that way."

"Where was the prisoner's bed?"

"In the open, about five yards from the back of the tent I shared with Lionel, Lionel Hughes."

"What happened then?"

"Soon after I went to sleep, I was disturbed by the shape of someone passing in front of the tent. That person was near to the little table, and I heard the rattle of teacups or such on the table where the gun had been left."

"Did you see who the person was?"

"The person then struck a match and I saw it was the prisoner."

"Would a person coming from the town to the camp have passed that way?"

"Yes, anyone would have had to."

"On the morning of the twenty seventh was the gun in its usual place on the table?"

"Yes."

"Thank you, Mr Griffith."

The judge sent an enquiring look in John Forbes's direction. John nodded, sighed internally, adjusted his gown, and stood up.

"Did you notice the gun missing from the table at any time between the 25th to the 27th?"

"No, I never missed anything from the table."

"Thank you, Mr Griffith."

John Forbes took his seat, a sinking feeling in his gut. Should have asked more—no time to think! And a match? Why would the prisoner strike a match if he was trying to put the gun back on the table unseen? Would that line of questioning have been much use?

The day dragged on, another witness, more questions, and

very little going for the defence. Trying to think ahead John Forbes decided he would have to emphasise the fact that it was a dark night. He would have to suggest that the deceased could not have seen who shot him.

"Mr Finbar Murphy," the official announced.

Another worker from the boring camp. Mr Rutledge puffed his chest and stepped towards the witness box. Mr Anthony bloody Rutledge, the big gun. Obviously, the crown was confident of a conviction.

John Forbes watched carefully as the prosecuting counsel introduced the witness—name, occupation, et cetera.

The gun in question was his, Murphy confirmed in a steady voice. He kept it on Mr Falconer's table. About mid-day on Friday, he had snapped two caps on the gun and found it was unloaded, both barrels were clear. Constable Doyle came twice to look at the gun on Saturday morning but about nine o'clock he, Murphy, took the gun to Mitchell with him. On Sunday he found a charge in one of the gun barrels. He drew the charge, put it in a piece of canvas and gave it to Sergeant Wright at the Mitchell police station. The other barrel of the gun was empty.

"Do you know who put the charge in?" asked Mr Rutledge.

"No, it wasn't me. I don't know who it was."

"Does the gun kick at times."

"Yes, a little, if you put too much powder in it," Murphy answered.

Forbes shook his head, no questions—no ideas.

Mr Lionel Hughes took the stand. He said he'd used the gun on Tuesday or Wednesday. The second shot had kicked a good deal.

"Was the gun loaded when you returned it to the table?"

"No, it wasn't loaded, I'm sure about that."

Sergeant Wright confirmed that he had examined Finbar Murphy's gun at Mitchell and found that the right barrel had been recently discharged and that there was something in the left barrel which was still there.

Mr Rutledge, the prosecutor, asked Sergeant Wright to fit one of the caps on the nipple of the gun, but it proved to be too small. The cap found on the prisoner was the same size, the Sergeant said, and also too small—but they can be put on by pressure, he added. He said that he examined the prisoner on the day before the committal, five days after the murder, and found that the prisoner's right collar bone was slightly swollen.

Senior Constable Doyle from Dulbydilla confirmed that he had examined the gun twice the next morning. He had found one cap and some shot of different sizes, some wrapped in newspaper, scattered over the prisoner's bed.

Mr Forbes did not cross examine.

Jimmy was surprised that the defence counsel didn't ask more questions. Someone was desperate to connect Hok with the gun. It seemed unbelievable that if Hok had shot Charlie he would leave incriminating evidence lying around. Would he be that stupid? There had been a lot of talk about the gun, and more about caps, shots, and charge, though no one had seen Hok with the gun. No one said that they had ever seen Hok with a gun.

Thomas Levy, a shop manager from Dulbydilla, was called, and he suggested another motive, jealousy over a woman named Kate.

Levy said he talked with Hok Siong the day before the murder and Hok told him that he had had a row with 'my missus,' because when he went up to her tent, he saw a man sitting on her bed. According to Thomas, Hok said: *Chinaman baker been there too, all the same, dead now. Thomas said: Dead where? And Hok replied: Tonight.*

Rubbish, thought Jimmy. Firstly, my missus? No one said that Hok had a wife, or even a girlfriend. He probably said the Missus, as in the Missus Kate. And secondly, dead now meant that the baker had passed out, was dead drunk.

Then 'dead where' and the answer 'tonight'? Jimmy was

suspicious. Did Hok answer the question he thought he heard: 'Dead when?' Or what? Was that part of the conversation a complete fabrication? Even if tonight was the answer, the conversation took place the day before the murder. So not tonight at all!

Jimmy looked across at Hok who was staring at the witness Thomas, his face half surprised, half angry. It looked like he wanted to say, where the hell did that come from? But straight away he looked down at the floor and his mouth pulled tight shut.

And what about this Kate? She wasn't even there in the court, as far as he could tell. Surely if jealousy was put up as a possible motive for shooting the baker, it should be established as true or false.

But now Mr Forbes asked, "Are you sure the prisoner referred to the baker when he said, 'all the same dead now'?"

"Yes," said Thomas.

Jimmy twisted uncomfortably in his seat, he wanted to yell out: it doesn't mean what you think it means. But he didn't.

Yung Kee blew out a match and swore to tell the truth. He confirmed that Hok Siong had asked Ah Fook to pay back the money he owed. They had had an angry conversation in his shop. The prisoner was very angry, but Ah Fook had denied it. He had said 'No, I don't owe him money at all'.

Constable Johnson, the watch-house keeper from Roma, said that they found a gun cap and some shot on the prisoner. He said the prisoner turned towards Constable Kelly as they searched him in the watch-house in Roma, and said, 'If me had known you were after me, I'd have cleared out when I done it'. Prisoner also said, 'He didn't see me do it, you'll have to prove it'.

Mr Forbes did not cross examine.

"Your Honour, I close the case for the Crown," said Mr Rutledge. The hands on the clock on the back wall showed it was 5 o'clock.

The late afternoon sun slanted in through the top of the windows and lit the twelve faces of the jury, turned as one toward the defence counsel. They were the usual collection, all men, all white colonials, and all looking as if they were too busy for this nonsense about guns, and shot, and dark nights.

Jimmy thought they seemed weary. He knew a few of them and felt sure that they wouldn't care which Chinaman shot who, or why. It was only two Chinamen after all, one already dead, and one soon to be headed for the gallows. People were always talking about the Chinese question, every newspaper in the country was full of it. The Chinese were not liked. They were expendable.

Mr Forbes stood. "I find myself in the serious and painful position of having to defend a man who is being tried for his life," he said. "I look upon all of the evidence, except for that of the two constables as to the statement of the prisoner, as circumstantial."

You'd better make a good case here Mr Forbes, thought Jimmy, because your heart hasn't been in it up to now. You are all there is between Hok and the gallows.

"The remarks made by the prisoner have been construed into an admission of guilt. But I desire to point out to the jury that the two constables were most likely mistaken in this matter. Everyone knows how apt constables are to try and make a case to the detriment of prisoners.

"The constables swore that the words the prisoner used were 'if me had known you were after me, I'd have cleared out when I done it.' I contend that the words the prisoner really used were 'suppose I done it I clear out.'"

What? Mr Forbes had as good as accused the policemen of lying.

"Mr Forbes." The judge interrupted. "I must remind you that it is not usual for the defence to give the words used by a prisoner unless witnesses are produced to prove them."

"Yes, Your Honour,"

Jimmy was bursting. How could Mr Forbes get that so wrong? It wasn't that the constables had necessarily repeated the words wrongly. It's that they had been mis-interpreted. Hok wasn't good at expressing himself in English, he might have used those words but what he meant was that if he had done it, he would have run away.

Forbes went on—again—about what a dark night it was, and that Ah Fook could have mistaken who shot him.

"The witness Carlsson had to use a lamp in order to recognise the features of the deceased," he said. "It would be a fair presumption that the deceased could not have so certainly recognised the prisoner as the man who shot him."

He paused as if to emphasise the point, and then carried on. "All Chinamen look very much the same, and in low light it would be impossible to distinguish one Chinaman from another. They are something like cats," he said, "which in the dark are always grey in appearance."

Jimmy swallowed his reply to the insult.

Mr Forbes cleared his throat. "The jury must be aware," he said, "that the Canton Chinese have a hatred for the Amoy men, and all in the town except the prisoner were from Canton."

He continued in a stronger voice. "This trial ought to be looked upon more as a persecution than a prosecution. And there is, in fact, every probability that it is a trumped-up charge."

A trumped-up charge? That won't go down well with the police or the crown, thought Jimmy.

Mr Forbes waved his finger at the jury and said, "I urge you not to be carried away by feelings of malice, but to review the evidence with intelligence and come to the conclusion that however strong the evidence might appear against the prisoner there are missing links which would justify you in acquitting him of the heinous crime with which he is charged."

And with that he was done.

Maybe Mr Rutledge for the prosecution thought that he already had enough of a case because he didn't take up the right of reply. Jimmy would be the first to admit he was no lawyer, but was it fair that there had been next to no defence? Why had they not asked Hok to explain some of the things said. Was there no one who could vouch for his character?

All eyes were on the judge as he sorted through the papers on the bench before him. The crowd started to chatter.

"Silence," said the official, and Justice Mein began his summation to the jury.

He reminded the jury of their duty to give the case their most serious attention. The prisoner had been charged with one of the most heinous crimes known to the law. He said that it was unfortunate that the prisoner was of an alien race, and that the jury must expunge all prejudice from their minds.

"The evidence," he said, "is of a three-fold character. First the confessions of the prisoner, second the statements of the deceased, and thirdly the indirect and presumptive testimony known as circumstantial evidence. There is no direct evidence except for the statements of the deceased."

Justice Mein advised the jury to regard with care the confessions the prisoner had made.

"The prisoner's statements may have been mis-understood as a confession," he said.

The judge has more sense than Mr Forbes, thought Jimmy.

"Secondly the testimony of a dying man is only to be given the same solemnity as an oath if it was made when he believed he was about to die.

"Thirdly," he said, "there is the circumstantial evidence, which is very often regarded as more satisfactory than direct personal testimony, since a witness could, for some reason, give false evidence—or could be mistaken in his belief. However it is improbable that concurrent circumstances sworn to by different witnesses would arise, unless they were consistent with the truth.

"In the prisoner's favour," Justice Mein continued, "he went voluntarily with the constable and straight away, and without hesitation, said that he didn't have a gun. On the several occasions when he was questioned, he had, again without hesitation or deliberation, denied both the shooting and his presence at the place of the shooting. However, the two constables have testified that he confessed in the watch house."

The judge acknowledged that the shooting took place on a dark night and said the jury must consider that two or three days previously an angry confrontation had occurred between the prisoner and the deceased about money. It was probable that a wounded person might at once think that the man with whom he had a quarrel was the most likely one to commit the outrage.

Regarding the circumstantial evidence, no one saw the prisoner near the deceased's house, and no one could confirm that he hadn't been at the camp at the time of the shooting. He commented that the conduct of Senior Constable Doyle with regard to the gun had been injudicious, to say the least of it, and that Doyle had no right to have handed the gun back to its owner.

Jimmy looked back up at the clock, it was nearly half past five. The judge gave a better defence than that so called defence lawyer, he thought. Let's hope that the jury take note.

Justice Mein's final advice to the jury was:

"If you think Ah Fook at the time he was dying was actuated by malice, or that he was mistaken as to the identity of the person who shot him, you will give the prisoner the full benefit of any doubt that may arise in your minds, but if you have no reasonable doubt, however painful it may be to yourselves, you must find a verdict of guilty."

Of course there is reasonable doubt, thought Jimmy. The judge took a deep breath, looked at his notes and then scanned the room before speaking again.

"In order to give the prisoner full justice, and to refresh your memories I will now read the evidence over to you according to the usual practice," he said. The assembled crowd shuffled their feet and stirred in their seats—not again! Haven't we already heard it all? But before the judge could begin, Mr. Lister, foreman of the jury spoke.

"Your Honour. The jury are hungry. Might we break for dinner?"

The court was adjourned till seven o'clock.

An hour and a half later the townsfolk shuffled back in. Darkness was falling and the lamps were lit. The court was full to the brim. People squeezed in together on the wooden seats yattering amongst themselves. It had been a long day but there was no way they were going to miss the verdict.

The court fell silent as Justice Mein read the evidence over. He talked for nearly an hour and Jimmy noticed a few heads in the jury droop. It was a warm night, and their stomachs were full of sausages and mash, the courthouse tucker.

Justice Mein asked the jury to consider two questions: Was Charlie killed by a gunshot wound? and: Does the evidence point to the prisoner as being the person who inflicted that wound?

And with that the jury retired. It was nearly eight o'clock.

Ten minutes later they filed back in. Guilty!

Guilty? Ten minutes? That's all it takes? thought Jimmy.

The judge asked the prisoner, "Do you have anything to say as to why the death sentence should not be passed on you?"

Jimmy readied himself to translate, but Hok said nothing. His eyes scanned the crowd from one side to the other, his face expressionless, and he said nothing.

The courthouse emptied. Hok Siong was bound for Brisbane and a date with the hangman.

It was all over.

EIGHT

Tao endures.
Your body dies.
There is no danger.

*Tao Te Ching by Lao-zi**

** No 16: Translated by Stephen Addiss and Stanley Lombardo.*

36: Boggo Road Gaol

Hok Siong: March 1886

Sentence of death was passed in the usual form.

Two days later, just before sunrise, Hok was shackled and escorted from the run-down gaol in Roma to be tossed into a closed carriage on the Brisbane train. He was not sorry to leave behind that miserable shanty town, Dulbydilla, nor the people from the Roma courthouse, all baying for blood, his blood.

More than fifteen hours passed before the sleepy prisoner was bundled off the train into the night, and into a prison van en-route to the Brisbane Gaol on Boggo Road. From inside the claustrophobic cramped confines of the Black Maria he could hear the snorts of the horses, and the precise clip-clop of their hooves on the hard beaten surface of the dark and empty city streets.

The heavy barred metal grille closed behind him with a note of finality, and Hok heard the key turn in the padlock. Peering out he saw one of the warders sit himself down on a small stool in the corridor outside the iron bars which closed off one side of the cell. Another settled a lamp on a shelf next to the door grille, then grunted and walked off. Inside the cell a sleeping platform and a tin can lay between the other three solid walls. Through a small metal-barred window on the back wall the night sky was pitch dark. Heavy chains still hung from the iron bands that had chafed his ankles raw.

Wide awake now, Hok heard faint shuffling sounds as the prisoners in the cells close to him shifted uneasily in their beds and rolled over. He heard an occasional moan and a sharp cry as one of the inmates tried to escape from a nightmare. The smell was new. The smell of one hundred and twenty-five sweaty men jammed into sixty cells, the smell of brick and cement, sweat and excrement. Sleep was the only escape.

He woke in the grey morning light to the din of a clamouring bell, followed by heavy footfalls and the clanking of cell doors being opened. But his door remained firmly shut until two turnkeys arrived and shoved a plate of food and a cup of water at him, before dragging the door grille shut again. They exchanged a few words with the warder on the stool—the same one as last night? Hok couldn't be sure. They all looked the same to him. He was obliged to scoop up the unidentifiable slop with his fingers and then lifted the plate to his lips to slurp the remainder.

From between the bars, he could see a platform and beyond that a big space, three stories high, with solid metal cell doors lined up on either side. Around the platform was a railing, and on the platform was a double-leaf trap door and a lever. Above was a heavy beam.

Five days went by in a regimented pattern of bells and footsteps, cell doors opening and banging shut, and cries in the night. On the sixth day, after a midday meal of yet another boiled stew, a large man appeared outside his cell. The warder on the chair touched his cap.

"Captain Jekyll, sir."

A tall heavily bearded man peered in at Hok.

"You have a visitor. Someone come to see you. Do you want to see him?"

"Who?"

"A gentleman. A Mr John Holland."

Fifteen minutes later Mr Holland was ushered in. Hok heard a familiar greeting, but it came from an unfamiliar face. Mr John Holland was a tall man in a grey suit and waistcoat with a clipped grey beard. Speaking haltingly in the Hokkien dialect he said that he knew Amoy, he had been there, and he had been at the trial in Roma. The first smile in many days crossed Hok's face. This was a good-hearted man and, however hard he was to understand, he spoke the language of Amoy.

"The Executive Council is meeting on Friday to consider your case."

"What is that?"

"Some important men in the city. They can decide to cancel the execution and change it to a prison sentence."

"You can help me?" Hok dared to hope. He pressed his hands together and bowed his head towards his possible saviour.

"I will try," Mr John Holland said. "Do you need anything."

"You have a Chinese priest here?"

"There is one at the Temple of the Holy Triad, at Breakfast Creek."

"Please ask him to come."

Mr Holland said he would ask; he knew some of the dignitaries. He took his leave with a few words of encouragement. But it wasn't long before he returned with the disappointing news that no one was willing to come from the Breakfast Creek Temple.

"Sorry. I tried, but no one will come. Some Christian ministers want to see you though," he said. "Will you see them?"

Hok nodded. Why not, he thought. What had Ba said? They are good men; they just don't understand us. He hoped that they could help him obtain a reprieve with the Executive Council.

The Christians came with their black books, and black clothes, and sorrowful eyes. They bowed their heads and muttered some verses from their books.

"Repent and the merciful lord will forgive your sins," they said.

"Repent? What is that?"

"Sorry for what you did."

Hok couldn't contain himself, "No! I did nothing. I not do it. I not kill Ah Fook."

The thin one looked at him with kindly brown eyes. The other looked down at his book.

"How can I say sorry for something I not do?" Hok pleaded, "Please help me, I did not do it. You can tell them … that council … please."

They murmured what may have been an agreement to help Hok, but may not have been. Hok couldn't understand what they were saying.

"You will help me? I am a good man," Hok appealed.

They bowed their heads again, clutched their bibles to their chests and said a few words, but they were non-committal, neither of them answered a yes, or even a no. And then they left.

A chasm of despair tore through Hok's heart. Seeing the Christians had reminded him of the village and of little brother. They were just a bunch of over exuberant village boys, but they had scared little brother, and left him to die in a cornfield, left him to the frightening fate of being mauled to death by a tiger. Hok repented that more than anything. Now he was facing his own fate, a tiger lay waiting in the shadows to claim his soul as well.

A few days later the warder unlocked his barred cell door and Captain Jekyll strode in. The look in his eyes told it all.

"Mr Tee, the Executive Council have met, and your appeal has failed." His eyes shifted to looking over Hok's shoulder at the wall behind. "I am sorry to have to tell you that the sentence of death will be carried out in nine days' time, on Monday, April the 5th."

Hok sank back down onto his bunk. There was no hope. He had no life—his destiny had been decided. The die had been cast. He too was headed for the tiger's mouth. He deserved to die. He would die bravely—only then would he be able to face little brother in the afterlife.

If there was one thing Hok knew, it was this: he would try his utmost to return to his family, if not alive then as a spirit. He asked the governor, Captain Jekyll if he might be allowed to inspect the scaffold. They thought it a strange request and thought it even stranger when he stretched out on the platform, crossed his arms, closed his eyes, and lay stone still.

Hok was willing his soul to leap from his body at the moment of death. He cajoled, he encouraged, he ordered it to obey. The Tao endures forever, he told himself, yet he could not rid himself of thoughts of revenge. He had obeyed nearly all the precepts but still he hungered for revenge. Would he fail because of that?

After supper one night Captain Jekyll came to talk to him again.

"The execution will take place in the morning," he said. "Do you have any last wishes?"

"Tell them I am innocent, tell the newspapers. I am innocent, I did not shoot Ah Fook," he begged the governor.

"I will tell them what you have said."

Captain Jekyll ventured a hand out and patted Hok on the shoulder. He looked as if he was going to say something else, but he didn't. He turned sharply away and marched out.

Hok was not afraid of dying, but he was still bitter. How could he have defended himself against such lies? All the time he said he was not guilty. He told them over and over that he didn't shoot Charlie. But no one believed him. Now it was too late. He would come back and avenge himself on those who had told lies about him. But then, who were the guilty ones? He did not know. All he could do was pray that the heavens would wreak justice for him.

The next morning Captain Jekyll noted in his journal that the prisoner had slept well and managed to eat breakfast, his last meal.

Five weeks and three days after Charlie Ah Fook was shot, at eight o'clock on Monday morning, on April the fifth, 1886, Tee Hok Siong was unshackled, pinioned, led to the scaffold, and hanged.

The press in attendance reported that he was precipitated into eternity in less than a minute from the time he emerged from the pinioning-room and that his equanimity never deserted him. They described him as a small, slight man, with straight black hair and an intelligent face and said that he walked steadily to the drop, looked around once or twice, but showed no emotion and did not speak.

Never was an execution more quickly and quietly managed, they reported—it was almost impossible to realise that a human life had been taken until the body was seen swinging by the distorted neck. Death must have been instantaneous, although the nervous twitching of the body lasted for almost ten minutes.

The corpse was lifted into a coffin with the white linen hood still drawn over its head. The lid of the coffin was screwed down and it was loaded onto a cart. The useless forms of ringing the death bell and hoisting the black flag were omitted. It was only another Chinaman after all.

Hok's body was taken to South Brisbane Cemetery, but his soul joined the other spirits—the hungry ghosts doomed to hover around the gaol until they could find salvation.

Wait for me little brother. I will come.

37: Charleville

An encounter in Charleville: August, 1890
In weeks following the trial not a few of the witnesses had felt uneasy about the part they played in the verdict. No one could deny that they heard Ah Fook name the prisoner. But could Charlie have been mistaken? He was taken by surprise while mixing his dough and it was a dark night, as all seemed to agree. Did Charlie really see the gunman, or did he just assume it was Hok retaliating after the argument about money?

All the while Edwin masqueraded as the epitome of an upright citizen, a prime witness. He surely was an important man now! But, much later, dark doubts set in. His nightmares didn't go away. He relived the scene night after night. First it was the moment, the thunderbolt, then Ah Fook falling back, his gasp of surprise, the grunt as he hit the ground and then that horrible gurgling sound.

As Edwin tossed and turned in his sleep, thrashing around in a jumble of bed sheets, a distorted yellow face peered at him out of the darkness and the apparition's outstretched hands threatened to grab him around the neck. Edwin woke up with a start when he heard the words, "I am come to get you." They repeated in his head like an ear worm, and he couldn't get rid of them.

He read of the execution in the papers. It's all over, he consoled himself. He's dead, they both are. But nothing could stop the uneasiness he felt every time he trotted out his honourable man mantra.

For Moll and Ah Sue things went well. The train line had been moving inexorably on to Morven, but they were one jump ahead—they left Dulbydilla, bypassed Morven and moved straight out to Charleville. They loaded every single skerrick of useful stuff onto a dray and walked all the way there. Moll could have perched on top of the dray for some of the journey, but, as she said to Ah Sue, it was too bleddy uncomfortable. She'd rather have sore feet than have her bones shaken around like that, sure enough.

They took over a patch of land on the township reserve, next to the Warrego River—some fellow was going back to China and sold them the lease. There was a cluster of gardens on the reserve, and Ah Sue was part of a community of market gardeners. They worked in harmony on the reserve, and together they built a platform out over the river; they drew the water up in buckets and shot it down the sluices between the vegetable rows. Hard graft, but it worked. Ah Sue was happy, he grew cabbage, potato, rhubarb, and lettuce.

They made friends. One was a man called Ah Que who ran a boarding house next to the reserve. He had a lot of strange guests of all persuasions. Most had a relentless liking for grog. They hung around from one binge to the next, lambed down, conned by the allure of women and grog, and drying out. Ah Que was a good man and fed them up with lots of Ah Sue's health-giving vegetables as they sobered up—no matter who they were, and no matter that as soon as the boarders were well enough to get a bit of money in their pockets, the cycle repeated.

As it happened, Charleville was the making of Molly and Ah Sue. Soon after they left that abomination of a place, Dulbydilla—Moll couldn't believe it—finally she was with child. Ah Sue was overjoyed. Moll agreed to marry him—well, her idea really—and he was on the way to becoming an Australian citizen. They named the baby Charlie after Charleville, and a year later another one came along. The second one they named Ellen, after Molly's friend Nell. Ah Sue gave them his own special names as well, but to Moll they were always Charlie and Nell.

One fine Sunday afternoon, Molly and Ah Sue were taking a stroll with the little ones, when they ran into Edwin, right there in the main street in Charleville.

"Fancy seeing you here," he said.

"Hello Edwin."

"It's been a while."

"Yes, we live here now."

"Still in the same business?"

"Yes, we're doing alright," said Moll. Edwin glanced across at Ah Sue. Ah Sue nodded at Edwin but stood silent.

"Seen anything of Kate? What happened to her?" Edwin turned back to Moll.

"No, I've not seen her. But I heard that she finally found a good bloke and they're living out near Surat. That stupid husband of hers fell off of his horse and died, leaving her a widow and free to re-marry."

"That's terrible."

"Maybe … but maybe not," Moll said, "I don't think she would have been too upset when she got that piece of news. He was a brute, leaving her like that. I do hope she's happy now."

He looked at her strangely, and said, "That Chinaman got what he had coming." There was something about the way he gave a sideways glance at Ah Sue as he said it, wary, but also condescending. Moll didn't like it.

"What do you mean … oh, the murder? Which Chinaman?" She was being deliberately obtuse; she wasn't going to let him off the hook so easily.

"Both," he said, and then abruptly changed the subject. Bowing over the baby carriage, he said, "What a pretty baby. Congratulations."

Burying her distaste Moll asked after his business and he told her he was going to make an offer to buy up the aerated water and cordial business in Charleville.

"They make the usual soda and tonic waters, ginger ale, and vinegar. But I have plans. I'm going to branch out and make Sarsaparilla, and Raspberry Balm, the ladies will like those, and even Peppermint Cordial," he said preening his moustache.

Moll hoped his offer came to nothing. Then she wouldn't have to run into him again. Charleville was a small place.

"Did you hear about that young fellow Finbar Murphy?" Edwin's pompous voice intruded on her thoughts. "It was his gun that the cook used."

"What about him?"

"You probably know that after the trial Mr Falconer sent him off to one of his private contracts, another bore," Edwin said. "Well, a month or so later one of the stanchions came loose and hit him on the head. Down like a sack of potatoes he went; they said he'd been drinking and got careless. He lasted a few days, delirious they said. Then he was gone. Pity. … Well, goodbye then. Ta-ta."

The sight of Edwin smoothing his waistcoat down over his fat watermelon stomach brought back bad memories for Moll. She'd never felt comfortable about him, there was something sly about that man. And she had never believed Hok did it. He was a good fellow. That was her opinion, then, and now.

Shortly after she'd run into Edwin in Charleville, Moll remembered something that had always troubled her. It must have been the day before Ah Fook was shot. She'd been cursing herself all morning for gossiping with Mary Carlsson, Kate was at her tub in the back, and she, Moll, was in the front serving a customer. Edwin had come striding by the side of the shop, moustache bristling, arms swinging, chest puffed out. He didn't have a bundle of clothes with him, but then Kate usually picked up and delivered when she could, so that wasn't unusual. Moll heard raised voices. Edwin's mostly, although it wasn't clear if he was being angry or just exuberant. The customer, Janet, her from the Albion Hotel, shot Moll an enquiring look. Then they heard Kate laugh, and returned to the task at hand, bargaining the price of some especially nice tomatoes.

At the time Moll thought Kate and Edwin were just joking around, but now she wasn't so sure, Kate's laugh had had an edge to it. More like a scornful laugh. And what did Edwin mean when he said that those Chinamen got what they had coming? Moll had always thought his testimony sounded a bit strange. And she wasn't the only one.

On the way back home after the trial, she had been nodding off to the rhythmic beat of the train when she overheard some of the others from Dulbydilla talking.

"You were there weren't you? That night?" said one.

"Yes."

"Did you hear all that, what Edwin said."

"No … I don't know what he was going on about. All that about potatoes, and who said what. All I heard was Charlie groaning *Me die, me die*. He was in no state to go on like that."

Bit late now, you buggers, Moll had thought.

"And another thing. What Finbar said was a bit odd."

"Shh he'll hear you."

They'd dropped their voices and, strain though she might, Moll hadn't been able to hear what they were saying. With a sick feeling in her stomach she'd settled her head back down to rest against the cold glass of the carriage window.

All in the past now, Moll thought. She sighed and finished setting up the stall with stacks of fat bright orange carrots, crisp green cabbages, and mounds of onions in their papery golden skins.

Molly never saw Edwin again. Jess mentioned in one of her infrequent letters that he'd moved to Brisbane, somewhere south of the river. He'd married again, she wrote, to a nice woman, a friend of hers … too good for such a blowhard. The wife, Ann, had confided to Jess that she was worried about Edwin's drinking, it had been getting worse and worse. He'd started to go a bit crazy, and had been seen roaming about Toowong raving about being chased—by what, no one knew.

Jess wrote again. She said that Edwin's demons had got so bad that Ann had been on the point of getting him sent to the lunatic asylum at Goodna. But then, a few days after Queen Victoria's Diamond Jubilee, there was a loud officious knock on the door. The police had fished Edwin's swollen body out of the river, dead.

Moll felt sorry for the wife. But did Edwin get his comeuppance? She always thought he had lied at the trial. And that argument Kate had with Edwin—she was sure, thinking back, that it was an argument—what was that about?

Ah Sue gave a knowing look when she told him about Finbar's accident and Edwin's fate. He nodded and said, "Good. Play with fire, get burnt."

"What do you mean?" she said, wondering if Ah Sue knew something she didn't.

"I know nothing," he said. "But I no like those men, I no trust them. And that Edwin Mallard, maybe he full of shame. He fear the wolf in front, fear the tiger behind. Inside he have his own devil."

38: On the road

Another encounter in Charleville: August, 2020

"We should go," I said to Dee over breakfast.

"Where?"

"Dulbydilla, where it happened. … The murder."

"Why?"

"I'd like to see where it happened."

"But why?" Dee repeated. "There's nothing there, I looked it up on Google maps."

And she was right. I'd tried too, and on screen there was nothing except the name. No matter how much you zoomed in, all you could see was the railway line and then the main road running parallel a few hundred metres distant. There didn't appear to be anything in between the line and the road, no buildings, no nothing amongst the green brown of the satellite view. There were two farmhouses, or maybe just one with outbuildings, beyond the railway line on the other side. Some areas were dotted with trees while others looked like sandy brown wastes.

"I still think we should go," I said. "If only to view the landscape and get the vibe of the place. Come with me—after all, we've never been out that way before."

I floated the idea of catching the train out west. The Westlander runs from Brisbane to Charleville, running through Dulbydilla, though it didn't stop there—nothing to stop for, I guessed. But it meant seventeen hours on the train overnight and into the next day.

"No way," said Dee.

"OK. Let's drive then. It'll take two days there and the same back unless you want to blitz it. We can take the ute and share the driving. We just need a few days leave either side of the weekend. Can you tear yourself away?"

"Alright but let's take my car, it'll be more comfortable."

I pointed out that the the roads might be dusty and rough. Her little sporty job may not cope very well.

"Better to take the ute," I said.

She agreed, but not without adding, "Don't know why you keep that dirty old thing."

"Can't get rid of Maud, she's a classic."

"Yes, well," said Dee, sounding unconvinced.

A few days later we were on our way, driving west from Brisbane. After six hours solid driving and a brief stop for lunch we arrived in Roma.

"I want to see the courthouse," I said almost before we'd dumped our bags at the motel.

"Dinner first," said Dee.

The courthouse was impressive in the dark with its four classic ionic columns backlit by a light in the entry vestibule. But it was a disappointment; it had been built in 1901 and the original courthouse, where Hok had been tried, had been demolished.

Next morning we headed for Dulbydilla. Two hours later we were in an unbroken sea of brigalow scrub—a landscape of never-ending black trunks and silver foliage broken only by a few muddy-brown creeks. I had a fair idea where the town was, but still managed to overshoot the turn off. At a hundred kilometres per hour an un-signposted road is easy to miss.

I drove gingerly along the winding sandy track, which looked more like a driveway. The mix of tall gum trees and scrubby undergrowth opened up and there was the railway line.

"We're here."

A tiny shed with a lean-to roof masqueraded as a railway

station. It stood between the two main tracks. The cream paint of the corrugated iron sides was worn and cracked. The front was slatted like a fence, with a half-height gate on one side. Dulbydilla—a sign with black letters etched onto a paint-flaked board proclaimed. The place had retained its ancient indigenous name, Dulbydilla, meaning black waterhole, or so I had read. It seems that the town had not been important enough to be renamed after some imported dignitary, or after a place on the other side of the world.

Opposite the shed was an old sheep loading ramp covered in weeds—it hadn't been used for some time. We walked down the track until the rails became a single line running over a bridge which was propped up by hefty round log piers. It spanned a completely dry depression, a dip in the land which was the only sign of what might once have been the creek—and might be again when the drought lifted.

A raised platform poked forlornly through the bone-dry yellow grass—possibly part of the original railway station. Dee found a few rusty old railway spikes strewn around; at least they evoked some sensation of the past.

I tried in vain to imagine the town as it was in its heyday. I'd read of numerous hotels, butchers, bakers, not to mention the water boring operation and the railway workers' camp. It was the end of the line and the springing point for the extension of the railway line to Charleville. The hotels thrived while venturous types waited for the Cobb and Co. coaches to transfer them and other essential goods further out west. But then one day it was no longer the end of the line, and the town's reason for existence faded.

"Just think, the artesian basin hides metres under this sandy wasteland."

"Hard to imagine," said Dee.

On the other side of the tracks was a farmhouse, and beyond that the land gradually rose to a gently mounded hill. We drove across the tracks and up the hill. Looking back, we could see what was probably the black waterhole—a body of dark murky water surrounded by a stand of trees.

To the original indigenous inhabitants the area had probably been a land of plenty, the dark still waters of the waterhole a welcome resting place after a day of hunting. I'd been amused to read that the first of the new settlers had called it Blacks' Waterhole, most not realising they were repeating a name already given. Speculations had been rife on the origin of the waterhole's name—a man named Black, frequented by blacks, or just black? Apostrophes had jumped around changing the meaning.

There didn't seem to be any way of driving to the eponymous waterhole and we were eager for the comforts of food and a bed for the night. We drove back towards the main road.

"You know what's strange?" I said, as we re-joined the highway. "That place had no presence, and no lingering manifestations of the hundreds of people who lived there. I can usually get some feeling of past lives. The marrowbones of history hidden under the veneer of the present. But there? I felt nothing."

"Yes, it's definitely gone. And probably forgotten," said Dee. "The good souls of Dulbydilla just up and left, never to return."

"Every last shack was probably broken up into salvageable pieces and carted away to be re-used at the next camp. And their spirits disappeared along with the buildings."

"Talking about spirits, do you think there's a cemetery anywhere?" Dee asked.

"I didn't see a sign. Did you?"

"No."

At Charleville we took a room each at the Hotel Corones in the main street. Our first priority was a wander around the town before darkness fell, and then we treated ourselves to a leisurely meal. After dinner, a drink in the historic Corones bar seems a must-do, and the bartender was friendly enough. "I'm Dan, pleased to meet you. You two sisters?"

I cringed inwardly, pigeonholed again! If it wasn't for our physiognomy, the colour of our skin and the shape of our eyes, we would never be taken for sisters. We were nothing alike. That week Dee's hair was cut in a short and shaggy pixieish style. Her heavy asymmetrical fringe was streaked with a dramatic, bleached-white lock of hair. And I, well as usual I had my long straight hair tidily tied back, and I dressed nothing like her! Dee shot me a look that said, there you go again being super sensitive. She knew me too well.

"What are you doing out here?" Dan the barman said.

"We came to find Dulbydilla, but it doesn't really exist anymore."

"No, it doesn't. That's a strange thing to do."

"Yeh, a bit strange," I said.

Dee gave me a meaningful glance, and I agreed—neither of us wanted to talk about the reason we had travelled all that way.

"This place has a bit of a history," she said looking around. "What's your favourite story?"

"You've heard of Amy Johnson?"

"The English aviator?"

"Yep. The first woman to fly from England to Australia, solo, in 1930," he said, swiping a questionable cloth across the bar's surface. He stopped mid-swipe leant on the bar and continued.

"She landed here a few days after touch down at Darwin. It was dark and the runway was lit up by the headlights of twenty cars. They carried her shoulder high to the Mayor's car and drove her here, to the Hotel Corones."

"Must have been quite something for an outback town."

"Oath! She appeared on that balcony up there," he pointed upwards, "like a queen. A crowd of one thousand people cheered for ten minutes. Continuously. Well, that's what the papers said. That night, Harry Corones, him in that picture over there, filled her bath with twenty four bottles of champagne."

"Bit of a waste. But maybe she got to drink some of it," I said.

"Never let a good drop go to waste, eh?" He laughed. "Rumour has it he re-bottled the champagne and sold it as souvenirs." Eyeing our empty glasses, he asked, "Get you anything else?"

We declined.

"What's with you?" Dee said as we climbed the stairs to our rooms.

"With me what?"

"You're getting a bit weird."

"Weird what?"

"I know you hate people thinking you're Chinese. But why do you hate people thinking I'm your sister?"

"Sorry." I stopped, my door half open. "It's just that stereotyping thing," I said at last. "We could be sisters, or we could be friends. I hate it when people look at us and lump us together because of the way we look."

Dee gave me a bemused look.

"Come on Sis, we can be friends *and* sisters too, can't we?"

"Yes … we are. But don't you hate being lumped into that Chinese basket?"

"I don't care what people think. Most of the time they're wrong, but when it's to my advantage, I'll take it. Like the assumption that we're total swots and super talented at maths, or music. Anyway," Dee added. "Once they get to know me the assumptions fade away. I just make a joke of it. Some get it, and the ones that don't are so fixed in their mindset that they're not worth worrying about."

"So, you don't feel Chinese?"

"Of course not. We're Australian."

"Not even the smallest bit?"

"I'm proud of our racial heritage, all of it, and not just from Frank's side. But I like to think I can take the best out of all those varied worlds, including the one we were born into."

"That's what Christian said."

"Sensible bloke."

As I drifted off to sleep Christian floated in to my mind. His face had that concerned look, the one he'd given me when I yelled at him all those months ago. Then his expression softened into a smile, I snuggled into the pillow, comforted somehow.

At breakfast bartender Dan from the night before was doubling as a waiter. He hovered above us as we looked at the country style expansive menu, then he cleared his throat.

"You might be interested. Old Barry MacBride, Baz, usually comes in of a morning. His family had some connection with Dulbydilla."

We looked up at him, our faces blank.

"He's got a truckload of stories. He'll be in the Thirsty Camel."

"The Thirsty Camel?"

"The liquor store out back. Opens at nine. He's an odd-jobber."

We looked at each other.

"Guess we could, we've come all this way," I said. Dee nodded.

"Great, wait for me by the back door, over there. Half past, okay?"

We nodded, and he took our order.

Baz came ambling out from the back of the shop when Dan called him.

"Baz, these two ladies want to know a bit more about Dulbydilla," Dan said. He turned towards us. "Sorry, I don't know your names."

I cringed at the 'ladies', but what can you do?

"I'm Eirene and this is Dee," I said.

Baz wiped his hands down the back of his overalls and gave us both a firm handshake belying his slight, bent figure.

"Give me a minute," he said. He wheeled his trolley to the the middle aisle, deposited two cartons on the floor and turned back to us, his eyes bright like a little bird's.

"Dulbydilla," he said. "My granny's uncle worked there way back when it was the end of the line. On the bore."

"Really," I said. "Do tell."

"Granny Annie, my gran, used to tell us stories. She wasn't born then, but she said her father always rambled on about it after he'd had a drop. Sounded like the wild west."

"There was a murder there," I said. Dee shot me a warning look.

"Yes, one of your lot."

Baz fell silent while we all contemplated the implications of that snippet of information. He looked down at his scuffed brown boots, wiped his hands on the back of his overalls again, and looked up at us.

"What her dad said was 'he didn't do it'."

"Who?" I asked. "Who didn't do it?"

"That Chinaman, the one that got hanged."

"Who did it then," asked Dee.

"It was all an accident, you see. He didn't mean to do it, and he didn't tell anyone, didn't want to be the one that hanged."

"Who?" Dee repeated.

"Annie's uncle. Funny thing was he caught it himself just a few months later. Another accident, on the rig. Told his brother, Annie's dad, just before he died. Confessed you might say. Too late for the Chinese fellow though."

"What was his name?' I almost whispered.

"Who?"

"Your granny's uncle."

"Well that's it, I don't know his name."

"Yes, but your gran, what was her name?"

"Grannie Annie? She was a MacBride, just like me."

"And before she was married," Dee said sharply, she was a step ahead of me.

"She was a Murphy, I reckon." His beady eyes darted from one of us to the other. He shook his head. "Probably said too much. Still it was a long time ago, and I'd better get back to work," he said. "Hope you two girls aren't going to have my great-great-uncle arrested—because he's well and truly dead." He chuckled and walked his trolley back, limping slightly. He turned at the doorway.

"I didn't ask you. Why'd you want to know?"

"Just chasing up the history of the expansion of the railway out west from Brisbane. Background information really," Dee said.

Baz seemed satisfied with Dee's answer. We thanked him and scooted back upstairs to our rooms ready to check out.

"Finbar Murphy," I breathed as we climbed the stairs. Dee cocked her head at me smiling, and I felt a weight lift off my shoulders. I waltzed into the room grinning widely and threw everything into my backpack.

We turfed our bags into the back of the ute, I fastened the tray cover, and we were on the road again. Black trunks flashed by as we drove along the highway. Every now and then there was a gap, whole paddocks of felled trees. Why? The question pushed it's way into the jumble in my mind, then disappeared, eclipsed by the import of Baz's revelation.

"I'm going to do that hungry ghost thing," I said, turning to Dee. "This is so exciting."

"Are you now?" Dee said. "When is it? And keep your eyes on the road, or I'll take over."

"Ghost month starts August nineteen, and September two is the full moon and the night of ghost festival."

"You'll have to get a move on then," Dee said.

I slowed as we came up to a small township—something-dilla. Means a waterhole I now knew. Although there wasn't much water to be seen anywhere. We travelled on along the unrelentingly straight road, back to Brisbane.

It was after eleven when we arrived and Dee went straight to bed. *Finbar, Finbar did it*, I channelled to the box.

Finbar Murphy?

I could almost hear a breathy voice, sad and angry at the same time. *Yes, and he died too. An accident not long after,* I said.

Aaah.

A waft of icy air seemed to swirl around the room, then it subsided into a still, dead, silence.

39: I am ready

Brisbane: August, 2020

Back home I couldn't wait to tell Christian the news.

"It was Finbar, Finbar Murphy," I shouted into the phone, and then told him about Baz and the Murphys.

"I'm going to get rid of that hungry ghost," I said. "The poor fellow was innocent. I'm going to set him free, and I'm going to reclaim the box as part of our family history."

Christian sounded impressed. I was grateful. He took me seriously, and didn't think I was some deranged, obsessed lunatic with a vivid imagination.

I buried myself in the internet and took notes. I had to follow tradition to the letter. I needed floating paper lanterns, incense, and joss paper. I made a list and headed for the nearest Chinese shop in Fortitude Valley. The woman at the counter was wearing a face mask, her black hair hung lank, and her eyes looked tired. I felt self-conscious, but she didn't give me a second glance as I laid the incense and joss paper on the counter. For once my looks didn't signal me as an outsider.

At my local shopping centre, I bought red tissue paper and string, tea lights and round coated-paper plates. I arrived home and, religiously following the instructions on the web, I managed to construct a beautiful lotus flower lantern. By the end of the week, I had fifteen. A good number. The squares of joss paper were printed in red and gold. I folded them following the instructions on YouTube. They looked like small boats but were actually replicas of the gold and silver ingots used as currency in ancient China. I was ready.

At the beginning of the seventh lunar month, ghost month, I placed some offerings on the table in front of the red box, bowls of cooked rice, beans, tofu, fruit and peanuts; some joss money; two red candles and two incense sticks. I added a glass of wine, and a few flowers—it felt right.

Thank you.

You're welcome.

The night of the full moon arrived, Wednesday the second of September. I arranged eight chairs around the table, six for the living, one for the ghost of Hok Siong, and although it broke my heart, one for Frank.

I lit the sticks of incense and the red candles on either side of the scholar's box. More candles went all along our long table and the room sparkled with a warm orange glow. Ronnie had driven up and was in the spare room getting ready.

Christian arrived, "All ready?" he asked.

"Ghost busters united," I said, and we exchanged conspiratorial grins.

Maddy and John were the last to arrive. My best friends at Uni who had happened to like each other enough to get married. A lot had happened since I'd last seen Maddy and all I'd said was dinner at mine, bring John. She had no idea about the reason for the occasion.

She looked around, "This looks pretty, all the candles and stuff." Her eyes swept over the box on the sideboard with all the offerings around it. "Is this something special?"

Time to enlighten her.

"Yes, it's a Hungry Ghost feast."

"Sounds spooky," Maddy shivered slightly. "But why didn't you tell us this before?"

"Sorry, it was just too complicated to explain over the phone."

"You're full of surprises," she said.

"Come and meet Christian, he'll tell you all about it."

Leaving Maddy and John to be educated by Christian, I rushed around in the kitchen, and soon the table was resplendent with a cornucopia of food. I herded them into their seats.

"Are you expecting anyone else," Maddy said.

"No. It's just part of the ritual. It's traditional to leave empty seats at the table for deceased members of the family."

"One for Frank?" John asked with one of those sympathetic how-sad looks.

"And one for the ghost," I said. "Well, for Hok, our great-great-great uncle."

"The one that was hanged?" said Maddy with a how-distasteful look.

I was beginning to wish I hadn't asked them. I looked over at Christian and met a pair of reassuring eyes. He came to the rescue, "Hungry ghosts can be people who have been wrongly killed. They are trapped on earth in a limbo, a state of un-death, or the Bardo, if you like. Or so it's believed. …Until someone releases them."

"The bridge between the living and the dead is strongest on the night of the Hungry Ghost Festival's full moon … and that's tonight," I added.

"So you plan to free the ghost of your uncle from the Bardo?" asked Maddy.

"Yes. We believe Hok was wrongly convicted, and we're going to free his soul."

"You think?" John said, obviously not quite ready for all this strangeness.

"We think," said Christian firmly with a nod and an amused smile.

"Cheers," I said, with a grateful look at Christian.

We lifted our glittering wine glasses in a toast as fragrant eddies of steam wafted from my best porcelain bowls.

"Help yourselves," I said. "This is soft tofu with chilli and spring onion, and these are mushroom dumplings in a ginger and shiitake broth. That one is spicy eggplant, and this is stir fry duck. Over there gai-lan, snow peas and rice."

I looked around the room at my favourite people enjoying themselves. Ronnie was at one end of the table, her face bright and alive, lit by the glow of the candles. She was wearing a red dress patterned with pale green palm fronds and her lustrous black hair was tied back in a loose knot. Her bold, ziggurat-shaped, silver earrings bounced around as she shared a joke with John and Dee. Maddy spooned the ginger and shiitake broth over her dumplings and beamed her enquiring blue eyes towards an ever patient Christian. And I sat there with a satisfied grin on my face.

"This duck is really delicious," Dee said, in her best stirring up mood. She knew very well that it wasn't real duck.

"It is," Maddy agreed, "But I thought you were a vego, Eirene?"

"Glad you like it. It's what the Chinese call mock duck. Made from flour."

"Mock duck? Is that a relation of the Mock Turtle?" Ronnie was the one to make the literary connection.

"When we were little," said Dee in a croaky wavery voice. "We went to school in the sea. The master was an old turtle—we used to call him Tortoise—."

I joined in, "Why did you call him Tortoise, if he wasn't one?"

"We called him Tortoise because he taught us," answered Ronnie. "Really you are very dull!"

They all laughed. I smiled. "Eat up, let's enjoy the land of the living!"

Maddy helped me clear the table.

"He's gorgeous," she whispered as she loaded plates into the dishwasher. "But I thought you were seeing Will?"

"I was," I said slowly. "It didn't work out. Who's gorgeous?"

"Oh, come on. You know … Christian." I blushed but bent my head to hide it.

"We're just good friends. A cliché, but there you are."

"Mmm, are you sure? Well, we must be going." She rounded John up and I walked them to the door.

"The food was gorgeous too," she said with a knowing smile as they left. "Take care now."

Ronnie gave me an uncharacteristic hug, "Thanks for the nice dinner … and everything. Good luck with saying goodbye to that ghost." And off she went to the spare room. Had she come around to accepting the supernatural then? Or was she just being accommodating?

Dee had an early start coming up, and soon Christian and I were the only ones left. It was nearly midnight. Celeste strolled out of the bedroom arching her back. Christian bent down to scratch her under her chin. She purred. And I almost did too.

"Let's go," I said to my partner in crime, putting that thought away for the moment. "I need to get rid of this damned ghost." I loaded the lanterns, the folded paper money boats, some tea lights, and the matches in a basket. Throwing a jacket over my dress, I shoved the red box under one arm, and we made our way down to the river.

The air was still and calm. Only the faintest lapping sounds broke the quiet as ripples of black water nudged the bank. I looked up and down the river path hoping that no late-night strollers would appear and think us strange.

And then I took courage. "Let's do it."

"Where?"

"Here?" We were on the river path in front of our building. He looked up at the many windows overlooking the river. I knew what he meant, too many windows.

"There's another place, a bit farther on. Not far."

We walked along the path, down a small slope. It was a clear night. Overhead a full moon blazed in the deep navy-blue sky, illuminating a few dark streaky clouds stretched out in rows low down near the horizon.

"Nearly there."

A few bats fluttered out of the fig trees, chattering and chirping, swooping here and there.

"This is it. There are windows here too, but we can launch the lanterns from the rocks in front of those pandanus trees. Do you think we can get over the fence?"

Christian put his foot on one of the horizontal wires of the rather posh stainless steel railing fence separating the river path from the river. He leapt up, scrambled over the railing and landed with a soft thump on the other side.

"Here," I passed over the box and the bag, grabbed Christian's hand and pulled myself up. I angled my body weight awkwardly over the top. "Bloody hell."

It wasn't easy. The top rail was offset inwards to stop any kid from drowning themselves. I braced myself on a pandanus trunk and leapt down to a thankfully firmly lodged flattish rock. It was high tide, and the water was well within reach. We hopped gingerly from one rock to another and squatted down by the water's edge. I pulled out my lotus flower lanterns and placed a tea light in the middle of each one.

"Are we ready?" said Christian.

"Almost." The last CityCat for the night came gliding around the bend heading for the Hawthorne jetty opposite. "When the ferry has gone," I said.

The ripples in the ferry's wake turned into black stripes flowing out behind it like a trailing skirt. A solitary figure stood at the stern, lost in contemplation.

The wash calmed. We burned the paper money, lit the tea lights, and set the lanterns afloat. They jostled in a clump by the edge dancing over the faint ripples. One by one, we nudged them out with a stick, and in slow motion they majestically drifted away in the direction of the ocean.

I rested my hand on the box and hoped that Hok Siong's spirit would find peace.

"Wouldn't it be nice if he found his way back home instead of going back to being a hungry ghost in some sort of limbo?" I said.

"It would."

Christian helped me clamber back over the railing. We gravitated towards a seat on the side of the path and sat down.

I go now. Goodbye... .

Goodbye, I repeated in my head, and then shot a quick glance across to Christian. But no, he didn't seem aware of the conversation.

I contemplated the night sky. The lotus-flower lights slowly drifted down the dark river. A lone runner and his dog jogged past. I felt a ghostly presence again.

Farewell.

One by one the lantern lights started to go out. I was about to break the silence when I felt an arm reach around my back and over my shoulder. I turned my face and Christian's eyes locked onto mine. Perhaps ... ?

He smiled. "Well," he said as he gave my shoulder a small squeeze. "Here we are, then."

再见⋯我先走

Goodbye ... I'm leaving ...

Soft as silk I glide along the moonlit muddy brown river, past the big brick buildings, past the spreading poinciana trees dipping their feathery leaves in farewell. The open sea beckons. My cold sad heart melts, I am happy.

Mama, Baba, I'm coming home!

Author's note

The story of Tee Hok Siong is based on an actual event in Australia's past. Around 1876 a young Chinese man, known here as Tim Tee, arrived in the country from Amoy, a city in south-east China. Ten years later he was hanged for murder at Boggo Road Gaol in Brisbane. He maintained his innocence to the end.

I was introduced to the story through Leonie Gane's book *The Hungry Ghosts of Boggo Road* and became interested in, not only the idea of hungry ghosts, but also Tim Tee and how he came to such a grisly end. Contemporary newspaper reports of his trial are available, and the witness statements I've used are almost word for word as reported at the time. There was at least one real person who thought Tim Tee might have been wrongly convicted, and his unattributed letter to the editor appeared in a Toowoomba newspaper of the time. In my book that person is the fictitious Mr John Holland.

My description of the town of Dulbydilla was helped by a series of newspaper articles entitled 'A Winter Tour in Queensland' by 'The Vagabond' and published in 1885. A number of the events, such as the bare knuckled fight and the Sunday cricket match, were experienced by The Vagabond.

Missionaries to China were prolific in describing their travels in the country, and I have relied on these accounts for creating the atmosphere of the city and villages of Amoy in the nineteenth century.

Some of the other characters and events in the book are real. The giant known in Australia as Choukiczee travelled out from China on RMS Singapore in May and June of 1876, and toured Australia and New Zealand. He was reputed to be anywhere between 2.2 and 2.4 metres tall and up to 180kg. The recounting of the voyage of RMS Singapore out from Hong Kong is based on Captain Peake's reports in the shipping news found in archived newspapers from the time.

Mr Falconer was a well known mining engineer and sometime entrepreneur engaged to bore for water in the real town of Dulbydilla. Richard Andrews, photographer and child sex offender, was convicted and sentenced in Roma in 1886 for interfering with two young children in Dulbydilla.

The fictional Billy sees his father being shot in the historical Bendemere Station massacre, on Yuleba Creek in the Maranoa, which took place in around 1860. My account of the massacre is taken from that of Konrad Nahrung (1838-1924).

Though based on historical records, *Tiger in the Blood*, the story of a murder and its aftermath, is an imagined one.

Many thanks to those who read the various draft versions of this novel. Your help and comments were invaluable and your encouragement was an incentive to keep going.